HEARTWARMING

Make Me a Match

Melinda Curtis
Cari Lynn Webb
Anna J. Stewart

ISBN-13: 978-0-373-36777-1

Make Me a Match

Recycling programs for this product may not exist in your area.

This edition published by arrangement with Harlequin Books S.A.

For questions and comments about the quality of this book, please contact us at CustomerService@Harlequin.com.

Printed in U.S.A.

Melinda Curtis is an award-winning, *USA TODAY* bestselling author who lives in drought-stricken California with her husband, where they hope El Niño comes to visit...soon. Their three kids are away in college, but their neighbors are empty nesters, too, the house is clean and the fridge unraided, so it's kind of fun. Melinda enjoys putting humor into her stories because that's how she approaches life. She writes sweet contemporaries as Melinda Curtis (Brenda Novak says of *Season of Change*, "Found a place on my keeper shelf"), and fun, traditional romances as Mel Curtis (Jayne Ann Krentz says of *Cora Rules*, "Wonderfully entertaining").

Cari Lynn Webb believes in life lessons. Her three older brothers taught her how not to act like a clingy, high-maintenance girl (their words). Her mother taught her how to laugh at herself and life. Her father taught her to follow her dreams and always be kind. Cari lives those lessons today. Her husband keeps her laughing, even when life is stressful. She's turned her dream of writing romance novels about strong heroines and the heroes who love them into reality. And she's grateful every day for all of her family's lessons that she now gets to pass along to her unsuspecting daughters.

Anna J. Stewart wrote her first romance (starring a certain hunky rock star) back in high school, and the rest, as they say, is history. A longtime fangirl and geek, this native Californian spends her downtime attending sci-fi fan conventions, avoiding crazy new apps for her phone and dealing with a serious *Supernatural, Star Trek* and *Sherlock* addiction. While her independent heroines don't need a man, when they find the one they want, that's when the fun begins. Anna is a *USA TODAY* bestselling author.

CONTENTS

I consider myself lucky to have two great friends
in Anna J. Stewart and Cari Lynn Webb.
Thanks for making Kenkamken Bay fun.
And to my family—especially Mr. Curtis—thanks
for always believing.

Baby, Baby

Melinda Curtis

Dear Reader,

Welcome to Kenkamken Bay, Alaska!

In K-Bay most men don't shave but once a year. And when they do shave? It might be because a spring trip to Anchorage is in the making. Most men in K-Bay aren't really pining for women. They like the isolation. So when Cooper Hamilton and his friends make a bet that they can successfully match six couples, no one really thinks they'll succeed.

But Coop has more than matchmaking on his mind. Last spring when the snow thawed, Coop made the drive to Alaska and met Nora Perry. Nora thought she might have met "the one." And Coop? He wasn't thinking along those lines. Now Nora has tracked Coop down before the most romantic holiday of the year—Valentine's Day! Too bad romance is not on Nora's to-do list.

I hope you enjoy Coop and Nora's journey. I love to hear from readers. Check my website to learn more about upcoming books, sign up for email book announcements and I'll send you a free sweet romantic comedy read, or chat with me on Facebook (MelindaCurtisAuthor) or Twitter (MelCurtisAuthor) to hear about my latest giveaways.

Melinda

MelindaCurtis.com

CHAPTER ONE

"A GOOD CAR is like a good life," Cooper Hamilton said to his friends over a beer on Friday night in Kenkamken Bay, Alaska's, Bar & Grill. "Make it affordable, make it practical, make it easy to trade in. And you're all set."

"A good car starts up and goes no matter how bad the storm," Gideon Walker added, tightening the knot on his don't-leave-home-without-it blue tie. "Nothing keeps a good car stuck in your driveway."

Ty Porter scratched his full, dark beard—the one that gave half the men in town beard envy—and channeled his inner cynic. "Unless it runs out of gas."

Coach, the bar's owner and bartender, rolled his eyes. And Coop couldn't blame him.

In their high school years, Coop, Gideon and Ty had strutted around town looking down their noses at K-Bay because they were destined to leave for better things in the Lower 48. Now they'd become a sad cliché. A fixture at the K-Bay Bar & Grill. Always taking up the three seats at the elbow of the bar near the kitchen.

As demoralizing as the 0–0 score of the hockey game.

There were other fixtures in the old bar, of course: the large brass bell that hung over the beer taps, the hand-painted sign above the mirror proclaiming it a Nag-Free Zone, and the other regulars at their regular seats. Mike and his fishing buddies around the pool table. Sam and other cannery workers in the booths near the front windows. Derrick and the cross-country truck drivers at the round wooden table in front of the big-screen television.

Coop supposed there was nothing wrong with being a regular and keeping to your group of friends. It was just that Coop hadn't expected to be one of them—the bearded, parka-wearing, windshield-scraping residents of a remote town in southwest Alaska.

The hockey game on the big screen ended. There were calls for a change of channel. Coach worked the remote with arthritis-gnarled fingers. Other sports played silently on smaller TVs around the bar.

Out of habit, Coop flexed his digits. His father had lost all the fingers on one hand in a fishing accident that had nearly killed him, right before Coop had planned to leave for college. Made Coop appreciate his limbs and everyone else's, arthritic or not.

A lifestyle report from an Anchorage station popped on-screen. The reporter was interviewing a woman wearing a turquoise business suit that looked as though it belonged in Washington, DC, not Alaska.

"The possibilities for matchmaking in Alaska are limitless due to the ratio of men to women here." Not one of the suited-lady's highlighted curls moved in the wind. "When I meet a female client, I intuitively know what kind of man she'll be happy with. You could almost say that love is guaranteed." She flashed a calculated smile at the camera. "If you hire me."

Jeers rose from the crowd.

Coop groaned. As a car salesman and used-car-lot manager, he knew a slick sales pitch when he heard one. "If that woman sold cars, she'd be doctoring repair records and rolling back odometers."

Coach found a basketball game and the patrons settled down.

"'There are no women in Alaska.'" Ty framed his statement in air quotes. "That's a myth."

"A myth everywhere but here," Gideon said. Since he worked as a loan officer at Kenkamken Bay Savings & Loan, he should know the area's statistics. "K-Bay is seventy-five percent male."

"And some of the females..." Coop didn't voice the rest of his opinion. The women in town were nice, but they weren't the kind you'd see in beauty pageants or in a Lower 48 big city. Heels? Glossy hair? Artfully applied makeup? Not in K-Bay. "Why would they put a story about matchmaking on the news?"

Coach slapped the lifestyle section of the *Anchorage Beat* on the nicked oak bar. "Because Kelsey Nash wrote an article about that woman."

Coop's gaze cut to Ty. His friend looked away from the paper and touched the scar on his cheek, the one half-hidden by that thick beard.

Kelsey was from K-Bay and had been the first to report on Ty's career-ending injuries seven years ago. That wouldn't have been so bad if she hadn't slanted the piece to make Ty look like an irresponsible, immature fool. Never mind the puck to Ty's face, detached retina, medically induced coma and the end of the man's pro-hockey dreams—of all their dreams. Ty wasn't a fool. He was just...Ty.

"It's a fluff piece. It's not as if matchmaking would be hard in a city like Anchorage." Coop tried to discredit Kelsey's story. "Let that woman try matchmaking in K-Bay."

"We could do better than her." Gideon was right there with him, adjusting the knot in his tie as if it was Monday morning, not Friday night. "I mean, come on. What does a woman like *that* know about what a man from Alaska likes? It's not worth the space in the paper or the airtime on TV."

"Listen to yourselves." Coach's voice rumbled like a logging truck speeding over rutted black ice. "Talking as if you had any idea about life or love."

"I just said life was like a good car." Coop sat up straighter. There was nothing that got his heart pumping like a good bar argument. "And women like a good car. Just look at me." He spread his arms. "I'm good-car material."

"Sure you are." Coach poured the sarcasm over Coop's belief. "You're cheap, boring and stuck in a rut. Just like my wife's snowbound sedan out on Old Paris Road. Won't get that out until spring. If ever."

And if that didn't deflate Coop's tires...

Ty was still lost in thought when Gideon jumped to Coop's defense. "Men know what they want in a woman. To make a match, you'd just have to dig down deep to discover what the heck a woman really wants. That matchmaker using her 'intuition' is farcical. If two people would just be honest about what they wanted—"

"Exactly." Coop leaped back into the fray. "If a woman would just say, 'I do want a long-term commitment from a man that'll likely lead to marriage and probably having babies,' it would cut through all the awkward, getting-to-know-you part." And transition Coop to the "sorry, that's not me, been nice to know you" part.

Coach chuckled, but it wasn't the sound of shared humor. "The three of you sit in my bar every Friday and Saturday night, and most Sundays, too. Sometimes you go to Anchorage to meet women, but you don't date anyone regular. What could you possibly know about matchmaking?"

"I bet we could make introductions with more success than that woman." Coop's voice rang with confidence. It wasn't as though he was actually going to have to prove his point.

"Look at all the single guys in this bar. There's a catch here for every gal."

They all scanned the bar's patrons.

Coop almost considered issuing a retraction. Scraggly beards. Scraggly hair. Scraggly flannel shirts. K-Bay wasn't exactly *Baywatch*.

But Gideon was back in the game. "I bet we could match more couples than her, too. And I wouldn't use my intuition."

"We'd have the Bar & Grill's bell ringing on the hour." Coop's statement might have been a little over the line. Whenever someone found The One, they rang the bell over the bar. The bell hadn't been heard in more than a year.

"I'll take that bet," Coach said, puncturing the wind from their sails. He leaned on the bar, capturing their attention the same way he had years ago as their high school hockey coach—with a steely-eyed stare that said he was done with small talk and ready for action. "There are three weeks until Valentine's Day. I'll bet you three can't get three couples to ring that bell by Valentine's eve."

"Three?" Coop scoffed, the first of their trio to find his voice. "We could do twice that."

Ty and Gideon stared at Coop as if he'd just told them he'd traded his truck for a minivan.

"Deal." Coach offered his hand.

Coop reflexively put his out, but Gideon arm-barred his hand aside. “We don’t know the terms. What do we get if we win this bet?”

“A hundred bucks.” Coach smirked, making his face as wrinkled as a shar-pei’s.

Again, Coop put out his hand.

Again, Gideon batted it down. “That’s not worth one match, let alone six.”

“Six hundred, then.” Coach’s grin said he thought they’d fail.

Heck, Coop thought they’d fail. *Six?* What had he been thinking?

Clearly he hadn’t been. Still, Coop kept his smile—the one that had helped him sell hundreds of cars—glued to his face. No reason to let Coach sense blood in the water.

Coop glanced at Gideon. Gideon glanced at Coop. It was too late to back out now. They nodded and extended their hands to seal the deal, but this time it was Ty who stopped them from accepting the bet.

“Forget the money. If we win, we want jobs on one of your hockey teams.” Ty had an expression on his face that Coop hadn’t seen in seven years—like a bull charging toward the china shop. He’d scowled like that during a high school championship and had defended four shots on goal in two minutes to ensure their team won.

Coop wasn't sure if the entire bar heard Ty's terms or not. For a moment everything seemed quiet. Or it could have been the ringing in Coop's ears that blocked out the clinking of glasses, beer-roughened voices and deep drifts of laughter.

Jobs in the Lower 48? It was all they'd ever wanted—to get out of town and work together in professional hockey.

Coach's gaze morphed from dismissive to appraising. He owned large stakes in a couple of farm teams in the contiguous US. He'd been a successful hockey coach at the highest level, retiring early due to a severe case of rheumatoid arthritis now under control with a change in lifestyle and diet. "You want to sell popcorn and pretzels at some of my games?"

Ty didn't flinch at the jab, although it hit him where it hurt because his thickly bearded chin jutted out. He'd gone from being a potential hockey superstar at eighteen, predicted to go high in the draft, to a jack-of-all-trades employee at K-Bay's run-down skating rink. "Coop can sell bottled sand in the desert. I'm sure you have marketing positions. Gideon can make money grow on trees—"

"Legally," Gideon murmured.

"And I know the game inside out." Ty's chin thrust halfway to Russia. "I could coach."

The stakes of the bet had increased astronomically. It was what the three of them had dreamed of as boys: escaping Alaska. Only, back then, Coop was going to be Ty's sports agent and Gideon his financial adviser. When Ty's dreams had fallen apart, so had Coop's and Gideon's.

Coop tried not to look as though he'd swallowed a fish bone. "Is it a bet, Coach?"

"You've forgotten one thing." The older man leaned against the back bar and crossed his beefy forearms. "What do I get when you lose?"

"We'll swim the Polar Bear Challenge naked," Ty offered.

Coach shook his gray, grizzled head. "You did that when you were teens."

"We'll bartend for you on weekends." At Coach's frown Gideon added, "For a month."

"I like tending bar," Coach said. "Gets me out of the house. Now…if you wanted to take my wife shopping in Anchorage every weekend for a month…"

They didn't.

Coop stared at Kelsey's article, at the suited

matchmaker, at Kelsey's postage-stamp picture. "We'll take out an ad in the *Anchorage Beat*. Full page. Stating we know nothing about life or love, just like you said."

Ty made a noise like a polar bear right before it dived under dark and stormy seas.

Coach's faded blue eyes narrowed. "I want pictures, too. And an article about why Alaska is the best place in the world to live."

Everything they stood against. Everything they complained about. Everything that made living in K-Bay as boring and rut filled as Coach had accused Coop of being.

It was one thing to be disappointed in his lot in life, another to be called on it. Coop didn't hesitate. "Deal."

They all shook on it and Coach left them to check on other customers. They each stared at their shaggy, bearded reflections in the glass behind the bar.

"Seriously, Coop?" Ty took aim with his hellfire expression. "An ad? This is worse than the time you convinced us to hitchhike to Anchorage our senior year. It's not as if anyone knows who you are. But me—"

"Coach wasn't going for a naked swim in the Bering Sea." Ty's anger didn't faze Coop. They'd known each other too long for him to take it personally. "And he wouldn't have gone for something simple like a case of rare whiskey."

"It is what it is," Gideon said, always the peacemaker. "But we can't tell anyone what *it* is."

Coop nodded. They'd be laughed out of K-Bay. "Where do we start?"

"Maybe we can get people to fill out an online survey." Gideon perked up. He loved anything techish. "I could design a program to pair them up."

The inner front door opened and a woman stepped in. She was wrapped from neck to snow boots in a reddish-brown parka that made her look like a stuffed sausage. Conversation in the room died away as every pair of male eyes turned toward her. She peeled off her knit cap, revealing shoulder-length, glossy blond hair and artfully applied makeup.

She was pretty, beautiful even. The kind of woman that men stopped and took notice of.

Coop sat up straighter. Noticing. "Here's our first customer."

She unfastened her jacket with small, delicate hands, revealing a small, delicate head covered in blond fuzz. A baby. Strapped to her chest.

The room heaved a sigh of regret. Conversations resumed, albeit not at their usual volume.

Slumping, Coop returned his attention to his beer. “And there goes our first customer.”

Boots rang across the oak floor.

Gideon tapped Coop on the shoulder. “She’s coming over here.”

Coop turned back around.

It was the weirdest thing. Coop was used to Alaska’s winters, used to the cold. But as the woman and the baby approached, the room took on a chill.

She stopped in front of him and arched a golden brow. “Cooper Hamilton?”

Coop nodded, rather numbly, because there was something familiar about the woman’s face, about her smooth voice, about the swing of her pretty blond hair across her shoulders.

She gestured to the baby. “I believe I have something of yours.”

CHAPTER TWO

"YOU DON'T REMEMBER ME, do you?" Nora Perry couldn't help sounding angry and embarrassed. She'd traveled more than one hundred miles on a bus. It'd taken six hours instead of two. She was tired. The baby was tired.

And the witty, handsome man she'd met ten months ago with the mischievous smile? He wasn't witty—he was speechless. He wasn't handsome—his dark hair brushed his shoulders unevenly and grew from his chin in short, thick stubs. He wasn't smiling—his lips formed a shell-shocked, silent O.

Coop led Nora to a tall wooden booth in the dimly lit, seen-better-days bar. She hung her parka on a booth hook, dropped her backpack to the floor and sat on the cold wooden bench too quickly, landing on her sit bones.

Zoe fussed, probably overheated from Nora's resolve-melting mortification.

Coop didn't remember her? Subtract fifty points from his man-appeal tally.

Last time Nora had seen Coop, he'd had a stylish, clean-shaven jaw, a stylin' opening line and a styled set of dance moves that would've qualified him for a spot on *Dancing with the Stars*, Alaska edition. They'd met at a bar in Anchorage last spring. Spring being a time when folks got a little nutty in Alaska because everything returned to "normal" for a few months. You didn't have to wear parkas the size of sleeping bags or shovel as much snow.

"You don't remember me, do you?" Nora repeated when Coop continued to be struck dumb. She was having trouble slipping off the baby-carrier straps. Her lower lip trembled, much like Zoe's did when her dirty diaper didn't get changed quickly enough. "Am I that forgettable?" Her pride and her stomach slid to the floor. "Don't answer that."

Nora finally got the straps off and settled Zoe in the crook of her arm. "You had no trouble with words that night in Anchorage." There. A clue. Perhaps the humiliation would end.

Coop couldn't seem to drag his green gaze from Zoe. "I…uh…"

Or not. More mortifying heat flash flooded her body. And when emotion flooded her hormonal, postpregnancy body, which was often lately, her milk came in.

Could things get any worse? "We met at a bar."

"Uh…" His gaze stroked her face and then dropped below her chin to the milk-production department.

"I didn't have these then." She waved a free hand in front of her now-tingling, melon-size chest and tried her best to glare at him. But it was hard to glare when the father of your child couldn't remember you.

Zoe squirmed then squinted and made a squishing sound in her pants.

So much for a classy, civilized meeting.

Still, it was hard not to love Zoe. Unless you were Coop. His gaze was still caught on the milk-production department.

"Excuse me." Nora scootched off the bench seat and rummaged in the backpack that served both as her purse and her diaper bag. Was it just last year she'd carried a budget-busting Dooney & Bourke tote? It seemed like a lifetime ago.

Nora tugged her diaper kit free and shot Coop another deadly glare. "Don't go anywhere."

Coop raised his hands slowly, as if in surrender, still in bachelor shell shock.

Nora was having a shock of her own. She wasn't just a one-night stand. She was a forgettable one-night stand.

Coop was just like her father: a happy-go-lucky drunk going through life in memory-stealing binges.

I'm not going to let Coop hurt Zoe like Dad did me.

Nora was in Kenkamken Bay for one thing and one thing only. Child support. She wasn't looking for a relationship with her baby daddy. Coop, being a self-centered bachelor, would probably be relieved that all she wanted was money. With direct deposit from his bank to hers, he need never see her or Zoe again. In fact, given who he was, Nora preferred it that way.

The ladies' room was a pleasant surprise. It was clean and had a drop-down change table. Nora made quick work of the diaper, enjoying Zoe's cooing nonsensical song. But the restroom lacked a place to sit and breast-feed. And boy, did she need to breast-feed. Given Coop's stupefaction, her breast-feeding in public would probably send him to an early grave, which—setting aside her own discomfort at the public airing of a private event—would be highly satisfying.

Spirits bolstered, Nora opened the door.

Coop was waiting for her, no longer looking like a man who couldn't believe he'd plowed his beloved sports car into a tree. His green eyes sparkled. His grin dazzled with straight teeth as white as snow. "Tangerine dress. Yellow heels. St. Patrick's Day."

She'd wanted him to remember her. And yet…Nora felt as if the unsalted nuts she'd eaten on the bus were giving her indigestion.

"You ordered white wine." His grin spread over his now handsome—despite the beard—face. Funny what a smile did to a shaggy man's looks. "We went back to your place and—"

"Please." Nora walked past him to the booth. "Not in front of the baby."

Everyone in the bar stared. She felt their eyes like a field mouse feels a circling hawk's calculating gaze, almost as if they were protective of Coop, more than ready to join him in rejection of her paternity claim.

Her steps quickened. A woman in a strange town accusing the local golden boy she'd had his baby?

It'd been a mistake to come. A desperate, stupid mistake. She'd find the means to get by without Coop's money. She'd get a second job. She'd trade babysitting services with other working moms. There had to be a way to raise Zoe without Coop's help.

He slid into the booth across from her, looking decidedly chipper. "The thing is, Nancy—"

"Nora." She resented his too-late chipperness and his too-false charm.

"I remember you." His voice dropped from light and pleasant to dark and repellent. "And I distinctly remember using protection." His smile never wavered as he tried to back her off from her claim.

Her father had a smile just like it, one that said he never worried about anything. And Dad didn't worry. Not when he'd lost everything because one of his many get-rich-quick ideas failed. Not when he had a baby with a woman he didn't remember meeting in a bar.

"You missed your weekend with the kids," Nora's mother would say. "It was three weeks ago. And your check—"

"Bounced again? I'll write you another." Dad would flash a minty smile meant to cover the alcohol on his breath. "Why waste time arguing? I'm here. And the kids want to have fun with their old man."

Nora and her brothers hadn't wanted anything to do with him. Not when he drank beer until he passed out and practically forgot their names.

"Protection?" Nora wanted to be sick. She swallowed back the memories and held on to her resolve because the bus wasn't scheduled to leave for another hour. "As my doctor told me…ninety-nine percent effective means one lucky woman in one hundred gets a golden ticket." She angled Zoe's sweet, innocent face toward Coop. "Here's mine." Not his. Never his. She'd never raise a child with this loser.

The wattage on Coop's smile never dimmed. "Why wait so long to tell me?"

"Since you didn't call me afterward, I figured you were just a beer-swilling guy looking for a good time, and I assumed I could afford to raise a child on my own." Diapers. Day care. The dollars added up far too quickly. "One of my assumptions was wrong."

His eyes narrowed, but that smile… "I'll want a paternity test."

She nodded, unfazed. "I brought one."

"SHE'S GOT YOUR nose, Coop."

Coop couldn't see what Gideon saw, maybe because a demoralizing thought kept buzzing in his brain. *You're going to lose your second opportunity in the NHL, even if you win the bet.*

It can't be mine.

The baby swaddled in neon pink in Nora's arms seemed like any other to him: round cheeks, tufts of blond hair, squinty eyes. Maybe the eyes looked like his after one too many beers the night before, but those days were few and far between now. As were his days of picking up women in bars.

A change made too late, it seemed.

He'd retreated with sluggish steps to the bar when Nora told him she was going to breast-feed. "It might not be mine," he said to his friends. His words didn't sound convincing.

Nora's words sounded convincing.

"Congratulations on a baby girl." Coach guffawed and set a shot of whiskey on the bar in front of Coop. "She's got the Hamilton nose. Won't be long before you're having tea parties and playing with dolls."

"Taking her to tap-dancing lessons," Ty said slyly, clearly enjoying this too much.

"Laying down the law with the guy who takes her to prom." Gideon grinned.

"Jumping the gun, as usual." A band of dis-appointment tightened around Coop's chest. If he was a dad, he had an obligation to stay where his child was. "Let's wait for the results of the paternity test. In the meantime, back to the issue at hand. Matchmaking."

Mary Jo, the bus-route driver, banged into the foyer and through the second door, shaking off snow that covered her boots and parka. She'd been a couple years ahead of Coop in school, but she looked as old as truck-driving Derrick, a crony of hers and ten years her senior. Lines had made permanent inroads on her forehead and from the corners of her frequently frowning mouth. Her divorce battle had aged her.

Nora waved to Mary Jo, buttoning up her yellow blouse. "Is the bus ready to leave?"

"The bus isn't going anywhere." Mary Jo clomped across the wood floor, tugging off her gloves. "That darn weatherman was wrong again. It's a blizzard out there. Service is cancelled for the day."

"But…I'm stuck?" Nora's horrified gaze bounced around the bar and landed on Coop. "Here?"

She'd taken the bus. She'd implied money was tight. There were hotels and motels in town, but could she afford a room? And how would she get there? Mary Jo wasn't offering a ride. Helio's Taxi was closed for the day. He was in the back on his fourth beer. Between the drifts of snow on the ground and the severity of the storm, it wouldn't be safe for Nora to walk anywhere with a baby.

Coop felt paralyzed.

Next to him, Ty was lost in thought, staring at the *Anchorage Beat*. Gideon asked Mary Jo if her divorce was final. Derrick tugged on a gray streak in his beard and made a joke about the fragility of buses on Alaskan highways. Trucker humor. Mary Jo gave Derrick a smiling gesture of disrespect. Bus-driver humor.

Just another Friday night at the bar.

A dark and stormy night. Near whiteout conditions. A woman alone. With a baby.

A baby that could be his.

He dropped his booted feet to the floor.

Ty's head came up. He assessed the situation with goalie-like speed. "Don't do it. Don't ask her to stay at your place."

"Why not?"

Gideon stepped into Coop's path, keeping his voice low. "Even the Moose Motel is better than your place."

Coop had expected advice about keeping his distance from Nora until he knew that baby was his. He hadn't expected criticism of his home. "Are you kidding me right now? Free accommodations? She'll be grateful."

“She’ll think you’re incapable of looking after yourself.” Ty made a sweeping gesture that encompassed Nora, the baby and then Coop. “Look at her and then take a good, long look at your scruffy, backwoods self.”

“If that’s a commentary about my beard—”

“Who cares about your weak attempts at facial hair?” Gideon had on his banker face, which was also his poker face, which was also his don’t-be-a-doofus face. “Your place is a dump. Duct-taped carpeting, leaky faucet, creaky floors.”

“It’s warm and dry. I can sell it or abandon it if I ever get out of this town.” That’d been the reason he’d taken it in trade for an RV he’d been unable to move on the car lot. “My place is free for Nora. Don’t forget free.”

“You’ll be amazed at what a woman won’t forget.” Ty’s gaze drifted back to the *Anchorage Beat*. “Whatever. That’s the second bad decision you’ve made tonight. Let’s just hope you don’t make a third.”

CHAPTER THREE

"HOME SWEET HOME." Coop opened the door for Nora and stepped aside.

Nora had been giving Coop points for a nice truck. No rust-eaten side panels. No dented fenders. No crumpled fast-food wrappers. And he'd driven competently on the snowy roads and through the storm.

But the house…

A dark and dated mobile home. Subtract ten points.

Duct tape across the foyer carpet and on the transition to kitchen linoleum. Subtract twenty points.

The shabby, sagging furniture and dreary lighting, the bigger-than-big-screen television, the mess of boots and shoes by the door, the stack of empty soda cans next to the sink. Subtract forty points.

Her backpack dropped to the ground. If Coop lived like this, how could he afford child support?

"That you, Cooper?" A scratchy, sleepy male voice erupted from the back at loud-speaker volume.

Zoe startled, jerking against Nora's torso beneath her parka. Nora slid the zipper down, preparing to get settled in. What choice did she have but to stay?

"Yeah, Pop. I brought home a guest," Coop shouted. He shoved a workout bag beneath a storage bench, nudged a jumble of shoes and boots against the wall, hung up his jacket and another that was on the carpet. "My dad moved in a couple years ago. He couldn't live alone after the accident."

The floor creaked in a back room. Coop's father appeared in the hallway, leaning heavily on a cane with a hand that had no fingers.

Nora gave Coop all his dark-mobile-home, worn-living-room and bad-housekeeping points back.

The older Mr. Hamilton had short, peppery hair and the spotted, leathery complexion of a fisherman. His steps were stilted—he walked with his gaze on the carpet in front of his feet—and he spoke like a ringmaster whose microphone had died. "If it's Gideon, I didn't get the dishes done today and the week's recycling is still on the counter. Got busy watching my shows and—"

"Pop—*Brad*, this is Nora," Coop said at baby-waking volume. He stopped cleaning. Stopped moving. Stopped looking like a man who made the world go around with his smile. He looked like a boy about to tell his father he'd been in a playground fight and broken his best friend's nose. "She's, um…"

Nora tried to shrug out of her parka so she could remove a stirring Zoe from the baby carrier. Coop helped her get free, allowing Nora to slide the carrier straps to her elbows and cradle Zoe.

"Well, I'll be," the older man said as he slowly worked his way to her. He laid the hand with a complete set of fingers on Zoe's head. "She's got the Hamilton nose." His sharp green gaze turned on Coop. "Haven't seen these two in K-Bay before."

"Me, either." Coop managed to sound both rebellious and repentant at the same time.

Nora resented them talking about her as if she wasn't standing there holding the next generation of Hamilton genes. "I'm from Anchorage."

"Forgiving my son and movin' here, I hope." Brad smiled, making Nora realize where Coop had gotten his forgive-me-any-sin smile. For some reason on the older man it didn't seem so slick. "Family should stick together. It's hard to raise a child on your own. I should know." He moved with a hitching gait toward a recliner.

"Paternity hasn't been proved." Coop cinched the bag of kitchen trash and tossed it out a side door.

"Have you seen this baby's nose?" Brad waved his arms, sending the chair rocking.

Nora gave Coop twenty bonus points for having a decent dad. But she had to be firm about things. "It's his, but I'm not moving here." She had a life in Anchorage: a secretarial job at a high school, benefits, brothers, friends.

"It's too early to say that. Newborns are easy. Wait until she's two." Brad sat in a grubby tan recliner with a breath-stealing, free-fall backward style. "Prepare the extra room, Cooper."

Coop had already disappeared down the hallway.

"Sit, Nora, and tell me all about my grandchild." Brad spoke so loud that Nora suspected he was hearing impaired.

She took a seat on the couch near him, placing the carrier next to her, and said in a loud voice, "This is Zoe. She's five weeks old."

"Wait a second." Brad held up his fingerless hand and bellowed, "Cooper?"

"Yeah?"

"I had a phone call earlier. What's this nonsense I hear about you being a matchmaker?"

Coop? A matchmaker? Shades of her father.

"It's not nonsense, Pop."

"What you know about love could be written on a postage stamp." Brad turned to Nora, his expression apologetic. "Best you know the truth, missy."

"Preaching to the choir," she murmured.

Zoe blew out a frustrated breath, perhaps sticking up for her father but more likely demanding Nora's attention since her little arms waved with rock-concert fervor.

"I'm not as clueless about love as you think." Coop appeared in the hallway, arms loaded with folded sheets and bed pillows. "I know you and Suzy Adams have a thing for each other."

"That's not a *thing*." Brad wrestled with the recliner's footrest handle, moving nothing. "It's a weekly lunch and occasional movie."

Coop cocked one dark eyebrow. "Do you pay?"

"What kind of a man do you think I am?"

Brad let go of the handle long enough to shake his fist at the heavens. "Of course I pay."

"It's a thing." Coop went into the other room.

"It's not a thing," Brad shouted louder than usual, finally moving the footrest out.

"It kind of sounds like a thing," Nora said apologetically.

Zoe made excited puffing noises of agreement.

"I can't have a thing. Just look at me." Granted, Brad was reclining, but he looked fine to her. He looked more than fine when he pulled out that Hamilton smile. No wonder he and Suzy Adams had a thing.

The heater kicked on with a house-shaking, window-rattling thud, reminding Nora of her father's run-down home and that, no matter how charismatic the Hamiltons were, this was no place for her baby.

"We need a game plan," Ty said to Coop and Gideon the next morning at the Bar & Grill.

Coach was open for Saturday breakfast to the citizens venturing out in the inclement weather. The blizzard had abated to heavy snowfall and the town's sole plow had been busy since the early morning. Many people in K-Bay regarded snowstorms as no more than an annoyance in their otherwise regular routine. Businesses that were open—including matchmaking—were going to get customers.

Coop and Gideon had wisely waited for Ty to finish his first cup of coffee before beginning the matchmaking strategy session. But that left Coop thinking about Nora and her baby.

Nora, who'd gotten more attractive since he'd last seen her, was nice to Pop and watched over that baby like a mama polar bear over its cub. She'd made a face when he'd first brought her home, but she hadn't complained or put down the place. Still, Nora hadn't said a word about what she wanted from him other than a reference to money. Thankfully, she didn't seem to be looking for a wedding ring. Because marriage didn't fit with Coop's lifestyle; the one that made it easy for him to pick up and leave.

Just last year, Becky Riney had turned up pregnant and demanded Wally Spitacker marry her, even though they'd never been serious about each other beyond being friends with benefits. That marriage lasted about two seconds and cost Wally a used minivan sold to him by Coop, a couple grand for the wedding reception and a couple grand in legal fees.

Until Coop was 100 percent certain it was his kid, he didn't want to talk child support or his visitation or…well…anything.

"I think we should ask people questions about what they want in a mate." Gideon tugged the buttoned collar of his polo shirt down as if he missed his uptight banker's tie.

"Can we not use the word *mate*?" Coop said, thinking of Nora.

"Significant other? Person of interest?" Gideon sounded testy and looked as if he hadn't slept well.

Coop couldn't cast stones. He hadn't slept well, either. Was he finally getting out of town? Or was this chance going to slip through his fingers?

"We need six matches." Ty's eyebrows had a grim slant. "Six, not three. For the life of me, I can't come up with a plan."

"Your plans weren't always good ones." Coop referred to choices Ty had made at eighteen that had scarred him for life. "When I want to get a sales boost at the car lot, I park the flashiest, most expensive car right next to the street. Doesn't matter if they don't buy it. Chances are if they come to look, I can get them to buy what they need. And the flashiest woman in town is—"

"Tatiana." A slow grin appeared in the depths of Ty's beard.

Tatiana Michaels was just back from college and in training to be the town queen bee. Men either ran to please her with the knowledge she'd chew them up and spit them out, or they ran from her because they valued their wallets and their pride. Either way, she was the flashiest, most notorious single woman in K-Bay.

Coach slid three plates loaded with campfire scramble specials in front of them. "Tatiana isn't going to ring that bell." The bar owner called out a greeting to Derrick before disappearing into the kitchen once more.

"Coach is right." Gideon peppered his food. "Isn't using Tatiana bait and switch?"

"If Tatiana agrees to sign up for matchmaking, who's to say one of our male clients wouldn't be the perfect match for her?" Coop really needed to believe his own sales pitch. "Once we let it be known Tatiana signed up, men and women will come to us in droves."

"K-Bay doesn't have droves of singles." Ty set down his egg-loaded fork, back to looking grim. "At least not singles I'd consider eligible."

"Work with me here." Coop needed his friends to jump on board. Granted, Ty had more of a reputation at stake than Coop or Gideon, but they needed to choose a direction and go for it, not snipe at each other. "Once they sign up, Gideon can give them his love survey."

"I wouldn't call it a love survey," Gideon mumbled. "Or even a survey at this point."

"Regardless—" Coop shot them with a look that had sent many a new hire racing out to sell a car "—we need to make a list of all the singles in town and get them down here. Now. Today, while nothing else is going on."

"Does Mary Jo count as single?" Ty nodded toward the door where the bus driver was entering. "Her divorce isn't final."

"Put her on the list." They needed all the single and nearly single females they could recruit. "How soon can you print up a survey, Gideon?"

"I need to do a little research." Gideon reached down and produced a stack of magazines from his computer bag. "These seem like a good place to start." He dropped them on the bar. "But if Nadine at the grocery store gives me any more grief about buying them, I'm going to say I was shopping for you two."

"I hope you told her what we're doing. She's single." Ty picked up the magazine on top. His grimness disappeared behind a wide grin. “Five Things He Wants You to Do in the Bedroom. Are you sure this is the right research material?”

“I’ll work on it.” Gideon swiped the magazine back.

“I have complete faith in your vision and geekiness.” Ty’s grin gave Coop hope. Short-lived as it was, because Ty excelled at poking holes in a plan. “Let’s just assume we have a list of singles interested in finding The One and a survey that helps us match them to potential soul mates. How do we get our clients to realize they’ve found true love in the same dating pool they’ve had available for years? I mean, they have only three weeks to fall in love and ring the bell.”

“Impossible.” Coach cheerfully refilled their coffee mugs. “You boys are going to lose.”

The three fell silent. Gideon pushed eggs around his plate. Ty sought answers in his coffee mug.

Coop clutched his fork, refusing to go down without a fight. Matchmaking couldn’t be harder than selling cars. With the right vehicle inventory, he could sell anything to… “We’ll draw from the neighboring towns and the university.” People drove for miles to find the vehicle they wanted. Why wouldn't they drive miles for true love? "And then we'll have the dates take each other for a test-drive."

Ty nearly choked on his coffee. "We're not running an escort service."

"I don't mean *that* kind of test-drive. I mean forcing them to spend time together." That didn't sound romantic at all. Coop squished his eggs into a chunk of potato.

The bar was slowly filling up.

"People lead busy lives," Gideon said. "Arranging these dates could take more time than we have. Unless..."

Ty and Coop turned to their friend expectantly. Being buddies since elementary school meant they knew better than to interrupt Gideon's thought process.

"We organize group activities. Preplanned. Pair people up in advance." Gideon had a gleam in his eyes that indicated he was on to gold. "Activities like a... I don't know. A boat trip?"

"It's dead of winter," Ty said before Coop could.

"Hiking? The views from the mountains are romantic." Gideon's cheeks colored slightly. "Or so I've heard."

"Again, dead of winter." Ty, Mr. Glass Half Empty.

"A test-drive..." Gideon's gaze turned distant. "Of course! An ATV excursion. Who doesn't love riding through the mountains on an ATV?"

Tatiana came to mind. But someone on the team had to be positive or they might just as well start listing reasons why they loved Alaska. "Awesome idea, Gideon. We could come to the bar afterward for—"

"If you say karaoke, I'll slug you." Ty pushed his plate away, scowling.

"A mixer." Coop gave Ty's shoulder an encouraging shake, hoping to get rid of some of his own doubts. "You said you wanted a plan. Now we have one." When Ty's scowl didn't lessen, he added, "We've always said we can do anything together."

"Coop's right." Gideon raised his coffee cup for a group toast. "Here's to our sunny, snowless future in the Lower 48."

Coop raised his mug. "What do you say? Are you in, Ty?" They'd be sunk without him.

"This is crazy." Ty blew out a breath. "Okay, I'll try not to let you down."

They clinked mugs.

"We're all in." Coop took a sip of strong

black coffee, feeling more confident than he had since they'd made the bet. "Now, about that list of singles..."

"I'M RALLYING THE TROOPS!" Pop entered the Bar & Grill with an unsteady shuffle, a gust of wind and Nora. "Since the snow's not letting up, I decided it'd be easier to create a baby command center here."

"Pop." Coop made a turn-down-the-volume gesture with both hands. "What is a baby command center?" And why did Nora show up every time Coop felt as if his dreams were within reach?

"The storm ain't moving. And my grandchild needs things." Pop tottered to a booth and claimed it with his usual fast, plunk-his-butt-down MO.

Almost immediately the door to the bar opened and married women began streaming in as if it was Black Friday at the mercantile. The invasion silenced the bar's regulars. They brought clothes for Nora and the baby, bassinets and car seats, curiosity and advice. Lots and lots of advice, which quickly turned to stories that made Coop's stomach turn.

"My baby had the worst colic," one woman

said. "He screamed so loud the neighbors thought we were torturing him."

"Talk about screams." Another built upon the building drama. "My Frank had an impacted tooth. Ruptured his gums like a seam ripping on my husband's pants. I thought he'd bleed out before we made it to the doctor."

Nora's smile looked strained. And who could blame her? This was just like the time Coop hired Bobby Evans to help him sell cars. Bobby knew a lot about cars and engines and manufacturer reliability records. He knew nothing about when to shut up. The only car Bobby had sold in his four-week tenure was to his mother.

The tension in Nora's expression, combined with the way she held the baby protectively to her chest, unleashed boundary-making, protective instincts Coop didn't know he had.

He crossed the bar and began negotiating a path through the crowd of perfumed women in parkas. They barely budged. At this rate he'd reach Nora by Valentine's Day.

There was nothing like a baby to attract a lot of women. It was like flies being drawn to honey. "Ladies, please step back. I'm a man who needs to see a baby." He very carefully didn't claim Nora's child as his own.

Worked like a charm. The crowd melted away like room-temperature butter for a hot knife. The women oohed and aahed and patted Coop's shoulder as if he'd done something truly wonderful.

Kind of made him feel like a cad.

"Cooper wants to hold his baby." Mrs. Begay topped her statement with a romantic sigh. She'd bought a SUV from him last summer and, on his advice, had special ordered the expensive snow tires that had no doubt carried her here.

Mrs. Harrison, who'd never bought a car from Coop, was a grandmother of five and had been his third-grade teacher. She moved slowly out of his way, watching him from behind cat-eye glasses as if he was still a troublemaking third-grader. "About time someone caught you doing something naughty."

Feeling kindly, Coop said, "You were right, Mrs. H. I was the one who replaced your glue with mayonnaise."

That brought a smile to her plump cheeks. "I knew it! Do you know? No little boy has caused as much mischief in my classroom as you did."

"I take that as a compliment." And he expected her next car purchase to be from him.

Mrs. Tsosie, who ran the local newspaper almost single-handedly and had purchased her last truck from Coop, produced a serious-looking black camera with a lens the size of a bourbon bottle. "I want a picture of this reformed bachelor holding his baby."

Reformed? That meant he'd be stuck in Kenkamken Bay forever.

"Oh, no." Coop's laughter sounded as hollow as his forgotten dreams. "We're not taking out a mortgage or anything."

In the booth, Pop frowned. Across from him, Nora rolled her eyes. Someone in the back of the group said, "I told you so."

Coop clung to his smile and his bachelor's shallow pride.

"It doesn't matter," Mrs. Tsosie said. "Now that you're a dad, we'll be seeing more of you in church and less of you in the bar."

Coach's laughter penetrated the crowd, penetrated Coop's car-salesman-thick skin, penetrated his normally unshakable smile. Coop resented the implication that his whole way of life would change with fatherhood, resented it with patience-snapping intensity.

But before he could say fatherhood wouldn't change him, Mrs. Tsosie said, "Go on. Hold your daughter."

Your daughter.

A small tremor passed through Coop's biceps and headed toward his hands. Probably, he'd lifted weights too hard yesterday morning. There was no way that tremor and the one that started in his quads and moved behind his knees had anything to do with nerves about trying something new. Coop was always the first one to jump off a bridge on a bungee cord or to test-drive a new vehicle in bad weather.

And yet…the baby in Nora's arms waved a tiny fist. It was the first time he'd seen the baby move.

Coop's step faltered. He grabbed on to Mary Jo's shoulder.

The almost divorced mother of two met his gaze with weary brown eyes. "You'll be fine."

Coop's gaze moved to Nora's. Her soft blue eyes were also dark rimmed, but there was something else in her gaze, something that caused Coop's hand to drop and his feet to move forward. That gaze said, "Stay away from me. From us."

Who was she to keep him away? Kids needed parents. If the baby was his…

Regret did a gut-stomping two-step with defeat, dancing right over his big plans.

Coop took a deep breath, trying to slow the

dance, trying to keep the dream alive, trying to shut up the annoying, upstanding side of his character that whispered about accepting responsibility for his actions. Finally, he reached the booth where Pop and Nora sat. "I want to hold her."

There was reluctance in Nora's eyes. He hadn't asked to hold the baby at all yesterday and now she didn't trust him. That look. She'd almost shot him down with it the night they'd met. She'd been hard to get—no playing. She'd made him work at winning her over, claiming at first that she only wanted to share some laughs and dance. But the more they'd laughed and danced, the more Coop had wanted. More conversations, more kisses, more Nora.

"Sit." She nodded toward the bench beside her. "If you must."

He sat, feeling weak and light-headed once more. Had to be the press of bodies and the four-inch-wide camera lens aimed his way. "I've never held a baby before."

"I'm beginning to think I raised you wrong," Pop announced loudly, as if Coop sat at the bar and not four feet away. "Playing the field all the time and not even knowing how to care for one of your own."

"Pop, please shut up."

Nora's cheeks were as pink as the baby's blanket. "It's easy. Bend your arms as though I'm handing you a football. Hold them a little higher than your breadbasket." Nora jiggled the baby so he could see how to position his arms. Her instructions were softly spoken, but her eyes… Her eyes warned of dire consequences if he dropped the ball—er, baby.

Mrs. Tsosie snapped a picture.

Coop held out his arms. "Football metaphors?"

"Two older brothers." Nora slipped the small pink bundle into his arms. "I could switch to truck engines or hockey if you prefer. I also throw a mean knuckleball."

Well, what do you know? Despite how she'd filled out her dress when they'd first met, Nora was grow-on-you gorgeous *and* a tomboy.

Coop couldn't seem to look away from her pert nose, her delicate mouth or her painfully truthful eyes. They were as blue as an Alaskan summer sky. Despite her tomboy declaration, she wore jeans and a yellow blouse that had style. She wasn't intimidating in her femininity, like Tatiana. She was approachable, like the girl you asked to help you with algebra homework.

The proverbial football he held squirmed

and waved a tiny fist toward his chin, demanding he give her some attention. The baby's tiny head rested in the crook of his elbow. Her body fit the length of his forearm, the pink blanket soft against his skin. Everything about her seemed like a perfect miniature of her mother. She opened dark blue eyes over a now familiar-looking nose and stared up at him, huffing and waving her fist once more.

"I didn't mean to ignore you," he whispered in a voice that was suddenly husky.

The women oohed and aahed again. Mrs. Tsosie snapped more pictures.

When he made eye contact with her, Zoe wiggled and blew spit bubbles.

"Show off." Coop felt something in his chest shift. He was used to women wanting his attention. What Coop wasn't used to was the feeling that this woman, this small female, was his. His to love by right. His to love by responsibility. His to love because she was so flippin' adorable.

"Dang, women," Pop said in his nearly shouting voice from the other side of the booth. "Give the man some space." He shooed them away.

Coop didn't see where his audience went. He only had eyes for the baby in his arms. His baby. He stroked her velvety cheek with the back of one finger and then traced the familiar Hamilton nose.

Zoe wrapped her tiny digits around his knuckle, blew out an I-wish-I-could-roll-my-eyes-at-you breath and squeezed.

Coop felt a corresponding pressure in his chest. In his heart. In the twisted strand of DNA that had passed on the good-parent gene from Pop. He had no idea what his daughter wanted, but whatever it was, he planned on giving it to her. "You don't need to pay for a paternity test. She's mine."

Nora reached for Zoe but Coop held her off with one hand.

Nora gathered herself, as if preparing for a score-stopping tackle. But when she spoke, her voice lacked its usual strength. "Don't get used to this. We're leaving as soon as bus service resumes. And then we're done."

Bachelor Coop… Car salesman Coop… Those parts of him felt relief.

But there was a new Coop in town. And that Coop felt a breath-stealing depression at the thought of never seeing Zoe again.

CHAPTER FOUR

THE WAY COOP had been giving Zoe a wide berth, Nora would never have predicted he'd fall in love with her.

But there was the proof in his lovesick gaze. In the way he held Zoe close. In the way he whispered, "That's a great grip for a hockey stick."

Fifty points for having a heart.

The crowd of mothers standing in the middle of the bar laughed and exchanged stories of moments when their men had realized being a father wasn't the end of the world. It was much preferable to their stories of sick, bleeding babies.

"Hey, Ty," Coop said. "Come check out my kid's grip." He spoke with pride, as if no other baby could possibly hold on to his finger as tightly as Zoe.

Nora wanted to snatch her baby back. She wasn't here to share Zoe with an irresponsible drunk. Coop had come to the bar before noon!

"She's just a normal baby." Nora brushed her hair behind her ear and tried to ignore the bitter taste of fear at the back of her throat. She wasn't about to let Coop get visitation and hurt Zoe with promises he never intended to keep and hopes that were constantly dashed. "That's enough."

But Coop had the new-daddy bug. He stood and walked around the bar, showing off Zoe to whoever would let him. And many did. The bar was filling up.

Nora cradled her forehead in her hands, staring at the scratched and scuffed tabletop. Fifty points for being a proud dad. Another fifty because he was acting on faith by claiming Zoe as his. Despite the positives, tension gripped her forehead with a vicious *pound-pound-pound.* She wanted to be taking points away, not giving them.

"Let him have his moment," Brad said at an abnormal—for him—normal volume.

Nora brought her head up, clasping her hands tight enough to crack a walnut. "This moment won't last. Coop doesn't realize that raising a child is about more than showing up on Christmas morning with a gift."

Brad's brow furrowed. "Cooper isn't like that."

"He is." Nora unknotted her hands. This visit wasn't about her. "He doesn't want to be a dad. He doesn't even know what that means."

"He doesn't know what he *wants*," Brad countered, still using that normal-volume voice, which probably served as his whisper. "You've had months to get used to the idea of being a parent. Give him time."

Zoe was becoming fussy, waving her fists and giving an occasional, demanding shout.

Coop hurried back to their table, dodging a bassinet and basket of baby clothes. "What's wrong with her? Did I do something wrong?"

"She's hungry." Nora dug in her backpack for a blanket, feeling her milk let down.

"That's my cue to leave." Brad edged out of the booth. "Suzy? When did you get here?"

"I'll feed her." Coop held out a hand.

He was clueless. He hadn't paid enough attention to either of them since they'd arrived. "Biologically, you can't feed her. She's breast fed." Although Nora had been intrigued by a breast pump one of the women had brought. It would be nice to have a spare bottle for those times, rare as they'd been—knock on wood—that Nora had been too tense for her milk to come down.

"Okay." Coop transferred Zoe into Nora's

arms and sat across from her. "I'll be right here when you're done."

"I'm not going anywhere." Nora slung the flannel blanket over her shoulder, draped it across Zoe and reached beneath it for the buttons of her blouse.

"You don't mean to do *that* here? Now?" Coop's gaze darted around the room, seeming to log every male in the vicinity. "I mean, you did it last night, but there are more people here today."

Sensing it was feeding time, Zoe kicked and gave an impatient shout. Coop stared at the undulating blanket and then leaped to his feet to stand in front of Nora, blocking her from the view of most patrons with his broad shoulders.

His Sir Galahad moment gave Nora pause, as did the way his long dark hair brushed his blue flannel collar. She remembered the texture of his hair. It was as soft as Zoe's. She remembered being held. His arms were strong and steady. Why did he have to be so sigh worthy?

Thankfully, before Nora lost herself to further fantasy, the mood in the bar seemed to shift. Conversation stalled. Footsteps approached their table.

"Hey, Tatiana," Coop said coolly. "Thanks

for coming down. Can you wait for me at the bar?"

A young woman with teased and curled black hair slipped into the booth and sat across from Nora. She was gorgeous, rail thin and seemed entitled, if her intense scrutiny of Nora was any indication. She was just the kind of woman Coop would want at his side. The kind of woman Nora had pretended to be the night they'd met: polished, sophisticated, feminine.

A shaft of jealousy pierced Nora's chest. Coop had asked Tatiana to meet him at the bar. She couldn't even subtract points. This wasn't about following her heart and giving up her body on a believe-in-love-at-first-sight whim. It wasn't about telling herself in a bar that the earth had shifted and the stars had aligned and by some twist of fate she'd met The One. Coop wasn't hers to be jealous over.

"A baby from the Heartbreakers' Trinity," Tatiana said in a voice as smooth as her cherry-bomb-red lipstick. "I had to see if it was an angel or a devil that brought you down, Coop."

Nora stopped peeking under the blanket to see if Zoe had fallen asleep or was just taking a break. "Excuse me?"

"The Heartbreakers' Trinity is what we local women call Ty, Gideon and Coop." Tatiana's smile wasn't lady-killer hateful. It was almost…wistful. "Three gorgeous, unattainable guys. Many have tried. None have succeeded. And yet here you are." She glanced up at Coop. "I'm disappointed."

Nora felt every extra pound of baby weight tackle her feminine pride and pound it into the mud. "He's not mine," she managed to say, feeling a cold draft swirl around her ankles. Did no one in this town stay home in a snowstorm?

"But you did catch him." Tatiana's gaze turned appraising.

"On accident, I assure you." Nora wished Zoe would finish, wished Tatiana would go away, wished the snow would let up. None of which happened.

Coop glanced over his shoulder. "All right, then," he muttered and then raised his voice. "Ladies, thank you for coming to the grand opening of Trinity Matchmaking. We're going to help you find your happily-ever-after. Who wants to sign up first?"

"That depends," Tatiana said slyly, still appraising Nora. "Are you an eligible bachelor, Coop? Or are you offering someone like Mike Lopes?" She pointed to a long-bearded man near the window. "Because if it's Mike, I'm out."

"Agreed," said a woman wearing the thickest pair of false eyelashes Nora had ever seen.

"Hey, I'm offended." Mike frowned. Or he might have frowned. Hard to tell behind his bushy beard.

"Let's not objectify each other based on appearances," Coop said with a surprising amount of authority. "We're going to have you take a survey that identifies what you're looking for in a soul mate and predicts who best fits your dreams."

"We're in test mode," Gideon admitted from the bar, avoiding eye contact with just about everyone. "So we may ask you to take the survey more than once as we refine the algorithm."

"And to make things less awkward, because we all know how uncomfortable dating can be..." Coop worked that smile of his for all it was worth. "We're planning group excursions where we'll pair you up with potential matches. Matches you should know today if you sign up."

Gideon frowned, looking as if he wanted to take that last sales promise back.

"And during our introductory period, sign-ups are free." Ty held up a clipboard. "What have you got to lose?"

Nora had the distinct impression that the would-be matchmakers were flying by the seat of their pants. There was something about Coop's smile that was strained, Gideon's gaze that was nervous and Ty's voice with its forced cheer. It was her father all over again. Still, they had some takers. People were moving toward Ty.

"Our first event is next Saturday morning," Ty was saying. "An ATV trail ride."

"Tell all your friends." Gideon smiled like a college intern giving his first sweaty-palmed business presentation.

"All your *single* friends." Coop broadened his still-fake smile.

Nora was almost sorry she was going to miss their event. Not the part involving ATVs, but the part involving these three bachelors convincing this group of set-in-their-ways singles that they'd found their perfect match.

"NORA, CAN YOU fill out a survey for me?" Gideon asked thirty minutes after they'd officially opened for business when, *miraculously*, they hadn't been laughed out of the bar.

The question left Coop feeling as though

he'd been checked from behind and slammed into a wall. "Not her."

"Why not?" Gideon glanced up from his laptop.

Coop couldn't look Gideon in the eye. "She's not exactly single."

"I am single and I'd be happy to fill it out." Nora had Zoe on her shoulder and was walking an imaginary track around the bar with a bounce in her step. She stopped next to Gideon's bar stool. "But it's only a test. I'm leaving as soon as the bus is cleared to go."

"You, too, Coop." Gideon handed him a sheet of paper.

Coop stared at the survey in horror. "Why do I have to fill one out?"

"Because if my survey matches you with Tatiana, we'll know the algorithm isn't working." Gideon left them to pass out more tests.

"Ah." Nora's smile was too knowing. "Tatiana broke your heart."

"It was more like a head-on train wreck. She's several years younger than me and sneaked into my bedroom one summer night minus a layer or two of clothes." He'd reacted to the ambush with horror and a firm rejection. "I haven't slept with the window open since." He watched Nora burp the baby the way he'd watched Coach demonstrate a new hockey move back in the day: with a keen desire to learn. "Have you ever had your heart broken?"

"Not by a guy." Nora must have realized how odd that sounded because she quickly added, "By my dad. He was a charmer, a frivolous dreamer and a drunk like…"

"Like me." Coop couldn't keep the bitterness from his voice. "You were going to say like me."

She almost looked remorseful. Almost. "What am I supposed to think? We met in a bar. You charmed my heels off and never called me back." She glanced around. "You hang out in a bar all day. And you probably think matchmaking is an easy way to riches."

"You don't pull any punches, do you?"

He almost wished she would. "You haven't even looked under my hood to see what kind of man I am." Lately. But it wasn't an issue of how well they knew each other physically. "First off, there aren't too many places to hang out in K-Bay, especially in winter. Second, you may have noticed I'm drinking water. And third, if I have anything alcoholic here, it's one light beer and only a couple of times a week." He sounded far too serious, as if he cared about her opinion. His habits were none of her business. And yet he didn't stop there. "As for frivolous dreams and matchmaking, I've always wanted to leave Alaska. I almost made it once on Ty's coattails. And I almost made it away to college."

"What happened?"

"Ty nearly died in a hockey accident and then Pop nearly died in a fishing accident. I couldn't leave either one." And now, when he was on the verge of leaving again, he was a father.

In Nora's arms, Zoe drew her little legs up and released them like a leaping frog. She made an indelicate grunting noise.

"What's happening?" Coop was filled with the need to comfort the baby. "Do you need me to take her?"

"She's about to mess her pants." The way Nora said it implied he had no idea how to change a diaper, not that he could argue with that. "I'd let you take her, but he who holds the baby when she goes," Nora said in a soft croon, "changes the baby when she goes."

Zoe repeated her frog-leg movements and grunted some more.

"Just because I hang out in a bar doesn't mean I can't change a diaper." Brave words for a confirmed bachelor. "I know how to properly strap in a car seat. I know the importance of a favorite pacifier." He didn't want to relive the day he'd learned that lesson at the car lot. "And I know moms need breaks." He held out his arms. "I'll risk it."

"It's a sure thing." Nora maneuvered Zoe for a transfer, but not before the baby pulled up her legs once more and made a sound that rivaled Pop after Beanie-Weenie night at the bar.

"On second thought." Coop took a quick step back. "This one's on you."

CHAPTER FIVE

"WE'RE IN TROUBLE." Gideon angled his laptop on the bar so Ty and Coop could see.

"What now?" Coop didn't think his nerves could take any more matchmaking drama. There was enough drama in his personal life.

Gideon tapped the screen with his pencil eraser. "Ty was matched with Tatiana—"

"No, dude." Ty hung his head. "No."

"—and Coop with Mary Jo."

There was a twang of something in Coop's chest. Disappointment? How could that be? Coop wasn't looking for love.

He glanced over at Nora, who was eating lunch with Mary Jo. She fit in easily with the crowd, as if she'd always belonged here. Zoe slept peacefully in a portable bassinet at her feet. The snow hadn't relented. Twenty feet in forty-eight hours. The single population of K-Bay that they'd managed to bring to the bar would be finishing up lunch soon. They'd be expecting to hear who their potential matches were for next Saturday. They'd want to leave, run errands and go home.

"The test was too shallow." Gideon clutched the placket of his polo as if it was a tie, stretching the fabric downward. "It didn't discriminate with enough precision."

"We're going to be the laughingstocks of the town." Ty chugged half his water.

"Nobody panic." Coop ignored the panic flipping through his stomach and removed Gideon's hand from its stranglehold. "We can say the computer crashed."

"What?" Gideon sputtered back to life. "That's like saying I'm incompetent."

Coop lowered his voice. "Then let's just announce their matches are a secret until the ATV event."

Nora brought her plate over to the counter. "Don't tell me. Let me guess. I was matched with Coach."

The elderly bar owner stopped filling soda glasses with ice and took Nora's measure. "You say that as if it's a bad thing."

"It's a bad thing because—" Gideon lowered his voice *"—you're married."*

"Then, you shouldn't have had me take the test." Coach flashed a mischievous grin at

Nora. "Keep in touch. Mabel could kick the bucket any day."

"And so could you if Mabel hears you talking like that." Ty glanced over his shoulder as if expecting Coach's wife to be there with a loaded shotgun.

"It didn't match you with Coach, Nora," Coop said wearily. It hadn't even matched her to him.

"That's a relief," Nora said with a pained expression. "I hate to tell you this, but your questions read like the ones from a list in a glossy magazine. I don't think I want to know who I was matched with."

Gideon snapped his laptop shut and glared at Ty, who did the back-away shrug and said, "They were your magazines."

"Ah, the sweet smell of disaster." Coach finished prepping his sodas and hefted his tray, leaving the trinity of matchmakers with Nora.

Nora considered their pathetic mugs far too long before saying anything else. "I told myself I wouldn't butt in. However… If you want to match people with their soul mates, maybe you need to think longer term than a one-nighter." At Coop's blank, shocked look, she added, "You didn't ask where I saw myself five or ten years from now. You didn't ask if I enjoyed cooking or gardening or puttering around a garage. Don't you think it helps if you have common interests?" Her gaze fell away from Coop's. "Women want fun, but in the end they all fall for a guy who does the dishes."

Gideon scribbled notes like mad.

"What about kids?" Coop blurted.

Ty stared at him as if he'd eaten a live goldfish.

"You need to be compatible there, too," Nora allowed. "Small family, large family, open to adoption. Do you want your kids to go to college? That kind of thing."

Gideon leaned forward, as intent as he'd ever been in Mr. Yazzie's algebra lectures. "What did you see in Coop when you met?"

Coop held his breath.

Nora surveyed Coop with a cool gaze that made him feel like an overpriced jacket in the midst of the clearance rack. "I went to the bar that night for fun. My mother had died and my father didn't show up for the funeral. Coop and I talked hockey and NASCAR. We laughed and danced. And I..." Her gaze drifted to Zoe.

Had Nora gone to the bar because she wanted a husband? A baby? Anything that would make Nora seem less than perfect? And ease the ever-increasing feeling that he'd made a mistake by leaving her that morning. "Go on."

"I wanted to feel special. And he did that." She met Coop's gaze squarely. "Until the next morning when he was gone."

Crap. She was a great person. Coop was the pathetic loser.

He'd given her a night that was exactly what she'd wanted, but he couldn't help but feel he hadn't come close to giving her what she'd really needed.

And he was now afraid he didn't know what that was.

"I COULD SIT HERE all night with this grandbaby," Brad practically shouted from his recliner. His volume didn't disturb a sleeping Zoe, even though he held her in his arms.

Outside, the snow still came down heavily, illuminated by streetlights.

Nora stood in the kitchen doing the dishes with Coop. "You're surprisingly domesticated for a bachelor." And she was entirely too comfortable being domestic with him. It was St. Patrick's Day all over again. There was just something about Coop that hoodwinked common sense. That urged her to trust. That said, "He's the one."

"When Pop was first injured, I had to make sure he had good nutrition." Coop washed dishes efficiently. He'd added the right amount of dish soap and had the proper sponge for the job. "Don't get me wrong. We eat a lot of meat and we only have a handful of vegetables we like." He handed her a plate. Their eyes met. Their hands touched.

Her heart beat faster.

Only because she nearly dropped the plate.

Wake up, common sense urged.

Her father was a drunk. He lied to cover his addiction. He lied to earn forgiveness for his insensitivity. He followed every promise of an easy buck, even if he had to spend ten to do so. But… Coop didn't seem to be a drunk. Sure, she imagined he exaggerated a bit to sell things, like cars and matchmaking services. But he wasn't an insensitive jerk. People in town cared for him. They watched his back. They wished him well.

Her trip here had seemed so simple. Show up, give Coop the paternity test, state her demands and make the last bus back to Anchorage.

But Coop was nothing like the man her broken heart had painted.

He was…

She was…

His gaze still held hers. "The snow may let up tomorrow." His eyes were full of promises that had nothing to do with babies and child support.

"And the bus will leave." She dragged her gaze away. "With us on it."

He washed the last plate. "How much time is left on your maternity leave?"

"I start back to work a week from Monday." There was too much longing in her voice. It was time to tell him the truth.

"I only came to find you to arrange for financial support. When my father was sober, which wasn't often, he felt it necessary to try to be a part of our lives, but he never fulfilled a promise. Not one." She took the last plate, carefully avoiding his touch. "Even so, every time he showed up, I was hopeful he'd changed. That he'd finally be the father I wanted." She forced herself to look at him, to make him understand why she couldn't listen to her heart and stay. "And every time, he broke my heart. I don't want that for Zoe."

Coop's eyes darkened to a stormy green. "I'm not some deadbeat who doesn't do what he says he's going to. Is that why you didn't tell me about Zoe?"

"You dumped me." She squared her shoulders. "Without so much as a text saying it was great but you weren't into long-distance relationships." Her throat was thick with hurt and battered hope, making it hard to speak, hard to be heard, hard to admit, "And then you didn't remember me."

"I'm not your father." Coop held her arms with soapy fingers, turning her to face him. "I'm just a guy who was dazzled by a beautiful woman and woke up scared."

"You?" *The man with the nothing-fazes-me smile?* "Scared?" The sharp edge of hurt she'd been carrying around in her heart for ten months dulled somewhat.

"We never talked about the future or our pasts." Coop lifted her chin with one wet finger. His eyes were soft and apologetic. His voice rough with remorse. "I had dreams of being a sports agent, making big bucks and living large. I had dreams of living in Malibu, driving a Porsche and being a man every woman wanted. And then Ty had his accident." He paused to clear his throat. "Now I'm a used-car salesman and a struggling matchmaker living in a mobile home with his dad. No woman wants that."

"In case you haven't noticed, you're a good-looking guy—" Overlooking the beard, which was growing on her. "With a steady job. Women give you points for that." Tatiana certainly did.

"Points? Like keeping score?" A hint of a grin teased the corners of his mouth. "I thought rating the opposite sex was something guys did."

Her cheeks heated. She stepped back and began putting dishes away. "I've heard some men rate women on their appearance at first glance. Don't even think about denying it," she said when he opened his mouth to do just that. "I've heard them. And..." She sounded guilty already. "Some women keep a running tally in order to judge a man's long-term potential."

"You do keep score." He released the sink plug. The water slurped and gurgled, taunting Nora as his laughter might have. "This is better than Gideon's survey."

"It's just a thing I do. It doesn't mean anything." There were no more dishes to put away. No more chores to hide behind.

"What's my score?" There was a teasing note to his voice, but there was also an underlying platform of seriousness.

Her hands knotted in the tea towel.

He slowly unwound the damp white material and replaced it with his now-dry hands. "Nora."

She stared at their hands, reminded of that night and of something she hadn't recalled, something she'd forgotten: his tenderness. "I don't actually keep score," she said, still in a place that was half memory, half here-and-now. "I give points when a man does something I like or admire, and I take points away when he does something I don't."

"My score, Nora." Resignation. He knew what was coming.

His deficit shouldn't have made her feel guilty. He was the one who'd run out on her. But there was his touch, his gentle smile, his broken dreams and his falling in love with Zoe.

"You don't have a score." She was a horrible liar.

His thumbs stroked the backs of her hands, an odd contrast to his jaw hardening beneath that scruffy dark beard. "I want a number."

"You don't have a score because…" She shouldn't tell him. They were getting along so well. Civility would help her negotiate child support. But a small part of her wanted him to know—with certainty—that his leaving had hurt her. "Because the amount of points you lost when you sneaked out the door is astronomical. I just can't trust a man like that." But she wanted to.

She expected Coop to release her. She expected him to turn away and scoff. She didn't expect him to pull her close, to look deep in her eyes or to press his whisker-fringed lips softly against hers.

She hadn't expected him to poke holes in her resolve to raise Zoe alone. But he did, with one too-brief kiss.

His point deficit was erased. Its use invalidated. The point system broken.

Coop stepped back. "I don't care about points or the past." He spoke in a low voice, one that set aside pride to make way for truths. "I'm responsible. And I won't run scared again. I could be responsible for—"

"Don't say it." Despite her words, she backed into the corner of the kitchen, waiting to hear what would next come out of his mouth.

"Stay, Nora." His gaze was guarded. His words as solemn as a wedding vow. "Stay until you're due back at work. Being a new mom is hard. Give me a chance to…to…spoil you a little."

To love you a little.

That was what Nora heard him say.

But she wasn't interested in loving a little. She'd had that with her dad.

And so she turned away.

But she didn't turn him down.

CHAPTER SIX

"I HAVE AN IDEA for your questionnaire," Coop said to Ty and Gideon the night after he'd kissed Nora.

The snow had let up but bus service had yet to resume. Nora had said nothing more about staying or going. Coop had told her the short version of his adult life, but he hadn't confessed the matchmaking was a bet. She'd chalk that up to one more bad behavior he shared with her dad. She'd dock him points. And he needed those points to qualify as dad material.

Coop rubbed his gritty eyes and scanned the bar patrons. "Let's ask them how they've been disappointed in love."

"Let me count the ways." Ty stared down a tall glass of ice water. "You'll blow up Gideon's program for real this time."

"I agree with Ty," Gideon said. "I can't just ask an open-ended question. I need a check box. A short list of check boxes."

"Why do you love Alaska?" Coach moved

toward the kitchen carrying a tray of dirty glasses and empty snack bowls. "That's easier to answer than the reasons for a broken heart. And you'll need to type that up when you lose this bet."

"He's right." Gideon sounded defeated.

"He's not. We're not losing." Coop showed them his phone and an article he'd found online. "Here are ten traits of a heartbreaker."

Ty leaned in for a closer look. "Too quick to make a connection with you. Doesn't call back after he scores. Can't remember your name after he buys you a drink. Doesn't remember you when he sees you again." Ty gave Coop an assessing look. "This could be you."

Coop tried to brush off Ty's conclusion. "It could be any of us."

Ty and Gideon shook their heads.

Okay, it was most likely Coop. Self-awareness sucked.

"I can't predict a man's behavior," Gideon pointed out. "And no man will admit to being a jerk."

"I will," Coop said, ignoring their dropping jaws. He couldn't be the only one remorseful about the past. "Where are we with the flyers for this weekend's ATV social?"

"I put some up at the grocery store and the

Laundromat." Gideon stared at Coop's cell phone, sounding distracted, which Coop took to mean the wheels in his brain were starting to spin.

"Ice rink. Sporting-goods store," Ty said. "But they aren't working other than to bring people in to see what madness we'll undertake next."

Coop had no idea what madness they'd do next.

"We've had about nine people sign up. Mostly guys," Gideon lamented. "For this to work, we need bachelorettes."

Coach came out of the kitchen and stopped in front of them. "I used to enjoy running this place with no one but my cousin Rafe and me. If you're going to consider this your home base, you need to help out." He handed Ty a roll of paper towels and a spray bottle of disinfectant. "Table four needs a wipe down."

"Why don't you hire someone?" The way Ty's chin was jutting, Coop bet Ty had more to say. He used to trash-talk with the best of them, but the former goalie was being civil.

"Because in three weeks you'll lose the bet and business will return to slow and steady. You and half the male population in this town will still be single."

"You might be surprised," Ty said tightly.

"Highly unlikely." Coach laughed and returned to the kitchen, but his lack of faith in them hovered overhead like a black rain cloud above Sky Hawk Mountain.

"I'd love to prove him wrong." Gideon wasn't one to start a fight. With a scowl and a determined edge to his tone, he certainly sounded ready to finish one.

As did Ty. "And then I'd love the three of us to take over one of his teams." He pounded a fist on the bar, but he might as well have been pounding his chest. "I'll make them winners. Gideon will make them solvent."

"Yep," Gideon said.

"And Coop will create a plan to sell more tickets than any other professional farm team." Ty's fist hit the bar one more time.

Nadine walked by wearing a hot pink sweater, which reminded Coop of Zoe, of Nora, of Pop and what he'd be missing if he left Alaska.

"Together. Right?" Ty slapped Gideon and Coop on the back.

"Right," Coop said with false enthusiasm.

"BRAD, WHAT EVER happened to your Mrs. Hamilton?" Nora was settled in the corner of Coop's couch, a sleeping Zoe snuggled in her arms.

Coop's father muted the big screen, looking as if he'd smelled one of Zoe's poopy diapers. "Kathy decided I wasn't the man for her. Then she decided Alaska wasn't the place for her. And then she decided being a mother wasn't the role for her." There was a coldness in his words that rivaled the below-freezing temperature outside. "I could have forgiven her everything but the last."

Nora brought Zoe a little closer. Poor Coop. "How old was he?"

"Nine." The older man cleared his throat. "He'd always been the outgoing, trusting type, but that…that changed him. He was only outgoing after that. Other than Gideon and Ty, he didn't let people get close."

"No one?"

"No one."

And yet he'd asked Nora to stay.

Because of Zoe. It had to be because of Zoe.

But there was that kiss…

The volume on the television went back up. Zoe blew a gentle bubble in her sleep.

And Nora couldn't stop thinking about a little boy with a broken heart and an infectious smile.

THE CROWD OF singles for the ATV social was promising: six women and nine men, including the three matchmakers. They had many other candidates that couldn't make the event. Talk and laughter greeted the dawn.

Gideon moved discreetly between their clients, mentioning names the refined survey had suggested might be their soul mates. With the supplemental test, Coop had been paired with Nora, which gave Coop an annoying feeling of warmth in his chest. Love and responsibility had kept him in K-Bay the last time he tried to leave. He wouldn't let a third chance pass him by, even if it meant risking a relationship with his daughter. Coop had to take this one last shot at greatness.

He and Nora had fallen into an easy rhythm during the week since she'd come to K-Bay. Coop made coffee in the early morning when Zoe awoke and wanted breakfast. After her feeding, he walked and burped the baby while Nora ate. The snow had let up enough to reopen the car lot. Coop came home for lunch. He cooked dinner. He took Nora and the baby to the bar for an hour or so in the evening for informal mixers. But there'd been no more kisses, no more getting carried away on Coop's part and nearly promising Nora more than he could give.

Nope. They talked about inconsequential

things, as if they worked in the same office together. He didn't admit he couldn't stop thinking about fatherhood. She didn't admit he continued to fall short of her fatherhood standards. And Coop was relieved because he didn't have to choose between his dreams and responsibility.

"Not him." The distaste in Tatiana's rising voice killed the positive energy of the ATV crowd. "I've dated beards like that. Never again will these cheeks receive beard burns."

Almost as one, the men placed hands over their bearded chins, even Coop.

A week. They'd been at this a week and no one had rung the bell. And no one would today if Tatiana kept this up.

Gideon drew Tatiana aside and spoke to her in a low voice. The women tried to pretend there was no tension in the air. The sun was out and the snow was melting, especially on the southern mountain trail they planned to ride today. Everything seemed promising except for Tatiana, who was playing Princess Pouty. And Ty, who was pacing.

Nora stood outside the Bar & Grill, shading Zoe's eyes from the bright morning sunshine.

Time to get this show on the off-road. "I need everyone in the Suburbans. Ladies, you need to sit with one of the men Gideon brought to your attention." Coop had taken two large SUVs off his lot and rented two large trailers, which he'd filled with every two-seater ATV he could borrow or rent in town.

The day wasn't all about matchmaking. He was hoping to sell a Suburban to Mike. It was large enough he could take all his fishing buddies in the eight-seater. Coop was also hoping for a kiss for luck from Nora. One without strings.

He had a better chance of selling a Suburban.

"What time will you be back?" Nora asked when Coop came to say goodbye.

"Worried about me?" The wind whistled between the buildings. Coop adjusted Zoe's stocking cap more firmly around her little ears.

"I'm a mother. I worry about everything." At his frown she added, "I worry this matchmaking thing is going to blow up in your face. And I'm worried someone out here is going to get their feelings hurt."

Mine. When you leave and take Zoe.

He had a thing for her. Couldn't she tell? The wind reached its cold hands inside his jacket and shook the material, covering up Coop's shock at the increasingly strong sentiment that he didn't want Nora and Zoe to go.

"If you and your friends are serious about matchmaking, you should charge for these things." She half turned away from him, sheltering Zoe from the wind.

"We're serious." About winning the bet and getting out of Alaska. "This kind of work can open doors for us."

"I hope you don't mean bedroom doors." Her smile sparkled as bright as sunshine on a snowdrift.

Would Nora want to leave? To go through that open door with him? "Have you ever thought about moving away from Alaska?"

"No." Her brow furrowed. "Why would I? My older brothers live here."

The hopes he hadn't acknowledged fell. Nora wanted to stay. He wanted to go. Yet he couldn't quite let loose the idea. "What if there was a job waiting for you in another state?"

Her gaze turned suspicious. "I thought you were serious about the matchmaker business, about building something and…"

"I am, but I'm also not close-minded about better jobs elsewhere." And then he made a tactical error. "We made a bet with Coach about the matchmaking and if we win…"

"You made a bet involving a job?" Clouds of frost emitted from her mouth and chilled him. "Is this a game to you?"

"No. Keep your voice down." He took her arm and walked away from the vehicles. "These are my friends. I want them to be happy."

"But there's a bet involved." Her face pinched, and not from the cold.

"Coop, let's get this show on the road." Ty climbed into the passenger seat of the lead Suburban.

Suddenly, Coop was all too aware that the clock was ticking on his and Nora's time together. "You'll be here when I get back? I'll explain everything then."

"Of course I'll be here. Mary Jo is going with you."

"Good." He leaned in and kissed Zoe's nose.

And then he kissed Nora's, telling himself it wasn't a final kiss goodbye.

CHAPTER SEVEN

"WE'RE GOING TO LEAVE, Zoe, and that's that." Nora fastened the baby's diaper tabs in the Bar & Grill's bathroom a few hours after the matchmaking group had left. "Your father may not be exactly like my father, but he's still a flake." *Matchmaking on a bet?* "Who needs him?"

Unfortunately her heart wasn't on the same page as her declaration. She enjoyed Coop's company. She wanted to talk about hockey and politics and Zoe's future with him. She wanted to dance and kiss and laugh and smile with him.

"But I want chocolate, too," she cooed to Zoe. "And I don't keep that around the house."

"I shaved my legs for this?" Mary Jo traipsed into the restroom, followed by a group of women. "I have mud up the legs of my jeans and down my backside."

Tatiana followed her in, took one look at her reflection in the mirror and shrieked. "I have helmet hair? Why didn't someone tell me?"

Nora snapped Zoe into her pink, footed jumper. The guys must be devastated. Not that they didn't deserve some devastation for playing with people's hearts. "I guess the trip didn't go well."

"Go well? Did you see my hair?" Tatiana pointed to the flattened hair above her ears with a comb. She began teasing it back to life. Soon it looked more like a lopsided dove's nest than a swanky hairstyle.

"Look at my jeans." Mary Jo showed Nora her mud-covered and unidentifiable-debris-spattered backside. "These were brand-new."

"My mascara iced over and my eyes nearly froze shut." Nadine rubbed at her eyes and then did a double take in the mirror. "Forget your hair, Tat. Why didn't you tell me one of my eyelashes fell off?" She held out her sweater, searching for the missing beauty accessory.

"You sat in the front seat." Tatiana went to work on the other side of her hair. "I couldn't see your face."

"Ah." Nora bit back a smile as she picked up Zoe. "That's what's on Mary Jo's jeans."

"Ruined," Nadine muttered, plucking the lash from her friend's behind. With a sigh, she carefully peeled off the other eyelash. "Can I borrow your mascara, Tat?" Nadine didn't wait for approval before digging in Tatiana's purse. "This was stupid. The point of a social is to look good, be social and talk."

"With hotties." Tatiana never paused her mad, fluffing rhythm.

Mary Jo grabbed a handful of paper towels and wiped at her butt. "A place where you can hear what a man says."

The three women stopped what they were doing and looked at each other. And then they all started laughing.

Nora missed out on the joke. "What's so funny?"

Tatiana edged Nadine out of the mirror space. "It was actually kind of nice not to hear them."

Nadine pumped the brush in the mascara tube. "All they talk about is fishing and hunting and hockey."

"And the weather." Mary Jo gave up wiping. She threw the towels in the trash. "And the road conditions. And…I don't know. Boring stuff?"

"What would you like them to talk about?" Nora asked, rubbing Zoe's back.

Silence. More exchanged looks, as if they were afraid to spill some mighty secret.

"Okay, I'll say it." Nadine turned to Nora, hand on hip. "I'd like to talk about me. And hear about him. What did he think of a movie we've both seen? What does he think about the roof that caved in from snow at the elementary school? It's like their conversational skills are buried beneath their beards."

The women nodded. Nora silently agreed. That described a lot of men she knew.

Except Coop.

"What's the point?" Tatiana gave up trying to fluff her hair. "The men in this town don't try. They can't even be bothered to shave beyond once a year. Ty and Mike don't shave at all. It's got to be better in the Lower 48."

Nora wasn't so sure.

"THAT WAS A DISASTER," Ty muttered, meeting Coop's gaze in the mirror of the men's room where Coop was cleaning up at the sink so he could hold Zoe.

"A mushroom cloud of disaster," Gideon added, leaning against the wall.

"I hear you," Coop said. "I might have salvaged the day if Mike made me an offer for that red Suburban."

"Are you giving up?" Ty's beard practically quivered with anger.

"No," Coop said carefully, unable to ignore the gut-twisting feeling of impending failure.

"But have you ever wondered if we were meant to stay here?"

Ty's expression turned mushroom-cloud dark. "You. Of all people." He flung open the door hard enough to make it bang against the wall.

"Seriously," Gideon said. "It's as though Nora came to town and you lost your edge. We need the shark who can sell a car to a guy who's got twenty." He stalked out.

Had Coop lost his edge? He looked in the mirror. Beard? Check. Flannel? Check. Hadn't he just taken an ATV through sloppy terrain? Yes, he had. There was no issue with his edge or salesmanship. Except…

He washed dishes. He changed wet diapers. He had a car seat in his truck.

It'll all be worth it if Nora stays.

His Y chromosome banged a protest in his chest, demanding the return of his maleness, of his drive for his dreams. Coop looked in the mirror. Twenty years he'd had this dream. He wasn't ready to give it up yet. Did that make him a bad dad?

Coop went out to face the music: twelve singles who'd complained bitterly about the cold, muddy conditions all the way down Sky Hawk Mountain and two good friends who deserved his all.

Nora stood by the bar arguing with Gideon and Ty. Zoe lay in the portable bassinet at her feet, cooing softly.

"She might have a point," Gideon was saying.

Ty had the fingers of one hand splayed upward through his thick beard, covering his mouth.

"What's up?" Coop draped an arm casually over Nora's shoulders. She startled, but didn't shrug him off.

"She wants all of us to shave." Eyes wide, Ty curled his fingers in his facial hair. "And it's not even March."

Nora wanted it?

The urge to say, "Take me to your razor" was almost overwhelming. Instead, Coop said, "*All* of us?" in a tremulous voice.

"Yes, all." Nora shrugged off his arm. "The women shaved. And ironed their clothes. And put on lipstick. What did you and your guys do?"

"We gassed up the vehicles," Coop said matter-of-factly, despite a very small voice in his head counseling him to shut up and shave.

"And?" Nora waited to hear more. When there was no more, she shot them a look of blue-eyed disgust. "My point exactly." She picked up Zoe and met Coop's gaze squarely.

"Where's the nearest barbershop? Maybe I can get one of the braver men here to shave, because if there's one thing I can't stand, it's half measures."

Translation: Coop had earned the same loser stamp as Nora's dad. How many points had that cost him?

"You mean, you want us to shave *now*?" Ty looked as though he might faint. His beard covered the worst of his scar. "That's not how we do things here."

"Look around." Nora gestured to the bar crowd. "The guys are sitting together by the windows and the women are sitting together along the wall. It's a social. Shouldn't they be socializing?"

Three men took in the situation. Three men remained silent. Three men who claimed they'd do anything to win the bet were balking over facial hair. And in Coop's case, it wasn't even good facial hair.

Mike stood, heading toward the door. Had he heard his beard—the longest in town—was at risk?

"Kiss your matchmaking hobby goodbye." Nora huffed. "It was all a stupid game to you anyway, but it was serious to your friends. I guess that proves what kind of friends you really are."

"We already knew about Coop," Ty muttered.

Gideon didn't speak or move.

But Nora did. She walked away, carrying Zoe in the bassinet. It felt as if she was leaving for good.

The bet was demolishing Coop's friendships and destroying his chance at being a father. If Coop didn't do something, his friends would never speak to him again. And Nora? She'd walk away tomorrow, taking Zoe with her. Forever.

"We're not losing anything." Coop found his determination, his pride. "Get your parka, Nora. This was your idea." He raised his voice. "This social isn't over. Guys, get your coats. Every man is coming with me. Ladies, you stay here until we return." Coop was on a mission. "Mike, I need you to open the barbershop."

"Mike is the town barber?" Nora was flabbergasted. "You're in more trouble than I thought."

"Where's the baby's snowsuit?" Coop plucked Zoe from the bassinet. "The men in this town are going to prove just how serious they are about finding their soul mates."

CHAPTER EIGHT

THE WOMEN DIDN'T stay at the bar.

And Nora couldn't blame them.

She stood inside the barbershop by the front windows, surrounded by six muddy, flat-haired, skimpy-lashed women. She could feel their excitement—in their hushed voices, repressed giggles and wide-eyed stares. It was unprecedented. Spring was coming early this year.

Coop was the first to go under the blade. His green eyes sought Nora's in the mirror. They blazed with a message: *Here's what I'm willing to do for you.*

Nora could barely breathe as Coop's cheeks and chin were revealed, stroke by stroke. Here was the face she'd fallen for on St. Patrick's Day, the one she'd cursed when she realized she was pregnant and the one she'd sent thoughts of thanks to when she'd first held Zoe in her arms.

Mike whisked away the barber's drape.

Coop stood, looking as though he'd fit in anywhere in the Lower 48, despite the flannel and the snow boots. Nora found herself in front of him. She touched his smoothly shaved cheek. "I hardly recognized you with the beard. And now..."

"You'd know me anywhere. Beard or not." He captured her hand and pressed a kiss to her palm.

She should pull her hand away. She should leave the barbershop. She did neither. How could she? She could barely breathe.

"You knew me when we met in the bar last year," he said. "You knew me the moment you walked into the Bar & Grill last week."

"It was your eyes." It had always been his eyes, so filled with laughter and warmth and desire.

"That's good. That's really good. Because my eyes don't get shaggy in winter." His smile reached past her defenses and made her legs feel unsteady.

"Uh, Coop?" Mike stood behind the empty barber's chair. "Next?"

Every man in the place had a sudden, urgent interest in their shoes.

"I knew it." Tatiana rolled her eyes.

"Gideon? Ty?" Coop searched for his friends in the crowded shop.

"Ty didn't come." Gideon separated himself from the crowd and eyed the chair as if it was a hibernating bear he didn't want to wake.

Coop went to Gideon's side. "Gideon?" The sharp doubt in that one ice-laden word could have punctured the hull of the *Titanic*.

It might just as well have been Nora who made the bet. She felt just as defeated as Coop looked.

A man in the back laughed. And then another. And another. Until the entire shop, with the exception of the matchmakers and Nora, was laughing with bullet-dodging relief.

Coop's shoulders sagged. A door seemed to close in his face, closing off his expression, shutting out his smile.

Gideon saw it, too. He touched the placket of his polo and sat in the chair. "I don't know what the big deal is. It's only hair. It'll grow back next winter."

The room filled with a different sort of laughter. Casual, friendly, accepting.

For the first time Nora believed Coop's matchmaking would work.

But the group's laughter rolled right over Nora. She had a steady, predictable life in Anchorage. She didn't gamble—not on cockamamy ventures or confirmed bachelor's hearts. Zoe needed her to make smart decisions, to be reliable, to put Zoe's welfare over the power of a man's grin.

Coop's laughter drifted from across the room and settled in her chest, near her heart. The same heart that whispered, *Stay. He's the one.*

Oh, no. What had happened?

Coop had charmed her. He'd charmed her the way he'd done the night Zoe was conceived. She'd never learn. Even now she could feel the yearning in her heart to go to him. Silly. She couldn't fall in love with Coop. She couldn't let him break her heart or Zoe's.

Nora returned to the safety of the women, where she watched man after man shed his facial hair. Finally they watched Mike shave himself.

Tatiana gasped. "Mike hasn't shaved for years."

"He could be hiding something gruesome beneath that beard," Nadine whispered.

"Not with those shoulders," Mary Jo murmured.

And he wasn't. Mike was rock-star handsome. All the men were.

The hair on the ground was swept into drifts. The matchmakers began pairing couples. This time there was no reluctance. No griping from the women.

And the men? Mike asked if anyone had seen the latest action movie. Derrick and Mary Jo talked about the repairs needed to the school roof. Another couple discussed the upcoming mayoral race.

Nora stood apart by the windows. Alone, with Zoe.

"It worked." Gideon slapped Coop on the back when they returned to the bar for the mixer and lunch. "They're pairing up."

"They're falling in love," Ty said, somewhat in awe. He scratched his traitorous beard.

"That's not love." Coop watched Nora settle into a booth in the back and adjust Zoe for a late lunch.

After he'd shaved, she'd stood with him—the same as any couple now—smiling up at him with accepting eyes while she'd touched his clean-shaven jaw. And then it was as if Nora flipped a switch.

If she loved him, she wouldn't have been able to walk away. He'd seen a woman walk away before—his mother. He knew what that closed-off expression meant. Nora was packing up feelings. Shutting down her emotions to minimize hurt.

That was essentially what Coop had done the morning his mother left. And the morning after Zoe was conceived.

A pit formed in his stomach, the same way it did when he sensed a car buyer was no longer interested in a vehicle. It was the feeling that made him reassess the truth behind the potential buyer's words. Did they really want the practical truck with snow tires? Had they dreamed of the fully loaded SUV with the tow package? Or deep down was their heart set on an impractical-for-Alaska minivan with the television screen in back?

He knew what Nora wanted: a dependable man to help raise Zoe. Someone who wouldn't hurt her child the way Nora had been hurt. That hadn't changed. And in her eyes, he still didn't fit the bill.

But something had changed.

Inside him.

Coop turned to Gideon, who was talking to a fully bearded Ty about the several hockey farm teams Coach owned in the States. Coop should be excited. He should jump into the conversation about the up-and-coming Portland team. He should be looking ahead to a life filled with everything he'd dreamed of: a career in professional hockey!

Instead, his gaze was drawn to Nora and Zoe.

Gideon interrupted his thoughts. "It's not working. Half the couples are leaving. And not as a couple."

Coop had a lifetime responsibility to Zoe. But his commitment to his friends had a deadline looming in two weeks. "You're wrong, Gideon. Not everyone is leaving."

Three women stayed to marvel at Nora's baby and perhaps dream a little.

And suddenly Coop knew. "We've been working the wrong angle," he told Gideon.

"NORA, YOU LOOK BEAT," Coop said that afternoon after they'd returned home and the baby had been fed and changed. "Why don't I take Zoe while you get some rest?"

A grateful smile flashed across her face, only to be quickly replaced with a suspicious one. "You're smiling. What are you up to?"

"Nothing." He tried to look innocent when in fact he was guilty. Zoe was the motivator to matchmaking, not clean-shaven faces or lipsticked lips.

"No, thanks." There was disappointment in her eyes behind the weariness. Disappointment in him.

He wanted to see something very different in her eyes. "Okay, I'll admit it. I was going to take her to the Shop and Sack. We need bread and milk." At her questioning gaze, he added, "Can't a man take his child to the grocery store?"

"You want to show her off?"

"No. No." He tried to look innocent again.

"Let the man have his moment," Pop said. "You look as if a northern wind could blow you over. Can't be good for you or the baby to be so tired, Nora."

"Okay." Nora relented. "But take her diaper kit and her car seat and her favorite bumblebee pacifier."

Coop grabbed the bag and lifted Zoe into his arms. "I've got this."

"I… You…" Nora looked lost.

"I'll be careful with her." Coop leaned in to kiss Nora's cheek when he'd much rather kiss her lips. "Get some sleep."

She wasted no time heading for the spare bedroom.

Pop trailed after Coop, following him outside. "What are you really up to?"

"Bread and milk, Pop. Bread and milk."

"I FEEL LIKE SCUM," Gideon said beneath the speaker playing pop music at the Shop and Sack. "What if Nora finds out what we're really doing with Zoe?"

"We're grocery shopping. Just…remind me to buy bread and milk," Coop said firmly, but he stared down at a sleeping Zoe propped in her car seat on the shopping cart and worried the same thing. "And if we run into some single ladies accidentally while shopping…"

"On purpose." Ty stroked his whiskers.

"Do you have to do that?" a clean-shaven Gideon snapped. No truer indication of his stress level existed than annoyance in Gideon's tone.

"What?" Ty tried to play the innocent, but he couldn't quite stop a smile.

"You know what." Gideon crossed his arms.

Coop tried distraction. "Did I hear a woman's voice?"

"No," they both said, exchanging the most reluctant smiles known to man.

Zoe stirred and made a mewling sound.

Coop put a finger to his mouth. "Don't wake her."

"I need to be back at the skating rink in thirty minutes for Pee-Wee league," Ty said in a whisper as he glanced at a display of cereal. "Remember when they used to put a toy inside the box? Life used to offer the promise of a toy inside."

"It's still offering a prize," Coop said. "That's the point of the bet. And Zoe."

"Just so you know, I'm not going to the bar tonight," Gideon said matter-of-factly. "You're going to have to deal with Nora on your own."

"I'm okay with that." As long as he and his friends didn't abandon each other now, in the trenches. Movement at the end of the coffee aisle caught his eye. "It's Shawntelle Kingman. Come on."

"We're going to burn in hell for this." But Gideon followed.

Coop stopped pushing the cart long enough to grab hold of Gideon's shoulder. "That's not true. I offer sales incentives all the time, same as you. I gave away microwaves with purchases last month. You offered a free toaster to anyone opening an account at your bank last summer."

"This is different," Gideon insisted. "Dads shouldn't use their kids like this."

Coop felt sucker punched. He shook his head. "Don't say that." He stroked Zoe's cheek with the backs of his knuckles. "I'm not a bad dad... I just... Don't say that."

"We lost Shawntelle," Gideon said, obviously relieved.

"She went to the beer aisle." Ty looked as if he'd rather have kept that a secret.

"I know this seems like a dumb idea, but we're here. Let's play it out." Coop pushed the cart into the beer aisle, flanked by his friends, who pretended great interest in the snack-food displays.

Another target appeared. Shy, single Eleanor Clambert crossed the center aisle and headed toward the dairy section. She was on their singles list, too.

But first things first. Coop approached his target. "Hey, Shawntelle. Picking up something to watch a game? Isn't wine more romantic?"

"Romance?" Shawntelle looked up and then did a double take. "Wait. It isn't March, is it? Your beards…"

"We shaved." Coop stroked his chin. "Along with several other single men in town." No thanks to Ty.

"Did you lose a bet or something?"

"You have no idea," Ty muttered and stroked his beard.

Her gaze caught on Zoe. "I'd heard you had a baby, Coop. Congratulations."

"Thanks." *Would you like one of your own?*

"And you know what? She's winning the hearts of every bachelor in town. Love is in the air."

"Get outta here." But Shawntelle didn't look away from Zoe's sweet, sleeping face. "You and that crazy matchmaking business."

"Hey, we crazies got eight bachelors in town to shave." That wasn't a disapproving glare Coop sent Ty's way. "People are talking."

Gideon handed Shawntelle a stapled survey. The list of questions had gotten longer. "This is our way of identifying what you want in a man. It's still rough."

"But we've had success with it." Fibbing, Coop gestured to the sleeping baby.

Shawntelle stared at the survey in her hand as if she couldn't remember how it had gotten there.

Bearded, burly Darryl Whitefeather turned the corner, saw them and made a quick U-turn. Coop bid Shawntelle goodbye and hunted Darryl down, leaving Ty and Gideon behind.

"Picking out some vegetables, Darryl?" Coop pulled his cart alongside the macho, muscular machinist. "Way to stay healthy. The ladies like that. I bet they notice you work out." More likely they'd notice he was so bulky he had to live at the gym. What kind of woman found that appealing?

Zoe began to fuss, drawing her knees toward her chest. Again? Coop only had a few minutes before he'd have to change a truly dirty diaper for the first time. He picked her up, hoping a different position would slow the process.

"Listen, Coop." The big man gave him a hard look. "I don't know what game you're playing, but I'm in Alaska because I want to be alone." His gaze fell to Zoe's face and his lips twitched enough to make him look less intimidating.

Coop glanced down. "Hey, she's smiling." He laughed. "Look at my kid. Gideon! Ty!" He pushed the cart back the way he'd come. "Sorry, Darryl. Come by the Bar & Grill if you change your mind."

Gideon skidded around the corner, Ty close on his heels. "What? What happened?"

"Look at her. Look at Zoe. She's smiling." She was smiling. At Coop. His chest swelled with love.

And then Zoe tensed. A familiar noise came from her. A foul smell filled the air.

"That's my cue to leave." Ty headed for the door.

"Coward," Coop called after him. He adjusted Zoe in his arms and tried to ignore the slam of trepidation in his gut. "Have you ever changed a diaper, Gideon?"

"No." Gideon had his hand over his nose and mouth. "And I'm not about to."

Zoe tensed again.

My cup overfloweth... It never rains, it pours. Stop with the platitudes!

"How hard can it be? We need the diaper kit and a flat surface." Coop walked swiftly to the front of the store. "I left the kit in the truck. Can you get it for me?" He tossed Gideon his keys as they reached the checkout stands. "Nadine, where can I deal with a diaper crisis?"

Nadine barely lifted her false eyelashes enough to look at Coop as she bagged Old Man Higgans's groceries. "There's a changing table in the ladies' room, but men can't go in there. It's against regulations."

Old Man Higgans squinted through thick lenses at Coop, sniffed and high tailed it to the exit on skinny, bowed legs.

Zoe started to fuss, whimpering and squirming. She did not like poopy pants.

"I'm not going to change my daughter's diaper in my truck when it's thirty freezing degrees outside." Coop pulled a wool, checked blanket off an endcap display and tossed it on the checkout counter. "I'll take this. Open it up and put it on the conveyer."

Gideon came running back inside with the diaper kit, dumping its contents on the checkout counter. "What do you need?"

"You can't do that," Nadine protested. "It's against regulations." She fixed Gideon with a false-eyelashed glare. "You'd know store policy if you read the signs and not women's magazines."

"I told you," Gideon said through limit-testing, gritted teeth. "I bought them for matchmaking purposes."

"Nadine." There were bigger issues at hand. "I either change her here or I go in the ladies' room. Either way, regulations will be broken."

Nadine had never looked so indecisive. Not even in the eighth grade when Coop and Ty had showed up on her doorstep at the same time to ask her to the same dance. She'd ended up going with Gideon, who didn't dance, not even the slow songs.

Coop couldn't wait for Nadine to make up her mind. Zoe was a ticking time bomb when it came to dirty diapers. "Nadine, that truck you've been driving has been in too often for service lately." Coop managed to unzip the plastic around the blanket with one hand and unfold it a time or two on the counter. "If you let me change Zoe's diaper here on this blanket I'm buying, I'll give you a good price on a low-mileage truck and Gideon will give you a good rate on a loan."

Nadine brightened. "You can change her here as long as you understand it's a one-time thing."

"Nobody plans on accidents, Nadine." Coop put the changing pad on top of the blanket and laid Zoe on it. "They just happen. Like life, sometimes." He set about freeing Zoe's leg snaps as if he might break something. Instead, his controlled unsnapping sent all the material on one pant leg free.

Zoe startled. Her face crumpled. A frail cry filled the air, a precursor of bad things. Very bad things.

"No, no, no. None of that, missy," Coop said in his best daddy-loves-you voice. "Your dad needs a little patience here."

"First diaper?" Nadine asked.

"Of this sort." First kid. First nasty pants. First love.

First love?

Ah, yes. It was love. Why not admit it? He loved both Nora and Zoe. Nora was everything Coop wasn't—brutally honest, brave and beautiful to her core. He cut corners. He fudged facts. And he certainly wasn't brave. If he had been, he would have left K-Bay long ago. Ty's accident… Pop's disabilities. They were excuses.

He couldn't let Nora leave tomorrow. Darryl pushed his cart within a safe viewing distance. "This I've gotta see."

"Viewing comes at a price." Gideon lurched past Coop. "You'll have to sign up for matchmaking services."

"And shave." Ty appeared in the doorway, shoulders dusted with snow. "Sorry, Coop. I panicked."

"I'm only signing up if Coop changes that diaper himself." Darryl smirked.

"This may be my first messy-pants change." Coop kept with the day-care-daddy tone of voice. "But it won't be my last."

"Bravo," Nadine said.

Shawntelle came up behind Darryl, surveyed his cart and then compared it to hers. "You're making me feel guilty about junk food and beer, Darryl." She smiled in a way that said she didn't feel incredibly guilty. "Here, Gideon. I filled out the matchmaking paperwork."

Darryl peered at the contents of her cart. "You're making nachos for the game tonight?"

Zoe shrieked, dragging Coop's attention back to the challenge at hand.

"Easy, girl." Coop laid a hand on her stomach.

"Nachos and sports are a must in my house. Hope you change that diaper, Coop." Shawntelle sounded as if she was smiling. "I'd like to see Darryl without facial hair."

"I'd like to see you eat a vegetable," Darryl quipped.

"I put peppers on my nachos," she shot back.

While Gideon handed Darryl a survey and Ty provided a pen, Zoe's lip quivered at the slow, inefficient style of Coop's diaper change.

Coop had adjusted carburetors and changed air filters in big-rig engines with the motor running and the drivers irate. He'd sold three vehicles at one time when he'd had a Christmas in July sale and both his salesmen had hopped on fishing boats the day before. He could change one little girl's diaper, especially when it was his little girl.

Gideon returned to the bagger's station just as Coop released the tabs holding the diaper closed. "Okay, then." He held out a hand toward Gideon. "Wipe." When no wipe was forthcoming, Coop glanced at his friend.

Gideon's face was a sickly shade of green. He had a hand over his mouth and nose again. "The deal was you change it alone."

Sophie Jennings walked in through the main doors. Gideon gripped the counter.

And wasn't that interesting?

Sophie paused, ready to come to someone's assistance. She was always willing to lend a hand. "What's going on?"

"We're watching history being made." Shawntelle had her cell phone out. "I'm gonna post this later."

"Go on." Ty's voice vibrated with laughter. "Take one for the team, Coop."

Gideon seemed struck speechless by Sophie's entrance.

"If I do this, Ty, you're visiting the barber," Coop said, getting down to business. A few minutes later, when he'd finished, he'd drawn quite a crowd. "Tonight, I want to see all you singles at the Bar & Grill. Everybody fill out a survey and everybody shave before you get there."

The crowd filled out surveys, even the town recluse, Eleanor Clambert.

Shawntelle eyed Darryl. Darryl eyed Shawntelle.

"When Coop said shave, I think he meant you, Darryl." Shawntelle's smile was positively wicked.

"Wrong." Coop wrapped Zoe in her hot pink blanket and strapped her into her carrier, thinking of Nora's words earlier. "I meant both of you."

CHAPTER NINE

"THERE'S YOUR BEAUTIFUL MOMMY." Coop's deep voice drifted into Nora's dreams.

Zoe's weight came to a gentle rest on her chest. Nora opened her eyes.

Coop's face was close to hers, clean-shaven and handsome. "Thank you," he whispered, pressing a soft kiss to Nora's forehead.

"For what?" She pushed herself to a sitting position.

His hand cradled Zoe's sleeping head. "For having her." He kissed Nora's forehead again. "For bringing her here." He kissed her nose. "For giving me the chance to be a dad." And then his lips settled on Nora's.

So tender. So gentle. So right. Like the night they'd met, but without the crazy spur-of-the-moment urgency. He kissed her as if they had all the time in the world and he'd be content kissing her until the end of time.

Nora wanted to slip her hand to the back of his neck, wanted to pull him closer, to deepen the kiss. But she had to think of what was best for Zoe.

And a father who picked up women at bars and played at matchmaker wasn't her idea of reliable.

And so she ignored her heart, heeded her head and drew gently away. A cold knot formed in her chest, loosely tangled loops of regret and sorrow.

Coop gazed into her eyes with all the warmth and tenderness she'd expected from him that disastrous morning after, with all the promise in his eyes that she'd ever dreamed of.

"I'm leaving tomorrow," she forced herself to say.

The warmth and tenderness drained, replaced by a cool expression she hadn't seen since she'd first walked into the bar over a week ago.

He stepped back. One step. Then another.

With each step she felt the ends of the knot in her chest tighten.

THE BAR WAS crowded that night, filled with more people than Nora had seen there before. She shared her booth with Tatiana, Mary Jo and a woman named Shawntelle, wishing this wasn't her last night in K-Bay.

"I wouldn't be here if it wasn't for your baby." Shawntelle stared at Zoe and sighed heavily. "She's beautiful."

"It was the shaving that did it for me," Tatiana said. "Have you seen Mike's cheekbones? I haven't seen them since high school."

"Wow. Simply...wow," Mary Jo said. "The men shave at all different times come spring, but we don't get the full effect since they all go out hunting as soon as the snow melts."

Nadine stopped at their table. She was dressed in tight jeans, a low-cut blouse and a fresh pair of false eyelashes. "Are you going to write a book, Nora?"

"About what?"

"How to train your man." Nadine turned on a heavily lipsticked, in-case-a-man-is-looking smile. "You did a great job with Coop. It gives the rest of us hope."

The women at the table nodded.

"Coop isn't mine." But how Nora wished he could be. If he changed and became someone else, someone more stable. Someone she could trust not to gamble away his paycheck or his heart.

Nadine kept flapping her cranberry-coated lips. "Coop changed Zoe's diaper right there in the Shop and Sack. Darryl didn't think he could do it."

For one brief, shining moment, Nora was proud of Coop. Zoe's poopy pants weren't to be dealt with lightly.

"I was there." Shawntelle joined in the storytelling. "Coop changed that diaper all by himself. On a dare."

That feeling of pride dissolved. The disappointment returned.

A dare. She should have known.

"Coop said I had to shave my legs, too, if I was coming here tonight." Shawntelle gazed at Zoe once more. "I had to buy a new razor."

Another woman came to stand next to Nadine. "Coop and Gideon came into the sporting-goods store today. Your baby charmed Nathaniel into shaving his beard, too." She sighed like a lovesick teenager. There seemed to be a lot of that going around. "I'd forgotten Nathaniel had dimples."

Every pair of female eyes at the table sought out Nathaniel's dimples.

"Mike's been busy." Tatiana couldn't seem to take her eyes off the barber. "Do you know? He didn't mind that I was sharp with him the morning of the ATV social. He said I have strength of character. He said I'd make a good mom." Her longing gaze turned to Zoe.

Coop had used their daughter as bait to draw in customers. Customers he wasn't serious about keeping. Matchmaking was just another amusement to him. A gamble. A dare.

She was no longer disappointed. Hurt and anger rippled through her veins.

Nora excused herself from the women shot by Cupid's arrow and carried Zoe to Coop. "I need to talk to you." She could barely contain herself until they got to the back corner of the bar nearest Coach, Gideon and Ty. The latter pair of men wouldn't look her in the eye. "You used Zoe. You let me think you were actually interested in being a father to her and you used her to bamboozle the town with baby fever."

Coop flinched. "I am interested in being Zoe's father."

A guttural sound rose from Nora's throat like steam from an overheated engine.

"Granted, she's the most effective advertising we've tried to date." No remorse. Coop showed no remorse at all.

It infuriated Nora. "What happens when the matchmaking stops being fun, Coop? What happens to all your friends' hopes about having a family?"

"I'm serious about matchmaking. I'm serious about..." He swallowed and looked away.

"Go on. Tell her." Coach stopped making a martini. "You love her." He hefted a tray of drinks and left them. "Is it that hard to say?"

Nora couldn't move. She couldn't believe. She

finally was able to shake her head. “It doesn’t matter if what Coach says is true. You pick up women. You place bets. You use your daughter.” She took a step to leave, but he caught her arm.

“I told you. We made a bet. But it wasn’t on a whim or made under the influence of alcohol.”

The two other musketeers nodded.

“All my life,” Coop said solemnly, “I’ve wanted to leave K-Bay and Alaska. All my life, I felt as if I could be more, if only I could get out of here.” He stroked a finger down Nora’s cheek. “First, my plan with Ty and Gideon fell through. Then my dad got hurt. And then there was you.” He stared deep into Nora’s eyes. “I’ve set up my life to be temporary, like a car I could always trade in so I could move on. But there was always a good excuse not to go. I don’t want temporary anymore. Proving we can take on any challenge—be it selling a car, fixing an ice resurfacer, figuring out federal-loan restrictions or making a love match—opens the door to professional hockey careers. Careers, Nora. In the Lower 48.”

He laid his palm over Zoe’s crown. “I was wrong to use Zoe like that. But it didn’t do her any harm. I’d never hurt her. I love her.” His gaze collided with Nora’s and he swallowed. “I love you. Can't you look beneath the hood and see past the dents, and see that I'm a better man every minute I'm with you? I only hope you love me enough to help me achieve my dreams."

Nora couldn't speak. Her throat closed up and the voices in the room faded away.

He loves me.

The idea of being loved by Coop and loving him in return didn't feel as scary as it had earlier in the day, because he wasn't placing bets on a whim.

He loves me.

Coop was working toward a future, one he'd dreamed of for years. He was a good man. He'd stood by his father when he could have gone away to college. People in K-Bay liked and respected him. He was so much more at twenty-five than her father was at fifty-nine. But he was asking her to veer off the stable, predictable path, to leave her established life behind, to take a chance on love.

The buzz of silence turned into a ringing in her ears.

Only it wasn't in her head. It was Mike, ringing the bell at the other end of the bar. His arm was looped around Tatiana's waist and she was smiling up at him as if he was the only man for her.

Nora was envious of that smile.

"We've had a crush on each other since high school," Tatiana gushed. "And neither of us knew it. Can you believe it?"

Mike swept Tatiana into his arms and kissed her.

Ty and Gideon high-fived. Coop stood in front of Nora, waiting for an answer.

Nora couldn't breathe. The bet. The abandonment. The blind faith needed to commit.

She took a step back. Then another.

Coop sagged against the bar, staring at Nora with hollow, defeated eyes.

Nora turned and worked her way through the crowd, holding Zoe tight. "I'm sorry, baby. But I've got to do this."

"Excuse me." She tapped Mike on the shoulder, edging around the couple. "There's more love in the room tonight than this bell can stand." Nora grabbed the bell and rang it with all her might.

Zoe woke and began to cry.

But there was Coop, encircling them in the safety of his arms, and laughing and smiling and finally, finally, finally sealing the bell ring with a kiss.

* * * * *

To my husband ~ your love and support mean more to me than you could ever know

Special thanks to my writing family, Melinda Curtis and Anna J. Stewart, for helping me reach my dream. You truly are the best! And thanks to my family for always believing in me. I'm so blessed to have all of you in my life.

The Matchmaker Wore Skates

Cari Lynn Webb

Dear Reader,

Family is the center of my world. My family can be supportive, loving, challenging and frustrating, but I wouldn't trade any of the moments I've shared with them. I'm a better person because of my family. And with them I know where I belong.

Just as it is for Cooper Hamilton, Ty Porter and Gideon Walker in Kenkamken Bay, Alaska. These childhood friends are family; they've dreamed together, failed together and stalled out in life together. And now they plan to change their futures.

But Ty Porter can't change the future without first facing his mistakes with Kelsey Nash. For Kelsey and Ty, revisiting their history reveals more than bitter memories and painful heartbreak. Turns out that true love never really fades, and sometimes where you belong is right where you are.

Ty and Kelsey's story was so much fun to write. I hope you enjoy this romance as well as the other two by my very good friends Melinda Curtis and Anna J. Stewart in this anthology.

I love to connect with readers. Check my website to learn more about my upcoming books, sign up for email book announcements or chat with me on Facebook (carilynnwebb) or via Twitter (@carilynnwebb).

Cari

CariLynnWebb.com

CHAPTER ONE

"If you want to play, you need to push." Ty Porter knocked his forehead against the steering wheel of the ice resurfacer at the outdoor rink in Kenkamken Bay. "Now."

"Or we could play around you." Stan tugged on his thick beard streaked with snowflakes and dropped a puck on the ice.

For love of hockey players worldwide, someone needed to save Ty from these amateurs. And weekly pickup games with ornery players. Ty squeezed the steering wheel and stared down at the six men watching him sit on his broken ice machine. "You can't be serious."

"Might be we are." Stan sent the puck skidding toward the far goal. The others nodded in agreement.

Ty closed his eyes and drew in a deep breath. The crisp bite in the air prevented a slow count to ten. "What do you want?"

"No matches." Stan swiped his glove across his red nose.

"What?" Ty's right temple throbbed.

"We push this box on wheels out to the parking lot and you agree not to play matchmaker for any of us." Stan tapped his chest and motioned to his buddies with his gloved mitt.

By now, the whole town knew Ty and his friends Cooper Hamilton and Gideon Walker had started a matchmaking business. What folks didn't know was that the business had only been formed as part of a bet.

Ty twisted in the seat and studied the guys: bearded, tobacco chewing, stained-shirt-clad men. The perfect representation of every male in K-Bay town limits. Add in the three-times-divorced Stan, the wet-behind-the-ears Tommy and a few with more colorful language than the most seasoned crab fishermen, and Ty's odds of successfully pairing any one of them descended into the negative. But these were hardworking, loyal, salt-of-the-earth men who'd give you the shirts off their backs, albeit stained from yesterday's BBQ sandwiches, without question.

Still, Ty and his friends needed to play Cupid four more times to win the bet they'd made with Coach. He wiped his hand over his mouth, covering his smile. "Are you sure,

Stan? Could be I located your soul mate and she's waiting right now at the bar."

"Only ones at the Bar & Grill right now are Coach and Sam," Stan said, referring to the bar's owner and one of the male regulars. Stan slapped the side of the bulky vehicle. "Only thing waiting at the bar is our empty pint glasses."

"Isn't that the truth," Tommy muttered, his shoulders drooping beneath his thick padded gear. Despite being only a year out of high school, Tommy's date options looked as bleak as him getting his empty pint glass filled in the next two years. Coach maintained a strict rule of not serving minors and threatened plain water to anyone who refused to abide by his policies.

"But, Tommy, Fannie is over there." Ty indicated the six-foot female who preferred her whiskey straight and belches unrestrained.

Fannie paused from sweeping off the walkway to the outdoor ice rink and glared at the men. "I won't be ringing no bell, either, Ty Porter, so aim those bedroom blues someplace else."

The bell Fannie referenced hung over the beer taps in the Bar & Grill and was sounded by those who'd found The One.

"Only bell I want to hear is the buzzer signaling the start of this game." Stan knocked his stick against the ice. His compatriots grunted in solidarity.

"Just to be clear," Ty said as he jumped down from the stalled resurfacer onto the ice, as sure-footed as the snow rabbit he'd seen race across frozen Lake Talbot last weekend. "You push and I don't match you up with any willing females." At their nods, he grinned. "Done. Now push, boys. Whoever gets to the bar first buys the first round." A safer bet than the one he, Coop and Gideon had made. They'd be playing here for hours.

The men got the bulky vehicle into the parking lot. While they pushed brooms across the ice instead of hockey pucks, Ty inspected the blown hydraulic hose and dead battery. He checked his watch. Given the time, the earliest he could order replacement parts was tomorrow morning. Add in several days for shipping and he'd be manually smoothing the ice on both this rink and the one inside the arena for the next week. Nothing like hand smoothing rinks to remind him just how far he'd fallen. But he'd played his cards seven years ago and had only himself to blame for the hand he'd been dealt. He rubbed his right temple and tried to block out the bad memories. Nothing good lay that way.

Shouts echoed behind him, dragging Ty from his past. He watched the guys cease pushing ice shavings to the edge of the rink and begin to pelt each other with snowballs. Even Fannie joined the fray, launching her ammo with her shovel like a catapult. So much for the weekly pickup game. Looked as if they'd be moving to the bar sooner rather than later. First round was going to be on him. Already his wallet seemed lighter. Why hadn't he quit while he'd been ahead—sort of?

His mouth seemed to be running faster than his brain could keep up recently. Case in point was the bet with his two best friends and Coach. Not only had he jumped in like an overexcited puppy diving into a ten-foot snowdrift, he'd upped the stakes. He'd blurted out what they all wanted, but never voiced: jobs in professional hockey in the Lower 48. If they won the bet, Coach had promised Ty a coaching job, Gideon a finance position and Coop a marketing role for one of his farm teams.

Ty wiped his face and tugged his gloves back on. The snowball fight had descended into more of a bench-clearing brawl complete with punches and rapid-fire snowballs to the face. Never mind that the guys didn't want to be matched. The real issue with winning the bet was the obvious lack of women to match men to. Aside from Fannie, his assistant manager, only testosterone filled the iceplex. And in the town of K-Bay at large, estrogen levels were severely limited.

But he'd failed his friends once and didn't intend to let them down again. He and Coop and Gideon would win this bet if he had to sell his soul to do it.

A red compact was backed awkwardly into the last stall in the parking lot, its rear end smashed into a snowbank. When had that happened? The iceplex's no-parking sign protruded like a bent tail from the compact's trunk. Ty pocketed the keys to the ice resurfacer, wondering where the owner of the rental car was—it had to be a rental because no one in K-Bay drove a vehicle that required chains. In fact, the two front tires had lost their chains. Tourists were like a rash beneath his beard, irritating until removed. Now he had one more thing to fix.

The driver couldn't have gone far. He glanced up and down and across L'Amour Street. Mothers and their kids rushed inside the Clipper Ship Coffee Shop, known for its hot chocolate. Win or lose, Coach had treated Ty's entire high school team to the steaming cups of goodness after every home game. He hadn't been inside in seven years.

A woman bundled from head to boots hurried, as much as a person could, given the salt and snow on the road, toward the coffee shop. She had to be the owner of the red, chainless compact. Only city tourists dressed like that in zero-degree weather.

Ty strode across the parking lot toward her, stopping at the waist-high snowbank that ate up almost half of the sidewalk. "Hey, stop! You can't park here."

The bundle spun like a sumo wrestler, moving with more bulk than grace.

"Iceplex employees only." He pointed at the mangled parking sign. "You need to move your car."

The puffed-up tourist came toward him and unwrapped a scarf so thick it looked as if his grandmother's handmade fleece throws had mated. She pulled off a gray wool cap, revealing familiar short blond hair that teased her ears as if daring Mother Nature to try to freeze her delicate, balanced features.

Kelsey Nash, the beautiful backstabbing columnist, had returned to K-Bay. The pretty looks belied an icy inner strength; the watered-down-bourbon doe eyes camouflaged a shrewd nature.

He'd never forget the headlines she'd written about him when they were both eighteen. The first article got picked up by hundreds of news outlets and launched an investigation: Gambling Ring Profits from Hockey Player's Greed for Fortune and Fame and Exposes Itself.

The second propelled a high school newspaper reporter into the national spotlight: Accidental or Intentional? Hockey Player Suffers Career-ending Injuries Hours after Investigation Begins.

Those headlines—those stories—and accusations that he would intentionally throw a game had contributed to the end of his professional hockey career.

Kelsey had ridden the red carpet of Ty's shame to Anchorage and her shiny new career before the first metal pin had been set in Ty's temple. Before the wound caused by her leaving had had time to heal.

"Kelsey Josephine Nash." Ty rolled his shoulders, trying to stretch skin that suddenly felt too tight for his body. "The *Anchorage Beat*'s best gossip columnist."

Her eyebrows lifted, no more than a flinch,

but he knew he'd hit his mark. She'd wanted to be a journalist, covering important news. She'd never progressed past the entertainment section.

"Tyler Ian Porter." Kelsey stepped onto the sidewalk, stopping on the other side of the snowbank. "K-Bay's iceplex handyman turned matchmaker."

Ty dug his fingers into the snowbank and scooped out a chunk, considered pelting her with a snowball like one of the guys from the rink. "My services benefit the community."

"And my columns inform thousands in Anchorage and the surrounding communities." Her guard came up with the speed of a winger winning the puck in a face-off.

"Entertain, you mean." He tossed the snowball from one palm to the other, testing the sting factor. "So I'm correct in assuming you're here for a story."

"I just needed a caffeine fix on my way through town." She motioned to the coffee shop behind her.

"K-Bay isn't a pass-through town. The highway ends here." Ty added more snow to his palm and packed it into a harder snowball, one that would sting for hours.

"Then, call it nostalgia." Kelsey clutched her scarf to her chest.

Once upon a very short time ago, her action with the scarf would have been his cue to wrap his arms around her for additional warmth, for additional closeness, for additional safekeeping. That she'd lived in Alaska most of her life and had never become accustomed to the cold baffled him. "Move your car, Kelsey. Move it right back to Anchorage."

"Look, I'll move my car after I get a cup of coffee." She lifted her gloved, scarf-clutching hands. "You can give me ten minutes."

And there it was: no apology. No "I'm sorry" for bashing into the parking sign. For the articles all those years ago. For the betrayal of friendship, if not young love. "You get five minutes till the tow truck arrives." He dug in his pocket for his cell.

"You aren't going to tow my car away."

"Don't test that theory. Like so many of your stories, it'd be proved wrong."

"I can give you what you need." She smothered her neck with the big wooly scarf.

He wanted a number of things. Perfect vision in his right eye. An end to his migraines. A shot at winning the Stanley Cup. But he didn't deal in harebrained wishes. He launched the snowball over her head, watching it splatter in the middle of the road. "You don't have anything I need."

"Don't be too sure." Kelsey stuffed her gloved hand into her pocket and pulled out a familiar neon green flyer. The one advertising the mixer at the Bar & Grill that Ty and his friends were scheduled to host the next evening. "Saw this at the Shop and Sack."

"You think I'd take your money to make you a match?" Ty asked, unable to smooth his gritty tone, as if he'd inhaled a mouthful of freezing water off the lake bed. The idea of partnering Kelsey with someone bothered him on too many levels to count.

"You think I'd seek your advice to find true love? You need women to make this venture of yours work." Kelsey waved the flyer at him. "Judging from my trip to the Shop and Sack, the mall and Page Turner Bookstore, there's still a shortage of single women in this town. And considering the talk at all of those places, you've been having trouble finding women to match with the outstanding male specimens in K-Bay."

Ty rubbed his right temple. "Why would you help me? There's no story here." But there were secrets. Ty still had secrets. Kelsey excelled at taking a confidence and building it into something more.

"There is a story here." Her slow, even delivery spoke of her conviction, yet that same assurance failed to spark up into her eyes.

She looked vulnerable. That couldn't be. A vulnerable Kelsey Nash was a myth.

"Reality TV shows have been built on weaker premises than male matchmakers in a small town. I'll bring some women to the bar tomorrow night…" She jammed her hands and the flyer back inside her pockets and straightened, tipping her chin up to meet his gaze. "As long as you talk to me about your business… and don't tow my car away."

That quick quiver of doubt in her voice scrambled every certainty he had about her. "The time and place are on the flyer. And, Kelsey, I'm not in a coma this time. Print the wrong story and your car won't be the only thing you need to worry about."

CHAPTER TWO

"SAW YOU OUTSIDE with Ty." The cashier, doubling as the barista at the Clipper Ship, poured milk into the frother. The half-dozen silver bangles on her wrist slid to her thin, pale elbow; her penciled-in eyebrows never twitched above her oversize sixties-style moon-colored eyeglass frames. "You know him?"

"I used to." But now…

Ty Porter was most definitely not eighteen and cocky. He wasn't buzzing from the thrill of dreams soon to be fulfilled. He wasn't being groomed for a long and successful career in professional hockey. And there was no way he was the same young man she'd had a high school crush on, chased around town and finally called her boyfriend for one summer when young love had trumped everything, even hockey.

He was taller than she remembered, more defined, harder, and not only from the scar slicing down his right cheek, disappearing beneath his thick beard. No man walked away from accusations of being a cheat without losing a part of himself. No man withstood the distorted rumors and speculation from articles written by his ex-girlfriend without becoming jaded in his fellow human.

Kelsey needed Ty to be jaded. She hated to admit it, but Ty's contradictions seven years ago had launched her career as a journalist. Now, to save her flagging career, one that seemed to be leading to the unemployment line, she needed another story like that one. But could she tap the same source twice?

The older woman switched the frother off and Kelsey leaned against the counter. "I'm curious about Ty's matchmaking business." She'd first seen Trinity Matchmaking mentioned on social media, but no one in K-Bay had replied to her direct messages or questions about Ty.

"I wouldn't know nothing about that." The crotchety barista set a coffee cup on the prep station. "I'm married."

Kelsey needed to find people who knew. She'd assumed she'd come back to K-Bay and look up some of her high school friends. She hadn't found any. Or any that she recognized.

Kelsey reached for her drink. But the uptight barista held the coffee hostage and stared down Kelsey. "You don't remember me, do you?"

Kelsey took in the woman's silver bob and slate-gray eyes, and then read her name tag. "Tilda?"

"So much plastic in that mountain house, protecting all that Park Avenue furniture. And that fancy white carpet covering every inch of space. It was a wonder your family needed my services, but I kept every bit of that place pristine."

Tilda Hopkins. Their housekeeper for the years she'd gone to high school in K-Bay. The chime of Tilda's bangles had broken the stifling silence in each room she'd cleaned. Nowhere else had seemed more like home—and her family had lived around the globe.

Tilda slid her glasses down her nose and looked over the rims at Kelsey. "People always said you were the same as that museum masquerading as a house—fake. One thing to look at, but something else entirely underneath. Then you threw stones at our poor Ty and ran off to your own glass house in the city. Disappointed me, and a lot of other people with long memories." The old woman welcomed the next customer.

Kelsey set her chin over the steam curling from the top of her coffee cup. Instead of the expected warmth, it seemed as if the warmth was chased away by Kelsey's inner chill. A frostiness that had nothing to do with arctic temperatures and everything to do with fear.

Kelsey was afraid she was going to disappoint the older woman again. If she couldn't find recruits for Ty's matchmaking business, she'd have nothing to write about. Her boss had given her two weeks to get a positive response from her readership. Ad revenue on her page was down significantly. The people of Alaska had always been the subject of her columns, and their story had always been told, though she'd made a name for herself by revealing the B-side of people, pointing out their flaws and opening a moral debate for her readers. Except there hadn't been an ethical angle in her last story. No questionable decision in the one before that. No edge in any of her columns for the past month.

"Did you pick up one of those?" A woman in an unzipped parka and light green scrubs pointed at a flyer on the counter with her ringless left hand. "Pretty unoriginal."

"I thought I'd give it a try." Kelsey sipped her coffee, hoping to dilute the pinch of guilt fluttering through her stomach. "You know Ty?"

"I've seen him around. He's a bit older than me."

Tilda began handing the woman several coffees.

The nurse poured two sugar packets in one

and pushed on the lid before adding cream to another. "You look familiar."

Kelsey set her cup down, grabbed a to-go tray and shoved the woman's drink order into it. "I heard they had success over the weekend. Matched two people." One of whom was Cooper Hamilton. How that playboy landed a woman brave enough to take him on was anyone's guess. Kelsey passed the tray to the woman. "Kind of gives a girl hope. Some of the guys in town shaved and it isn't even spring. Can you believe it?"

Doubt was there in the woman's hesitation, but Kelsey noticed the interest in her soft smile. "Maybe I'll see you there tomorrow."

Yes! Score one bachelorette for the investigative reporter.

After the woman left, Kelsey might have fist pumped the air if not for Tilda and her hard stare.

"You'll be going tomorrow night?" Tilda asked. "If so, make sure you sit between Stan and Derrick at the bar, the warmest seat in the house. I remember how you were always a cold one, even in summer."

"I don't plan to be there long enough to sit down." Only long enough to get her story and head back home. She just needed a few more recruits for the mixer to get that interview with Ty. "And fortunately, I'm warm enough now thanks to my down-filled jacket and fur-lined boots." Kelsey took her hot coffee back to her car, pausing to take in the mangled parking sign, thankful she'd added rental-car insurance. If only she could add heart insurance as easily. She was afraid she might need some if she was going to get the real story out of Ty.

"READY, GIRLS?" KELSEY STOMPED her feet, shaking snow from her boots outside the Bar & Grill, hoping to encourage blood flow. Surely not every part of her had been flash frozen in the ten minutes she'd waited outside.

Her recruits had finally arrived, all five of them. Not bad for one day's notice. The nurse from the Clipper Ship still wore her scrubs, but she'd released her hair from its braid, letting the waves curl past her shoulders. The pair Kelsey had cornered at the gas station tossed their empty fast-food containers into the trash can, wiping their hands on their skinny jeans. The cashier from the Shop and Sack armed her car while the last straggler from the produce aisle of the same grocery store rubbed lip balm over her mouth.

Kelsey stepped inside the tavern, stuffing her

gloves into her coat pockets and unbuttoning her jacket, wanting to rush to the nearest heating vent and hibernate beside it. The women crowded in behind her, introducing themselves to each other as they hung their jackets on the hooks lining one wall of the entrance.

"I thought you said they'd shaved." The nurse frowned at Kelsey and tipped her head toward the bar.

She'd seen a picture of Coop. He'd shaved. Kelsey surveyed the patrons. She'd never seen the Bar & Grill so full on a weeknight. A half-dozen men lingered nearby, each showcasing a messier version of an unkempt full beard. And one empty stool jutted out between the mountain men. Tilda's hot seat.

Gideon stepped into her path, guiding the women toward a couple of unoccupied tables. "Ladies, welcome. We have a brief survey we'd like you to fill out."

The cashier accepted a pencil from Gideon. "Can't you use the one I filled out last week at the Shop and Sack? I still don't want to debone my own halibut or skin a deer."

"Nadine, it's a new day. New questions." Gideon thrust a paper at the woman.

"New men, too, I assume." Nadine high-fived her produce-aisle compatriot.

Kelsey waited while the women filled out the updated surveys. Ty maneuvered through another group of men gathered around the weathered oak bar like a practiced politician coaxing constituents to renounce their party and join his rogue revolt. But unlike a sleazy politician, nothing in Ty's interactions was false or forced or insincere. His handshakes included the grip on the shoulder as an added measure of contact. There was camaraderie. Good-natured ribbing. Laughter: quick bursts, gusts and low rumbles.

And answered prayers. Several clean male faces appeared, if she included the two with stubble and the one goatee over at the pool table.

Once the women finished the surveys, Ty came by, moving into her space.

The air shifted around her, brushing the back of her bare neck, forcing a quick shiver. "Looks as if you needed me after all, Ty. I don't see another available woman in here."

Ty leaned down to whisper in her ear. "Let's be clear, K.J., we've seen these ladies before. They've taken our survey before. You've done nothing for me."

But he did something for her. The rasp in his voice skated through her, carving a path of warmth over all those chilled places within. Caution flags snapped.

He turned away, his tone ratcheting from a rich rumble to a good-natured greeting. "Ladies, welcome to the Bar & Grill. Shall we see where this evening takes us?"

The women Kelsey had invited swelled around her, snared no doubt by the hint of temptation in Ty's warm voice. And like that, she was dismissed.

Too much heat made her light-headed anyway. Better she was cold. She could always add more layers. Kelsey rubbed her hands together and moved to the bar to get a drink.

A gap in the mountain men huddle opened and a familiar dry voice cut through the noise. "You look as lost as a newborn pup."

Tilda. "You can't be here for the matchmaking—you're married."

"My other half, Clarence, is teaching those whelps to play a proper game of pool." Tilda patted the empty stool beside her, her silver bangles colliding on her wrist. "The second-warmest seat in the house."

Kelsey glanced at the other women. They were giving Ty their drink orders.

"Didn't see you fill out a survey, so you can't be joining in over there." Tilda sipped her dark beer, watching Kelsey carefully. "That's the rules. Now sit before you scare the lot of them out of here with your reporter's face. You look as if you got a microphone stuffed in your bra."

"At least I'm not wearing an infomercial grin and oozing lies through my dimples." Kelsey nodded to Coop, who was circulating through the men at the opposite side of the tavern. "He looks as if he's trying to convince that behemoth next to him that his masculinity won't disappear if he trades in his lifted SUV for a minivan." Kelsey twisted the stool beside Tilda's to face out into the room.

Gideon sat at one of the tables, looking from the surveys to his laptop and back again like a spectator in a tennis match set on Fast-Forward.

"That one was here last week." Tilda tipped her pint glass toward the supermarket cashier. "You can't freshen up your hair with a store-bought bottle and expect it to bleach out the bitter inside you, as well."

"She was friendly enough when I was at the checkout."

"Nadine's paid to be nice to every customer," Tilda said. "A person's true colors are muted at work."

Except for Tilda's. Hers seemed to be on

display 24/7. "Maybe one of these guys can sweeten her up."

"Look at them." Tilda nudged her shoulder against Kelsey's. "Like scared rabbits stuck in a fox's den. Poor Coop can't hold all their hands, although he's trying."

Kelsey leaned forward, trying to hear Coop's sales pitch to the men.

Tilda leaned with her. "You remember those jawbreaker candies you loved as a kid? That's what you invited tonight. Those women are hard all the way through, not that I blame some of 'em. But these boys, well, they're like soft taffy. When you mix the two, you get nothing but a sticky mess."

"Good." Kelsey's impression was that this was an informal mixer. Like the ones she'd witnessed in the city. A night of drinking and dancing and… Wasn't that the rumor about how Coop had met his bell-ringing bride-to-be?

Gideon snapped his laptop closed and motioned for Coop to lead the men over to the women. Gideon pushed a burly red-haired giant wearing a firefighter T-shirt and untamed beard toward Ty, who stood beside the nurse. Gideon mouthed the word *soccer* and framed an invisible ball with his hands.

Ty picked up the cue. "Collin, this is Paula,

who works at K-Bay General and considers herself somewhat of an expert on soccer. Paula, meet the soccer federation's walking vault of facts."

Collin snapped his fingers and pointed at Paula. "Where was the 1994 final game played?"

"Pasadena." Paula twisted her hair up into a loose bun. "Your turn. Who won that same year in overtime?"

Collin tugged on his beard and grinned. "Brazil. And it was scoreless in both regular and overtime. It was decided by a shoot-out." Paula laughed and slipped her arm through Collin's when he offered to get her a refill.

"Not bad." Tilda rolled her empty glass between her palms. "Score one for our boys."

Score none for Kelsey. This was nothing her editor wanted to read.

A burst of laughter erupted from the foursome that Coop gathered at the table across from where Kelsey sat. One of the men slapped the wooden tabletop and shook his head. "Little T's Pizza is the best in the county."

The produce shopper didn't look convinced. "That's good, but the sauce is better at Romano's." An argument ensued over the correct sweetness for the best sauce, the ideal thickness of pepperoni slices, the perfect crunch in a thin crust. Finally, all parties agreed to a taste off later in the week.

"The boys are doing better tonight. Must be those improved questionnaires." Tilda spun her stool around and ordered two beers.

Kelsey surveyed the gathering. Where was the sticky mess? Why weren't potential couples making out in the corner? Why wasn't one of the mountain men tossing a woman over his shoulder to take her to his man cave?

Right now Kelsey's tagline read Local K-Bay Boys Make Good on Promise of Love. The vision of her packing up her cubicle into several boxes solidified in her mind. That she'd need only one and a half boxes for her stuff after almost ten years at the *Beat* made her frown.

Tilda pressed a pint glass into Kelsey's hand. "Maybe you're the only jawbreaker here."

She was career focused like her mother and father. And if that made her hard, so be it. "Then, it's good I didn't fill out a survey."

"These boys might have the secret sauce to find the one meant for you." Tilda tapped her pint against Kelsey's glass. "Never discount the power of making a real connection."

Kelsey shook her head and then drank her beer. Real love couldn't be trusted. She only had to read the interviews she'd done for her column to know that. Or simply look at her own family and her parents' shell of a marriage. "I think I'll leave love's pain and misery to the lost souls here tonight."

"That's only what's on the surface. Get to the center and there's the good stuff." Tilda pointed at the brass bell over the beer taps. "That's the stuff worth ringing the bell for."

Kelsey wasn't interested in the bell or discussing love's complexities with Tilda. But the older woman reminded Kelsey that good never existed without bad. It was her duty to discover the nasty inner core and reveal the truth inside. That was what the *Beat* promised their readers.

The story wasn't here with Tilda on her warm seat surrounded by her mountain men. And it wasn't going to be discovered among the couples now debating puppy potty training at the table behind her. But Kelsey wasn't giving up. She'd been raised surrounded by perfection; she knew firsthand that nothing was ever as it appeared. And tonight's event was too perfect not to have a catch.

Ty set a bin full of empty glasses onto the far end of the bar and stepped behind it as if he belonged there. He had always been a contradiction. Maybe if she confronted him, the story would reveal itself.

Kelsey stood and picked up her beer. "Thanks for the drink."

She made her way to the empty stool at the bar's corner. Ty filled an order from a waitress, moving with the ease and grace of a seasoned bartender. He only acknowledged her once to offer an abbreviated introduction to Coach, the owner of the Bar & Grill. Coach offered a measured smile, as if she were a star recruit and he didn't believe the hype, before moving toward Tilda and her mountain men as they placed bets on the most likely matches in the crowd. Several were convinced there wouldn't be any.

Ty set a highball glass on a waitress's tray and finally turned his full attention on Kelsey. A shadow passed through his expression.

Kelsey's reporter instincts pounced. She'd seen that look hundreds of times before. Shadows meant secrets. Kelsey brought forth her most easygoing smile. "So you work at the skating rink. You're a matchmaker, and now it seems a bartender, too."

"Among other things." He tore off a mint leaf and stuck it in his mouth. The shadow was gone.

"Do you have time for that interview?"

"How did you like your beer?" He motioned to her half-empty glass.

"It isn't as good as a mai tai."

He nodded to someone who called for another beer and drew it from a tap. "You're out of luck, Kelsey. Paula over there just told Collin that she's too busy for a relationship now." His gaze narrowed and for the first time she noticed the irritation threading through his gaze, the small twitch at the edge of his right eye. Even his scar appeared deeper, more crimson, more pronounced. "All deals are off."

"Wait." Too late. She knew he'd heard the desperation in her clipped tone. Inhaling a deep breath, she tried to push serenity through her limbs like her yoga instructor had drummed into her. She purposely slowed her words, striving to sound indifferent. "I could bring in different women, better women."

"I don't know how." He picked up her glass, poured out the beer and set the glass upside down in the stainless-steel sink. "Besides, it doesn't matter. You came. You saw. There's no story here."

That serenity chant ruptured into a scream, complete with double fist punches against the bar top. She squeezed her hands together in her lap. "I'll decide when I have enough facts."

"You use facts now?" He set his elbows on the bar and leaned toward her. "And here I thought you finally wanted to write something with more heart."

Get to the center and the bell-ringing good stuff. Her gaze tripped over Ty's face as she tried not to linger on his full mouth or notice the mint on his breath. Or wonder if the good stuff was still there, beneath that thick beard, deep inside him, waiting for her to uncover it.

His smile angled slyly. He was wondering about the good stuff, too.

She shoved her thoughts aside. This mutual wondering wasn't doing her any good. She clenched her teeth together, reminding herself she was the jawbreaker. Tilda had that right. And she wasn't far enough along in her career for soft centers. "And here I thought you would've let the past go. Your name was cleared after all. Isn't that what this is about? A fresh start? New career? Plastic surgery for your—" her gaze drifted to his cheek "—image."

"Leave it, K.J." He drew back and pressed his thumb into his right temple, no rubbing, no gentle massage, just a force of pressure to stop whatever pain pulsed there. And then he began mixing a drink.

She'd touched a nerve, a deep one from the finality in his voice. She knew everything about his past injuries…didn't she? "I came for the matchmaking story, but I'm guessing the backgrounds of the matchmakers are much more interesting."

He didn't rise to the bait, but his gaze darted to his friends. He set the cocktail on a coaster in front of her. "I've got another customer. Take care."

She played with the straw and stirred her drink. "Is it last call, then?"

"For you, it is." Then he turned his back on her and walked away.

"Do you know what the real test of true love in Alaska is?" Coach picked up a remote and aimed it at the TV hanging in the corner. A hockey game filled the screens on each of the televisions scattered around the bar, snaring the men's full attention.

Coop lunged across the bar and attempted to grab the remote from Coach's grip like a parent snatching his child from an alligator pit. But Coop hadn't been fast enough. Snubbed—in some cases, almost midsentence—a number of the women moved to a table near the door.

Gideon and Ty hurried toward Coach.

"Taught you boys to react better than this." Coach shook his finger at them. "What did I used to tell you about game plans?"

Gideon drummed his fingers on his laptop. "Hockey is a graveyard of the best-laid plans?"

"Any breakdown can be corrected with ice experience, not diagrams?" Coop captured the remote, changed the channel to the news and tossed the device into a cupboard beneath the bar.

The three men turned to Ty.

"Never underestimate the power of teamwork," Ty recited, as sullen as a schoolboy.

Coach's laughter burst out in one blast like a low-budget hockey horn. "Game experience is different than any plan or diagram you might have. You'll continue to fail until you understand what it means to win and lose at love." He went into the kitchen.

"The game isn't over," Coop stated.

It certainly wasn't. Kelsey was thrilled. Ty's reticence. The matchmaking team's tension. There was more to the story. She was betting her future on it.

CHAPTER THREE

"STILL LOOKING TO prove love by the book works?" Coach asked the next morning at the Bar & Grill. "There is no manual on love, fellas. No fancy equation. No mathematical formula." Coach wiped down a blue vodka bottle and set it back on the shelves. "Take note for that article you have to write when I win our bet, boys. Fresh, clean air. That should be in the top-ten reasons to love Alaska. Can't get air like this in the Lower 48."

Clean or not, Ty couldn't breathe. The last he'd seen of Kelsey, she'd had that look in her eye, that mad-scientist gleam that said she'd shifted into the express lane.

"But our surveys work." Gideon dropped his laptop bag on the empty stool beside Ty. "The logarithms paired up our soccer couple, Paula and Collin."

Ty picked up his bowl of mixed nuts to give Gideon more room to spread out his surveys. Gideon shuffled through his papers and pulled two from the pile. "They match on every question."

"Perfect on paper." Coach wrapped his white towel around the neck of a bulk-size whiskey bottle. "Then, why haven't they rung my bell?"

"They're perfect, apart from the fact that Paula doesn't want to be in a relationship right now." Ty chose a few spicy peanuts from the bowl. "Maybe there needs to be a header—participants must be willing and open to being in a relationship right now, not ten years from today."

"Here's another tip. Do you know what you can see later this month in Alaska?" Coach asked, grinning. "The World Ice Art competition. That should be on your list, too, of why you love living in Alaska. Don't take the easy way and include all them obvious tourist places. We're more than cruise-ship ports."

Coop walked out from the kitchen, waving a clean pacifier. His infant daughter was strapped to his chest in one of those baby-carrier contraptions. The days of chest bumps, fistfights and all-nighters were gone for his friend. Coop kissed his daughter's head. Not that he looked the least bit miserable or remorseful. Still, the whiplash lifestyle change his friend had made confounded Ty. Fortunately, he intended to never make that kind of game change.

Coop gave Zoe her pacifier. "We don't need to write that list yet. We just need women who are ready to settle down."

"But we don't need any more repeats, in women or survey questions." Ty tossed a handful of peanuts into his mouth and chewed. The spices hit his stomach and rolled around like the ball on a roulette wheel. It'd been days since Trinity Matchmaking had made a match.

Gideon opened his laptop and started typing. "Only some of the questions were the same from last week."

"Find last week's questionnaire from our cashier, Nadine." Ty set the bowl down and scanned the previous night's surveys until he found the one he wanted. "I bet she gave different answers this week when we paired her with Derrick. Last week was...Wendell." One guy was a truck driver and the other a restaurant owner. The two men couldn't have been more different.

Coop grabbed the two surveys and held them above Zoe's head. "Last week she liked beer and spending her weekends fly fishing. This week it's wine and preferring to be at home on the couch watching the sports channel. Nice attempt at gaming the system."

"Still didn't work." Gideon shrugged, his fingers tapping a rapid beat across the keyboard. As the town's banker, and the guys' financial guru, he certainly dressed the part. Now all he needed was a chance to run a professional-hockey outfit. "She wasn't matched on the computer, this week or last week. We assigned her somebody last minute."

Didn't that make them sound like losers?

"So we agree that we need new fish for our matchmaking pond." Coop stroked Zoe's cheek. "Yesterday the beauty parlor on Birch Street refused to put up a new flyer for me."

"We've exhausted our contact list and our goodwill in town." Gideon never looked up from his laptop. "And I swear someone in Bitzy's Bling nail shop put the closed sign in the window just as I was heading over there with new flyers."

Coop cooed at Zoe, his voice sugared in baby goodness. "Kelsey Nash can find us more women."

No. Obviously all of Coop's cooing had mucked up Ty's hearing. His friend was on serious baby overload. Not every woman was as angelic as Zoe or as trustworthy as Nora,

Coop's fiancée. "Why would you say that? Look what she produced last night. Fish we'd already thrown back in the water."

"Kelsey has connections." Gideon never slowed his keystrokes. "Here and in Anchorage."

"I think she understands now what we're hoping for," Coop said.

She understood nothing. Or perhaps she understood too much. It didn't matter. *Kelsey Nash didn't matter.* Ty couldn't allow this to happen. "She wants a feature story. You know what that means." *Him.* She wanted a story on him.

But his friends didn't know that Ty still had a secret. One that would give Kelsey the headline she wanted and sever the guys' friendship. A friendship forged on the third-grade playground during a dodgeball war against Randy Lee Jenkins, fifth-grade bulldozer.

"Then, give her our story in exchange for her help." Coop played peek-a-boo with Zoe.

"It's never that simple with Kelsey." Ty shoved his stool back and stood. He washed his hands in the sink, willing his stomach to quit roiling as if he was out on a crabbing boat in a storm-tossed sea. "She has a way of getting people to tell her things." And by people, Ty meant himself.

Gideon stopped typing and followed him behind the bar and slung an arm around his shoulder. "At least this time she can't make things up. Besides, she exposed all the skeletons in your closet years ago."

But she hadn't.

And once discovered, this truth would leave Ty more alone than he'd ever been. And that included the time his father's body had washed up near the pier. Exactly one week after his father had conned his grandparents and several friends into investing their life savings in a mining venture. In three days his father had gambled and boozed away all the money. In three more days, he'd doubled his debt owed to a loan shark. On the seventh day, that debt had been paid.

And Kelsey? Ty had been young when he'd spilled his guts to her. He'd have told her just about anything when they'd finally stopped fighting and teasing each other and put their lips together.

He could stonewall one woman for two weeks until the bet with Coach was won. Once Kelsey left town and his friends had moved to the Lower 48, the truth wouldn't matter. It'd stay buried for good. All Ty had to do was stay one step ahead of Kelsey, go on the offensive, call her out before she called him.

Ty got out his cell phone and dialed the Sky Hawk Mountain Lodge. The receptionist connected him to Kelsey's room. Two rings later and her sleep-tinged voice filled the silence.

"It's your chance at redemption," Ty said. "Tomorrow night. Iceplex. Seven o'clock. And invite women comfortable outdoors. We've got an ice-fishing event planned for the next day." He paused and rubbed his temple, trying to get rid of the image forming in his mind. "And, K.J., sharpen your blades. Your participation is required."

He clicked the end-call button before he heard her reaction. Before the picture from the past came into full focus: midnight on a frozen lake, ice skates and stolen kisses.

CHAPTER FOUR

"IF YOU WANT to return skates, you're in the wrong line."

Not again. Not here. Kelsey tossed the end of her crimson scarf over her shoulder and leaned around Eleanor Clambert. Sure enough. There was Tilda working behind the outdoor ice-rink snack counter. The woman was like a slice of red bell pepper: overpowering, strong flavored and hard to digest.

Tilda stared back at her through those wide, round sixties frames, her eyes like twin magnets, always tracking Kelsey. "This isn't the skate line."

The women in front of her—Eleanor, the shyest girl in their high school class; Summer, the earth-tuned woman Kelsey had tracked down at her health food store, Lately Lettuce; and Holly, the elementary school music teacher with lavender-dyed hair whom Kelsey had discovered working the evening shift at the gas station—shifted as a unit to the other line.

Kelsey stepped up to the snack counter. "You work here, too?"

She should do a column on the K-Bay residents and their adaptability in the workforce. The town wouldn't lack for qualified employees if all of the residents were as versatile as Ty and Tilda.

"My other half likes to ref." Tilda held a thick soft pretzel between stainless steel tongs. "And I like to help wherever I can."

And by *help*, Tilda meant sharing her numerous opinions without restraint. Kelsey assumed Tilda would opt for a job at any venue that granted her such freedom, even if it meant having to filet salmon in the harbor in her bathrobe.

Tilda pointed at Kelsey with her tongs. "Unless you have skates stashed in that oversize tote you haul everywhere, and I doubt you do, you need to get in that line."

Kelsey had skates. In her closet. In her studio. Back in the city. Not that it was Tilda's concern. Besides, Kelsey had invited more than enough women to grant her a no-skate pass, despite Ty's orders last night. "There's enough participants. I'd like a hot chocolate."

"Only the pretzels are ready." Tilda dunked a pretzel into a bowl of melted butter and shook her head. "I can't believe no one has taught you how to have fun."

Kelsey squeezed the wide shoulder strap on her tote. She knew how to have fun. She just didn't have time for fun. *Hello, big difference.* Her focus had to be on her career. Fun would come later. And if it never came, so be it. She'd had fun, in a once-in-a-blue-moon memory kind of way. In a different time. On a different ice rink. With a different boy. Her gaze found Ty. "The city is fun."

"Oh, my little lost lamb, fun isn't sitting on your balcony alone, watching the crowds rush in and out of the bars and restaurants on the street below." Tilda dropped the hot pretzel into another square pan and used the tongs to smash it into the salt. "Sometimes you just gotta let go, dive in and let the fun stick to you."

She'd tried that before and ended up just plain stuck. Now she let go in her columns and kept herself safe. "Thanks. As terrific as this has been, I'm going to find Ty and see if there is anything else he needs from me. I'll come back for that hot chocolate."

Ty waited behind the counter in the skate bay beside the snack bar, holding on to several pairs of skates. Of course. Was there anything he didn't do?

Kelsey stepped around several of the women seated on the benches, removing their boots, and moved to Ty's station. "I don't need those."

"Right. You already missed the free skate portion. And besides, broomball is more fun without skates."

Ty's tone brought Kelsey up short. Because he wasn't being short with her. He sounded almost…glad to see her.

There was something wrong here. "I'll pass. I'd rather hear the story behind Trinity Matchmaking." Kelsey crossed her arms over her chest.

"After the game." Ty held out a broomstick to her, handle first, with the bristles duct-taped.

Kelsey didn't move. "You never mentioned anything about a broomball game."

"You don't need a ref for free skating," Tilda called out from behind the soda fountain. "See my Clarence out there?"

"Have you forgotten how to play?" Ty nudged the broomstick closer to her.

"If I'm honest and say no, can we please forget about my participating?" She could blend in with the crowd during free skate. But broomball meant teams. She'd always been picked last for teams.

"Why? Don't city girls skate? Don't city

girls have fun?" Ty scratched his beard. "Did the city take your laughter, too, K.J.?"

Kelsey grabbed the broom handle and gestured toward Ty. "The city didn't take anything I hadn't already lost here in K-Bay."

"Maybe it's time to find some of those things again." There was a challenge in his voice, as if he was testing her.

"There's nothing in my past I want found," she said. Nothing she wanted found by Ty.

"Then, we understand each other. The past remains where it belongs…in the past." He released the broom. "Women against men. One game. Drinks and appetizers by the fire pits after the third period."

"And then we talk?" That had to happen first before she would decide where the past belonged.

"If you brought new women interested in making real matches." Ty tipped his chin toward the stick she held. "If you participate. Oh, and one more thing. If you're going to write an article on us, we insist you take our matchmaking survey." He handed her a paper and pen.

Kelsey scowled. "Let me get this straight. No broomball, no interview. No survey, no interview."

His smile broadened enough that she could see his white teeth. "Now we're on the same page."

Grumbling, Kelsey filled out the survey. No, she didn't know the time she wanted her wedding to occur. Anytime from dawn until dusk when she could get the groom to meet her at the church would be ideal. That answer wasn't an option. No, she hadn't given much thought to pets before or after children. That would imply she'd planned… That was the next question. No, she didn't know at what age she wanted to have her first child. Anytime after her upcoming June birthday and before menopause sounded about right. Again, that answer wasn't listed. She glanced through the next page, checking boxes at random. Surely the guys didn't really believe these questions would help them pair folks into happy couples?

She pushed the pen and paper across the counter and asked, "Aren't you playing, too?" Ty loved being on the ice almost as much as he loved to have fun.

"I'm working." His lips disappeared within his beard again, but his scowl was there in his tone and the stiff set to his shoulders.

Again, Kelsey had the feeling that something was wrong. "I don't imagine there'll be much matchmaking required while the game is in progress."

"I don't skate anymore." He pressed his

thumb like a fingerprint against his temple. "Haven't in years."

Seven, she'd bet.

"Can't or won't?" Her hands tightened around the broom handle; her breath quieted. And yet her blood pounded in her eardrums, and her nerves sparked as if she'd just received an injection of pure caffeine. The reporter inside her imagined sharpening her pencil. Some called it a hunch, others a gut reaction. Whatever it was, Kelsey paid attention. And she knew, like she knew the Sunday edition of the *Beat* went to bed at midnight every Saturday, that the real story hovered in the silence between them like a pin against a balloon. "Because of your injuries?"

She let her gaze drift over Ty's strong shoulders. She had yet to see him rub his neck as if it was sore. She'd bet if she could run her fingers beneath his pullover, she'd count a six-pack. And he hadn't limped, not in the parking lot when they'd first met, not in the bar and not now. Only that subtle wince, the press of fingers to his head and the thin scar on his right cheek gave away that he'd been injured.

His cheek tensed. The edges of his eyes narrowed.

Story gold revved, zooming through her. "Why deny yourself the only thing you ever loved?"

"I've loved more than one thing." His voice dropped low into that deep rumble that came from somewhere inside the chest, close to the heart. But he didn't move; his hands fisted at his waist, his feet remained spread apart. He was braced as if anticipating her attack. As if waiting for her to probe. Waiting for her to find his secrets.

Because he had secrets.

She was so excited, she could barely keep from hopping over the counter and grabbing on to his coat lapels. "Why don't you skate anymore?"

"Ty, I'm ready to trade skates for a broom." Stacey Logan stepped up to the counter in her pink socks and set her skates on the counter.

"Sure thing, Stacey." Ty took her skates and disappeared into the storage bay.

So close. Kelsey had been so close to him giving her the info that could make this feature fabulous.

Stacey leaned her hip against the counter and smiled, unaware of her poor sense of timing. "Thanks for inviting me." Stacey had a soft voice, a kind smile and a casualness about her that would make it easy to call her a friend.

"Sorry about broomball. I didn't know participation was a requirement." Obviously. Although Kelsey was curious whom she'd be matched up with.

"I think it's going to be the best part." Stacey was another one of Kelsey's intentional finds. She was the daughter of Ty's physical therapist. And a potential story source. "I wouldn't have had the guts to come alone, but I'm glad I'm here."

"Maybe you could persuade Ty to join in. That is, if he's still physically able…"

"I did my ice time years ago." Ty had returned with Stacey's hiking boots. "Speaking of years ago, Stacey, you were in our freshman class, right?"

"Yes. Kelsey and I had precalculus and British literature together with Mrs. Bristow." Stacey touched Kelsey's arm. "You haven't forgotten Bad Breath Bristow, have you?"

"Nope."

"Remember, we took up a collection and gave her a jar of mints for Christmas." Stacey was as sweet as those mints. If she knew anything about Ty's recovery years ago, she'd never tell.

"Right, and she claimed she was allergic

to peppermint." Kelsey shook her head. "She never touched the jar."

"Sounds interesting." Ty laid a broomstick on the counter and started duct-taping the bristles. "But it's not the freshman memory I like to recall. I have many, but one in particular is my favorite." Ty flipped over the broom and chuckled. "It was at summer training camp."

The rich, deep sound of Ty's laughter curled through Kelsey like spiked hot chocolate, warming and delighting in all kinds of forbidden ways. He did still hold a fond memory of her.

"Remember the time camp was closed to the public?" Stacey fluffed her hair. "I know because I had a crush on Nathan Daniels and I wanted to bring him lunch or a snack or even water, but I couldn't."

"That's what I was referring to, Stace. The camp was closed after a particular freshman crashed our practice." Ty's tone conveyed a shared secret.

If Ty said one more word, Kelsey was going to kill him.

Kelsey desperately motioned toward the rink. "Isn't the game about to start?"

"When I blow the whistle," Ty said. "And

besides, we have one man down with faulty equipment." He smiled at Stacey.

"You're almost done with her stick," Kelsey said, trying to sound as if Ty's detour through the back alleyway of high school memory lane was no big deal. "I'm sure Stacey wants to get ready. Maybe find a man out there to bring water to."

Stacey leaned against the counter, content to let Ty finish repairing her broom at his own pace. "Wait, I remember a rumor about a freshman flashing the hockey team."

It hadn't been the team. *Team* implied multiple players. It had been only one. The goalie. Ty. Kelsey was certain the red dye in her scarf had leaked into her cheeks.

Not that Stacey had a clue. She'd body blocked Kelsey out of the conversation as if she was no longer necessary. This was why Kelsey didn't join in.

"But that was high school lore. A myth." Stacey reached out to Ty, wide-eyed. "Oh, no way. Did it really happen?"

"It's burned in my memory as if it happened yesterday," Ty said.

"Wonder what that girl was thinking," Stacey ventured.

She'd been thinking she wanted Ty Porter's

attention. She'd been thinking she wanted him to see something other than a puck. She'd been thinking if she let go and embraced the spontaneous, she'd discover a different life. Instead, she'd been grounded through hockey season, listened to Tilda's bangles after school every day and eaten jawbreakers.

"It's in the past." Ty handed the stick to Stacey. "Could be I'm remembering it all wrong. Maybe that's what I wanted to happen."

"Ty Porter, you're making me want to gossip like a teenager again, which is just fine. I need something to talk to the nurses about when my treatments start up again in a few weeks." Stacey laughed, cradling her boots in one hand, her broomstick in the other. Ty squeezed her arm. Stacey stretched her smile wider, shook her head. "Tonight isn't about that. Tonight we beat the boys."

Stacey bumped her hip against Kelsey's as she passed. Kelsey glanced down at Stacey's pink socks, noticing for the first time the familiar ribbons printed all over them. Unfortunately the *Beat* didn't want an article about the nearest clinic being a hundred miles away. Or what it was like to drive home from chemo in a snowstorm. And Kelsey wanted Stacey's insider information on Ty, not her real-life story, even if it was one that needed to be told.

Ty stopped Kelsey from leaving with a hand on her arm. "K.J., you don't have any Mardi Gras beads stashed in your pockets, do you? I want this to be a fair game. No talismans. No tricks."

Kelsey wanted to swat his touch away with her broomstick and brush off his hopeful-sounding voice. "If I had any now, I'd use them to wipe out your memory."

"Hey, I was an impressionable young man."

"And I left an impression," Kelsey muttered.

"Indelibly." When Kelsey leaned across the counter to try to slug his shoulder, Ty jumped away, threw his head back and laughed. This time his whole body was involved—it was that rare, unguarded kind of laughter released only in the safety of trusted friends.

A warmth swirled through Kelsey along with the bitterness from questioning whether she'd ever let go like that. If she'd ever been that secure. Perhaps once. With Ty.

But all they shared now was distrust and bylines.

And she wasn't here to change history. Or even repeat it.

Kelsey pulled her phone from her back

pocket and snapped a picture of Ty before he frowned at her. She knew without reviewing the photograph that she'd captured the money shot for the feature. Ty Porter: chin tilted up, head tipped back, openmouthed grin, laughter in the lines fanning his eyes. Pure pleasure. Pure joy. One carefree moment captured and later twisted.

Kelsey strode over to the bench, away from Ty's laughter and her memories of him.

She uploaded the photograph of Ty to her social media app, adding beneath the caption, Should your #matchmaker wear #skates? Do credentials and history matter in your matchmaker choice? Or are looks enough? Inside scoop Sunday. Then she hit the publish button.

She ignored the roiling in her own gut. This was nothing more than she'd always done. She made headlines.

At the snack bar, Tilda dropped steaming pretzels into the salt bath, one after another. She glanced at Kelsey, slowed her movements and released another pretzel into the pan. "Time to dive in, little lamb."

Kelsey shoved open the door that led to the outdoor rink. She'd join in. This one time. If only to prove it wouldn't change anything.

CHAPTER FIVE

KELSEY MOVED INTO the left forward position. She expected a clean game, and instead what ensued was a competitive one with dirty plays and trash-talking. Five minutes into the second period, the coed melee had exploded.

Kelsey wasn't certain if it had started when gigantic Trent picked up Summer, or when Jason, the lumberjack, had stolen the ball. Or when Holly had tossed her glove on the ice, bent over with an extra thrust in her chest area to retrieve it, and Charlie, charming because he was clumsy, had tripped over Holly's stick. Either way, Trent had refused to put Summer down, so Kelsey had swatted him with her broom. Charlie's stick had slid into the goal, prompting Eleanor to pick it up.

"All's fair in love and hockey, boys," Stacey shouted before she and her new pal, Holly, grabbed Jason's belt from behind, tugging him away from the women's goal. He managed to shoot before spinning and wrapping the pair in a bear hug as Ty stepped onto the ice to help Charlie up.

A shrill whistle finally broke through all the laughter and shouting.

"Trent, you need to put that girl down. This ain't a pairs skating competition. You're in the box for five." Clarence then sent bear-hugger Jason to the penalty box for interference, followed by Charlie, who'd come out of his goal to join in the chaos. The men protested the loss of their goalie, prompting Clarence, the ref, to point directly at Ty. "You're in the box in his place."

Kelsey set her hands on her hips. "Ty isn't even playing."

"He was on the ice when the penalty occurred." Clarence winked at her. "You're in there, too, for hitting, and you can take your goalie's time with you."

Kelsey walked to the women's penalty box. "Whose rules are these?"

"Mine." Clarence chuckled before blowing the whistle to begin play.

Ty joined Kelsey in the women's penalty box.

"Your box is over there." Kelsey jabbed her broom handle across the ice.

"No room." Ty dropped onto the bench beside her and stretched out his long legs, crossing one ankle over the other.

"How long are we in here for?"

Ty stacked his hands behind his head. "Until Clarence lets us out."

"Aren't there time standards? Two minutes? Five?" Kelsey leaned her broom against the wall and wrapped the fleece blanket that someone had left on the bench around her legs. "Those were minor penalties."

"There was holding, hooking, tripping and high brooming that I saw." Ty's breath came out in long puffs. "And I believe at one point Eleanor held two brooms and the ball. Add those together and you're here for more than ten minutes."

"I only hit Trent to get him to put Summer down," Kelsey said, enjoying their banter more than she should.

"And he's over there in our box," Ty said. "Punished, as well."

"Holly dropped her glove. It wasn't her fault Charlie—the smoothy—did a somersault over her broomstick when she went to get it." Kelsey tucked her hair up inside her hat. "I suspect he'd trip on flat pavement with no one around."

Ty chuckled. "No doubt."

"But Holly got his attention." Kelsey smiled.

"As planned, I'm sure," Ty said. "Like you planned to get my attention at training camp."

"I was young. Stupid," she said. "One very bad decision that is in the past. Forgotten."

"So you forget bad decisions and move on?" he asked.

"I try not to repeat the mistake," she said. "I don't know that I ever forget."

"There're things I can't forget," he said. "And things I don't want to forget."

"That's rather convoluted."

"Not really. I don't want to forget that afternoon. One of the few times I witnessed you embrace your free spirit." Ty's voice had lost all its teasing. "And all for me."

She'd always felt more like a trapped animal. A forgotten trapped animal, maybe. But a free spirit?

Did he really think of her like that? "Enough about me, Ty. What can't you forget?"

His gaze tracked to her and locked on so that she held her breath, wondering if she'd crossed one of those imaginary lines again. It was something she always seemed to do with him. But she knew his history, knew his dark past, not because she'd researched his father, but because he'd told her that summer when they'd dated, when she had been more important than hockey.

"All of my bad decisions." Ty reached over and adjusted her scarf up around her chin. "Remind me that I can't have what I want. I didn't deserve it then. And I don't deserve it now. I've made peace with my lot in life."

If that was the truth, then why was there a wistful note in his voice?

"What do you want, K.J.? Besides my story," he said, turning the tables on her, taking her hand and tucking her glove up under her jacket sleeve. "What does that carefree girl I used to know want? I figured you'd be living in the Lower 48 and traveling the world like your family."

"We don't share the same definition of *stability*." Or *home*. She'd never fit into her family's lifestyle. "I have an apartment in the city with a view of the bay."

"City reporter. City apartment. City life." Ty pulled away from her, leaned back and stacked his hands behind his head again. "Sounds as if you have it all."

"Not yet." But she would when she made her next headline. "You should try life outside K-Bay."

"What's out there that I don't already have here?" Ty asked.

Me.

A traitorous thought, immediately discarded. Kelsey blamed it on the ice and the star-dusted sky and the man sitting next to her.

"You were meant to be more. So much more." They were meant to be more. There had to be more than this. For him. For them. There had to be more than one moment in a penalty box, one moment on the ice every seven years.

What was she thinking? They didn't even have this moment. She needed to expose his secrets to save her hide. This would become one of Ty's need-to-forget moments. She huddled beneath the blanket and watched the players on the ice.

The whistle cut into her thoughts. Clarence shouted, "Ty, you can get out of there."

"Views good in here," Ty called back with a sly half grin that sent Kelsey's heart sliding across the smooth ice along with the ball.

She had to recover her focus. Be the heartless reporter with killer instincts. "You should be pleased at the potential matches."

"Who do you think has potential for a second date at tomorrow's event?" Ty asked.

"Holly and Charlie," Kelsey answered. "But it won't last more than a week."

"Because he'll trip and give himself a concussion." Ty grinned, a full one this time.

"That could happen, or more likely they'll realize they have nothing in common beyond good physical taste. They both appreciate fine-looking, well-toned bodies."

"Wow, that's shallow." His grin faded.

Despite being a closet romantic, Kelsey was a glass-half-empty pessimist. Didn't he read her column? "I'm not saying they don't have lovely personalities. They're just hung up on the image of what their significant other should look like."

"Who would you pair Charlie with?" Ty asked.

"Summer."

"The whimsical 'I listen to harp music and look for fairies in the forest' Summer?" Ty rolled his head to stare at her. "You can't be serious."

"Yes, very. Charlie took over his family's logging business—he could use a bit of Summer's whimsy so he doesn't have an early heart attack like his dad. And Summer needs him to keep her grounded. They'd balance each other out." Kelsey crossed her arms over her chest and flopped back onto the bench. "And I'd put Eleanor with Trent."

"No." His reply was swift. Instant.

"Why not?" Kelsey twisted to look at him. "Eleanor puts in more hours a week at the day-care center than anyone else. She needs someone to take care of her. Trent lost his father last year. He could use a break himself."

"Eleanor needs someone who won't tire of her quirks within a year." His mouth was firm. His chin was set. Every part of his body broadcast end of discussion.

She gave him this one. "You've really put some thought into this."

"I'm a matchmaker. Isn't that my responsibility?" Ty's voice had *boundary* ruffling all over it.

"Why the sudden interest in playing Cupid?" Kelsey watched Tilda lean over the sidewall and give Clarence a kiss on his papery cheek before he blew the whistle.

"Because I'm a romantic at heart." Ty stood. "Your time is up, Ms. Nash. Thank you for the interview. You know the rules. If you want another, you need to find more bachelorettes."

He exited the penalty box, leaving Kelsey to speculate how he'd managed to get the upper hand.

She stared at her duct-taped stick. Had she just been charmed out of an interview? Had any of what he'd said been real? Her heart wanted to believe there was something between them, but she was a Nash. She was more likely to believe in the bottom line. And yet, she was smiling.

The game ended in a tie, according to the ref. But the women decided one of their goals did in fact count and declared themselves the victors. The men declared a forfeit and called for the game to be rescheduled the following week. Same time. Same place.

Brooms returned and no injuries reported, the group gathered around the fire pits located inside a massive open-walled lodge that offered some protection from the elements. Tilda brought over chocolate bars, graham crackers and several bags of marshmallows that she set on one of the picnic tables. The long skewers she set on the rock ledge surrounding the fire pit. "You're all old enough to assemble these on your own."

The group offered a collective thank-you and crowded around the table, everyone offering their suggestions and tips on how to make the perfect s'mores. Gideon strode in, his customary tie in place, laptop in one hand and a stack of papers in the other. Coop and Ty announced their computer-generated matches. Kelsey's name wasn't among them.

Kelsey backed away, away from the warmth of the second fire pit. She pulled her cell phone from her back pocket. Her editor had favorited the post about Ty. Not only her editor. Several others at the *Beat*. Even the editor-in-chief.

She was reclaiming her place in her world. But for the first time, she wondered if it was the life she wanted.

CHAPTER SIX

TY LEANED BACK in the office chair he'd wheeled out from the iceplex and set his boots on the rock wall of the fire pit, propping one ankle on top of the other. He pulled the last marshmallow from the bag and popped it in his mouth. One less thing to clean up before tomorrow morning and peewee open skate.

"I kept hoping Kelsey's story was about Trinity Matchmaking." Coop tore apart Tilda's last pretzel and dipped the pieces in hot mustard at the picnic table. "She posted about you on social media."

"You know what she was really after." Ty still felt a step ahead of her. Although sitting in the penalty box, he'd noticed a few distracting things. He'd noticed the small dimple in her left cheek peeking out when she laughed, the clear brown of her eyes when he teased her and the gentle tone of her voice when she spoke of their past. He tossed a twig in the fire and watched the flames consume the branch, wishing it was as easy to incinerate his mistakes.

"Anything Kelsey writes is old news." Gideon unwrapped a chocolate bar and snapped off a piece. "Let her write about Ty. She can't hurt him or us."

She could if she uncovered Ty's last secret—the reason he'd been injured. And that tidbit would undermine his friends' dreams of hockey careers in the Lower 48. He rubbed both hands over his face, wishing he could erase his fatal fascination with Kelsey. "Old news, new twist, wider audience. Look how many hits her social media posting got. That was only a teaser."

"She could surprise you and write a success story." Obviously Coop was still in happy baby mode. "A column about how you rose above your past and helped us all achieve our goals and ambitions."

"You need to get your head in the game. Not everyone holds hands, skipping around the campfire while singing nursery songs." Ty's boots smacked against the stone foundation. He stood, letting the chair roll into the picnic table.

"People change." Coop shrugged and stuffed another bite of pretzel in his mouth.

"Not people like Kelsey." Or himself. If he had really changed, he wouldn't still want Kelsey Nash. He'd always craved the things that were bad for him. Like father, like son, he supposed. Ty paced around the fire pit.

"Maybe we can make the matches before Kelsey's column breaks." Gideon spread the surveys across the picnic table. "We have some very well-matched couples this time."

Ty walked over to the table, reading the names until he found his whimsical fairy chaser and Charlie. He compared the two surveys. Not one of their answers matched. Their compatibility factor: a resounding zero. And Kelsey wanted to match them? He crumbled up the surveys and tossed them both in the fire.

Gideon frowned at him. "Did you have to do that? Those are our records."

"You have the information loaded on your laptop." Ty picked up Eleanor's survey. They'd find her a match, but it would not be Kelsey's suggestion. Kelsey knew nothing about K-Bay people. "Which couples does the computer recommend we match up?"

Gideon opened his laptop and tapped on the screen. "Collin, from the mixer, and Stacey ranked a compatibility factor of 8.75. And tonight, Charlie and Holly."

"Perfect on paper," Ty muttered.

"I saw Holly and Charlie together earlier." Coop rubbed a napkin over his face. "There's a good possibility in that pairing."

"It won't last." Ty tossed candy wrappers into the fire. "If they ring that bell, it'll be only for show." Coach would see through it. And Kelsey would have the last laugh when they ended it the following week.

"It might be worth putting them together again," Gideon said. "Just to see."

"No, find another pair." He wasn't about to explain that Kelsey had already mentioned their incompatibility for the long haul. Or that he agreed with her assessment.

Coop gave him a funny look. Thankfully Gideon was too occupied with his survey results to notice. Coop asked, "How about Jason and Nadine?"

"Fine. Send them invites to the ice fishing." Ty stared at the fire. "We need more women."

"If you hadn't chased Kelsey out of here, we could've asked her where she found the women she invited tonight," Coop said.

Ty already knew that answer. "From my past. I took Summer out to dinner once. Holly and I went to the movies."

"Wait." Coop leaned forward. "All of them?"

Ty nodded.

"But..." Gideon looked stricken. "Eleanor?"

Ty shrugged. "She asked for my help fixing her fence. We had coffee." He didn't mention Stacey's dad had been his physical therapist after the accident. If Kelsey could figure that out in one day, what would she find in his past given two weeks? That marshmallow seemed to have stretched from his throat to his stomach, making his voice stick as if he'd swallowed glue. "We need to find our own pool of women from now on."

"Unless Stan has a sister we don't know about or Fannie has a cousin we haven't met, we're stuck with the women we know." Gideon gathered the paperwork.

"Add Charlie and Holly to the fishing invite list." Coop shot his crumpled napkin into the fire and looked at Ty. "We need to even out our odds."

Ty checked his watch. "Gideon, can you create a flyer tonight?" At his friend's nod, Ty added, "I'll drive over to Cove Creek in the morning and hand them out."

"Aren't you opening here tomorrow?" Coop asked.

"Fannie can handle it until I get back." Ty rubbed a hand through his hair. "I need to get away. If only to do a little solo fishing before tomorrow night."

His friends agreed.

"Then, we have a game plan. Not even Kelsey Nash can stop us," Coop said. "Here's to reeling in more love than fish."

CHAPTER SEVEN

KELSEY'S TEASER POST had been seen, liked and shared by hockey fans and Alaska residents alike, casting doubt on Ty's matchmaking ability.

Women in K-Bay weren't answering Trinity phone calls. The female-oriented businesses in Cove Creek had stopped accepting Trinity flyers. The fish had stopped biting. And Ty had stopped hoping. In that order.

In the space of twelve hours, Kelsey was ruining Ty's chance to redeem himself. It was time to reclaim the lead and get a step or three ahead of her.

He searched through his tackle box, looking for a different color lure. He heard the car coming up the one-lane road to his house. Even if he hadn't already known who it was, he would've guessed it was her when he heard the scrape of tire chains on the pavement.

He never moved from his chair beside his fishing hole in his very sparse, very small fishing hut on Lake Talbot. He didn't stand when the door opened. And he didn't offer his guest a warm welcome.

"You issued an invitation for an exclusive interview." Kelsey stepped inside the hut. "And yet I haven't recruited any more bachelorettes."

The door swung closed behind Kelsey, the thud similar to the sound of his stick smacking against the goalpost. Game on. "I figured you'd be out interviewing K-Bay residents to get dirt on me. Why not take off the gloves and let you at me? Your post last night has basically shut down our business, and the people who were serious about matchmaking are now crushed." That was an exaggeration.

"You make it sound so…mean. And me… I'm from K-Bay, too. I care about people here."

"You were never from K-Bay. You visited K-Bay. You came through K-Bay." Ty picked up a knife and sliced through a tangled fishing line. "You observed, took notes and then passed judgment."

"Don't forget I also took down its only rising star."

"I'm sorry, that one isn't yours to claim," he said. "I took myself down. You simply let the world know."

"Funny thing." She moved farther into the

hut. Her key chain flopped from one hand to the other. "This town refuses to talk about you, other than to sing your praises."

Ty spun his reel, working on the knotted line. Her keys continued to clink in her palm, a reminder that her stay, and this interview, were temporary. He could relate to the mangled iceplex sign he'd replaced yesterday. Kelsey twisted him up and then she drove away.

"I shouldn't be surprised." She paced the short distance of the fishing hut and returned to stand beside his chair. The keys dangled from her fingers. "You won't talk about you."

"Maybe there's simply nothing left to say." The truth pressed at the back of his throat.

"Why am I here?"

"I was hoping you could answer that question."

He thrust his arms wide, his wrist connecting with her hand, knocking the keys from her grasp. The car fob skidded to a halt near the second ice hole. "Why did you come? Matchmaking? It's not your kind of story. There's no sex, no violence, no incriminating evidence." Thankfully.

"Matchmaking is small-town," she admitted, sitting on an overturned bucket, the only other chair inside his fishing hut. "Why would three bachelors—employed bachelors—begin a business that sells happily-ever-afters?"

"You didn't used to lie to me." Ty knotted a new lure on his line. "The truth."

"Maybe I want to help."

"By ruining me again?"

"By setting you free." She laid a hand on his knee. "From this place. Give me something, Ty. My article can create new avenues for you. Three months ago, a woman in my column was offered the job of a lifetime. A year ago, a man I featured had his name cleared."

"And the rest of them? There are fifty-two weeks in the year."

"I won't let you make me feel guilty."

"You? Feel guilty?" His laugh sounded hollow as if it rattled around inside his ribs, knocking against the emptiness. "How did two kids with messed-up parents end up so messed up? You'd think we'd know better."

"You think it's that apple-and-tree thing." She picked up the skimmer and swirled it around in the hole he'd drilled into the ice. "We just didn't fall far enough away."

"Or we never fell at all." Like father, like son. He tugged on the line, checking the lure.

"I would've had to be with my parents to become like them."

The flat pitch in her tone emphasized the bitterness in her words. He paused and looked at her.

"It's like with every column I write, I'm trying to get a seat at the family dinner table." She hugged her knees as if she didn't trust herself not to run. "As if that will make me a part of the family. As if we had dinner together around a table like a normal family."

He set the fishing pole on the ice beside his chair. "I'm not sure I could tell you about normal families." But he had a dinner table in his house, hand carved by his grandfather for his grandmother as a wedding present. Seating for eight. He hadn't sat there in years.

"Pathetic, isn't it?" She dunked chunks of ice under the water with the skimmer as if she was stabbing at memories from her past.

"And when you don't get that invitation?" Ty leaned forward in his chair.

"I write another column. And then another one after that. And then another." She stopped drowning the ice and rapped the skimmer on the water. Small rapid pats that perhaps beat back the pain. "Business associates, friends, even the guards at their security gate, they mention my weekly columns to my parents. For that moment, I'm a buzzword among

Mother's financial report. I'm remembered before my father's mergers and acquisitions meeting. For a moment I'm as relevant as their company's stock price."

"Why does it matter?" he asked. The force of his words plowed through her, pulled her attention back to him. Just like he'd intended.

She scrambled up, knocking the bucket backward, dropping the skimmer on the ice. "Haven't you wanted to matter? To someone?"

"Every day." He pushed out of his camp chair, stepped toward her. They weren't so very different after all. He wanted to matter to someone. Her. "Why do they still matter?"

"I have to matter." She thrust her hands into her hair as if that action alone would contain the truth. She watched him, her brown eyes wild, unsteady. "I have to matter to them because then I'll know I wasn't a mistake."

He crowded into her, sliding his arm around her waist, pulling her against him. Her hands dropped to his chest, fisting against his sweater. "I cannot be a mistake, Ty."

Ty set his hand beneath Kelsey's chin and tipped her face up. "You were never that."

And if he hadn't taken a puck to his head for all the wrong reasons, he would have framed her face with his hands. Captured her mouth beneath his and devoured her in his own way, in his own time. He'd make the longing in her heart match his own. Beat for beat.

But he had taken the puck.

Kelsey stepped back, as he'd known she would. "I have a different voice with you. I'm different. With you. Or I was."

Maybe she could be again. Maybe he could actually get things right this time, if not for Gideon and Coop, then for her. He hadn't meant to give up his last secret, but perhaps she could use it more than he could. The matchmaking was a bust. Whatever happened from here, he couldn't blame it on his past. "You came here for a headline. Let me give you one."

Her eyes flashed with need—the need for her parents' approval. But there was something else there. Reluctance. No matter what had happened between them, what had gone wrong, they had a bond.

She was better off without any ties to him. She was destined to be an investigative reporter. And his confession would give her another career boost.

The need in her eyes gave way to confusion, then clarity. Anger edged her tone; defiance stiffened her stance. "I don't have a headline."

"You will now." He scrubbed his palms over his face, trying not to see something more in her gaze that wasn't there: longing that matched his own. "I had a different experience in junior league when I left K-Bay. You remember when I left. We shared a few texts, maybe a phone call or two after I first arrived."

She gripped the back of the chair and squeezed her eyes closed. The reporter in her wanted his confession no matter how much the woman in his arms didn't want to hear it.

"I had a family legacy to defy." He'd gotten out of K-Bay and cut all contact from home, thinking it was his one chance to make it. "I met a bunch of new guys. They warned me I'd never turn professional without juicing. And the PEDs I injected into my veins, well, those would be my insurance."

Her head jerked up; that whiskey color swirled through her eyes and settled into something harder, less welcome.

"There's the reporter. Hard to contain her, isn't it? Ever hungry for the corrupt parts." Ty bent down, picked up her car fob and stuffed it into his pocket.

Silence settled around them. Not a calm like watching the world wake inside the first snowfall of the season, but more like that pause before a fireworks launch on the Fourth of July. Anticipation charged the air; promise pulsed through the plywood walls.

"I was out before I was ever in. I refused the surprise drug test I knew I'd fail." Coop and Gideon weren't around to watch his back. No one had told him to store his clean urine. No one had told him to stay away from bars and bad guys when he was on steroids. Not to mention a couple of women whose closest acquaintances included a known bookie and die-hard gamblers. "My coach might have given me a second chance on the drug test. But the rumors had started about me and cheating, and those my coach couldn't overlook. I couldn't even say for certain that I wasn't guilty of agreeing to throw a game or two. Everybody knew I needed the money. Still, steroids, beer and any type of booze I could get into a shot glass tend to muddy one's mind and distort one's memories."

Kelsey had slapped him that night. She'd wanted to surprise him and found him instead in a bar with his former teammates. She'd called him a drunk like his father. Accused him of infidelity like his father. The only person Ty had cheated on that night had been himself. But Kelsey had yelled. Cursed. Railed.

Now she held herself still like a deer before a gunshot. The stiff set to her lips blocked her voice. But it was the pale cast to her skin, as if his words punctured so deep inside her it made the rage clutch his own throat. Man, he hated himself.

"Which brings us back to my accident. After I was released from the team, I went to the bar and provoked several patrons into a pickup game of sorts. I had to prove I wasn't the cheater everyone believed I was." He crammed his hands into his pockets, smashed her keys in his fist. "I bargained with fate that night. Bargained with any deity that'd listen. If I stopped the first shot, I was meant to be in the pros. If I stopped the second, I was innocent. If I stopped the third, I wasn't my father." Except he was just like him. He'd gambled that night exactly as his old man had. And like his old man, he'd lost. "The first bounced off the ice and shattered my right temple, the second broke two ribs and the third left a hairline fracture on my shin."

He hadn't seen that forlorn expression on her face since her parents had left her alone with the housekeeper on Thanksgiving. That night she'd reached for him. Tonight she reached for the chair.

"Later I told myself you betrayed me with your articles. But the truth is much more simple than that. I betrayed myself."

"Now I know." Her voice dipped low, part rebuke, part disbelief. "And the matchmaking business?"

"All about a bet." Ty crushed a chunk of ice beneath his boot, grinding it beneath his heel. "Winners get jobs in the Lower 48 with one of Coach's farm teams."

"So that's it."

Her steady gaze locked on to him as if she'd sighted him through a bow-and-arrow scope. Now he was the one hunted.

"Your life is lies and illusions, Ty. You're a shadow of a man, surviving instead of living, and all inside the ghost of your father."

"The matchmaking isn't about him." Ty kicked a bucket out of his path, knocking his fishing pole into the hole. He'd knock the hut into the lake if it'd stop her pursuit.

"It's always been about your father," she said. "How come you don't get a job in the Lower 48 if you win the bet?"

Ty watched his favorite pole bob in the water. "I never said..."

She cut him off. "Coach will offer you a job.

You don't intend to take it, out of some type of misplaced penance."

He lifted his chin. "That isn't the point."

"No, the point is that you never intended to tell them the truth. You'll win this bet, send Coop and Gideon on their way and make some excuse as to why you can't go."

She knew him too well. "What's the problem with that?"

"Nothing, except you've just become the man you swore you'd never be—your father." She circled the ice hole and stepped toward him. "And I don't think you ever want to be free."

"Then, take the headline, Kelsey. Take it and take me down with it."

"I'm sure you'd like that. You'd have someone to blame again," she said. "Wouldn't want failure to be your fault and have everyone know it." She thrust out her hand, palm up. "Give me my keys."

She held his stare, her expression as set as the frozen lake he stood on. He didn't move. She didn't flinch. No parting shots were volleyed. Ty dropped her keys into her palm. She pushed him out of the way and raced outside.

The wooden door slammed against the frame, bounced open and slammed shut once more. The sound like the *thwack* of a puck leaving the blade of a stick. Except this time the puck hadn't leveled him. Kelsey's words had pummeled him enough.

She'd wanted him to forgive himself. She wanted him to be free of his past.

He scrubbed his fingers through his beard and tugged.

Now she'd given him a choice.

CHAPTER EIGHT

COOP HAD PREACHED that the guys in K-Bay needed cleaning up. The men had paid for shaves and haircuts and received a new outlook as a bonus. Ty had gone to the barbershop after Kelsey'd left the ice hut, even sat in the chair, but he'd stopped before completely losing his identity. As for his outlook, he planned to pick that up after he'd faced his two best friends and Coach.

He pushed open the door to the Bar & Grill and stepped inside, stopping to roll his shoulders and shake out his arms. Hoping to dislodge the doubt and focus his courage.

He went to the end of the bar and claimed one of their usual lunch-hour seats. When he pushed away the jar of bar mix, the one he normally devoured by the handful, his friends exchanged questioning looks.

"Did Kelsey fall in the ice hole this morning?" Gideon smoothed his red tie down the front of his dress shirt.

Ty blinked, rubbed his chin. "What?"

"You look like you did that time when Janie dumped you right before our tournament game and the Muskies scored that buzzer beater on you to take the whole thing." Coop tossed some bar mix into his mouth and chewed, cocking an eyebrow at him. "Not one of your better days."

"Neither is this one." Ty scratched his cheek. The scrape of his nails against his almost bare skin was going to take some getting used to. Clearly his friends weren't ready to comment on his changes. But he had something they'd react to. And it was a blow best given direct and swift. "Kelsey left this morning with her story."

"Knew you'd control the situation." Gideon opened his laptop, seemingly unimpressed. "Did she tell you where we should look for different women?"

"It's not the story you're expecting." Ty rubbed his stomach, his muscles tightening as if readying for the counterpunch he knew was coming. One tap to the goalpost had always set his position on the ice. He'd learned to trust his peripheral vision. Even now, without a goalpost, he knew Coach was readying his shot just outside the crease.

Coop lowered the glass jar of bar mix. "What story is it?"

"You told her about the bet." Gideon peered at him over his laptop screen, his eyes narrowing. No doubt he was already running the angles and equations to keep their bet in good standing with Coach.

"I gave her the truth." Ty rolled his shoulders again and touched his face. God help him, his skin felt cold beneath his fingers. Almost clammy. Like the touch of a ghost. *You're living inside the ghost of your father.* Not anymore. Not if he could help it. "Now I'm giving it to you three."

The volume was lowered on the TV behind Ty. *Read and react, boys.* Coach was reading, but not yet reacting. Coop wiped the back of his hand across his mouth and looked as if he was going to speak.

Ty pulled a weathered letter out of his pocket, the one that said he'd violated the drug policy and had been released from the team. He slapped it against the bar between his friends. Cold air drafted around his face, sliding beneath his chin and finger walking a chill across his chest. Coop and Gideon leaned forward to read. Other than several muttered curses, his friends remained silent. Coach picked up a beer stein to dry, but never reached for the paper, never looked.

Gideon sat back, crossed his arms over his chest. "You never mentioned anything about drug use when you came home to recover from your accident."

"Not exactly the sound bite I wanted to lead with." Ty faced his friends, flexed his fingers. He'd never felt this uncomfortable in his skin. Even when he'd watched his father fish from the bay, he'd never felt as if he'd been wrapped in a thousand barbs.

"Does Kelsey have a copy of this letter?" Gideon asked.

"Kelsey," Ty said and shook his head. Hadn't he given her enough? Those cold spikes sank into his chest, squeezed around his heart. He hadn't given her everything—like his heart. "No, but she knows the truth about the failed drug test."

"Still, anything she writes is only conjecture without proof." Gideon tapped his finger on the paper, again seeming to work through a solution in his mind.

Coop rolled the glass jar between his palms, glanced from Ty to the letter and then back to Ty. "But that isn't all of it."

Ty gripped the bar, stiffening against those

barbs coiling into his muscles. He met his best friend's gaze, readied the next slap shot. The next direct hit. "The accident wasn't an accident. I challenged some guys at the local bar to take the shots on me."

Gideon's palm flattened on the paper as he said, "You're telling me you planned on getting pummeled with three pucks at over sixty miles per hour without any gear."

Ty grimaced; even his scar pulled tighter against his cheek. "I had to show I wasn't a cheater. And I'd planned to block those shots."

"At the same time?" Coop set the jar on the bar top with a decided smack. Ty refused to let his head drop onto his chest as Coop put two and two together. "You convinced them to shoot at the same time."

Gideon frowned and looked over at Coach. "Pour us a round of something from the top shelf."

"You never came to us," Coop accused.

"I'd ruined our futures and became a possible cheat and criminal in less than seventy-two hours. What was there to talk about?"

"We would have stopped those shots. Pulled your wasted butt off the ice and brought you home," Gideon said.

"I know." Ty risked a glance at Coach. He

was relaxed, his arms loose, his expression passive as he set three whiskey glasses out. He'd be like that every time they lost a game because of their own stupidity. Until they'd gotten into the locker room, and then he'd react.

Ty looked back at his friends. "I can't change the past, but I can change the future. Coach, I want to alter the bet. They go to the Lower 48 with four matches."

"The bet stands." For the first time since Ty entered the bar, Coach met his gaze.

But this wasn't locker-room Coach. Yes, the anger in Coach's scowl and the challenge in his unwavering stare were the same. But the force behind Coach's words punched into Ty like a well-placed uppercut cracking his ribs. And Coach had one more blow.

"No, Ty Porter, you don't get to use a newspaper story to cheat your way out of our bet."

"But I am a liar and probably a cheat and definitely a former steroid abuser. Those aren't exactly the best qualities in a matchmaker." Or best friend. Or partner. Kelsey agreed—she'd taken a bunch of words and a byline over him.

"Too bad." Coach poured whiskey into a tumbler, then added several ice cubes. "Nobody cares about your past but you. It's what you do in the now that matters, just like you said."

"When Kelsey runs that story, the old charges and the old rumors are going to surface." Ty slammed his fist on the bar. First Kelsey and now Coach. Why wasn't anyone doing what he expected today? He noticed Gideon's tie, making sure it was red. Gideon only wore red on Thursdays. Everything in K-Bay was as it should be. "No one wants a morally bankrupt matchmaker."

"Then, you best get your matches made before that story hits the front page of the Sunday edition." Coach pushed into his space, chest to chest. "Or do you intend to let your boys down again?"

"Coach, enough," Coop said, his voice a plea and also a warning.

"The bet stands." Coach smacked his open palms on the bar. "Any questions?"

Ty stuffed his frustration back down his tight throat. Yelling at Coach only ever earned another dozen push-ups. And he ached enough already.

Gideon rubbed the back of his neck and looked around the group, his gaze finally landing on Ty. "You in?"

And like that, everything inside him settled.

Those barbs retracted. He drew his first decent breath since he couldn't remember when. And his anger stalled like a puck shot without enough momentum.

Only two words, but likely the most meaningful throughout Ty's life. They'd first been issued during their fateful dodgeball war against their fifth-grade nemesis. And they'd thrown down the dare at every challenge and every obstacle since then. The night of the accident had been the only time Ty hadn't looked to his friends for help. Only now did he truly understand his mistake. These were the words that said, "I have your back. You're family. I forgive you." Nothing more was ever needed.

Ty remained still, shifting only his eyes toward Coop.

Coop repeated Gideon's words. "You in?"

"Let's do this." And finally he released his grip on the bar.

"Last I checked, this was a bar, not a therapist's office." Coach pointed at each one of them. "Now if you need to hug it out, take it outside so I can get ready for the evening."

Coop rose, slapped his palm on Ty's shoulder and squeezed. "I call dibs on taking the next slap shot on you."

Ty straightened, met his friend's gaze. "Name the time."

Coop studied him. They both knew Ty hadn't been on the ice since his accident. "Let me check my calendar and get back to you."

"Ty Porter back on the ice." Gideon rubbed his hands together. "Let me know when so I can take a few shots."

"Has to be after this Saturday." Ty grinned. "Seems we have an ice-fishing event this evening and a bet to win."

Coop and Gideon started talking about potential matches as they walked outside.

Ty followed behind his friends, but stopped when Coach called his name.

"Own your past, but live in the present. Live in the present, but command your future." Coach tossed a hockey puck at him. "Now if you'd stop seeing your father when you pass by the mirror, you might have a chance."

"I share his DNA." Did everyone think like Kelsey?

"Bloodlines can sometimes mean less than the ice in this whiskey glass." Coach picked up a tumbler. "Your family is made up of those boys outside. Family are the folks you grab on to and don't ever let go. In your case, your kin have got nothing to do with it. Trust, faith and love... That's all that matters. Family trusts you're going to screw up again. They have faith you'll ask for their help to make it right. They'll forgive you when you don't. Because it isn't family without love."

Ty studied the puck. He knew this one. It was his first save. Coach had given it to him at his father's funeral, told him, *Bad blood only defines you if you let it. You want something different, be at morning practice.* Ty had left it in Coach's office when he'd signed for the junior team against Coach's advice. "I'll make it right."

"See that you do." Coach nodded toward the door. "With their help."

"What about Kelsey's story?"

"Seems that comes down to you," Coach said. "Is she family or not?"

Ty grabbed his coat from the wall and hurried to catch up with his friends. Coop stopped him with a hand to his chest when he reached them. "You were serious when you said Kelsey was leaving?"

Ty zipped up his jacket. Now he understood Kelsey's fascination with thick scarves. He almost needed one himself. "That's what I said."

"But you shaved." Gideon adjusted his tie beneath his thick wool trench coat.

Ty patted his cheeks. "And here I thought no one noticed."

"We haven't seen your full face in seven years," Gideon said. "It's hard not to notice."

"I still have a beard." Not the thick one he'd worn for the past seven years. But enough not to reveal all of his scar.

"Adolescent teenagers have more of a five-o'clock shadow than that." Gideon pulled out his phone and started typing. "When did you say Kelsey left?"

"Why'd you shave if not for Kelsey?" Coop asked.

Ty squeezed the hockey puck inside his pocket. "Felt as though it was time."

CHAPTER NINE

KELSEY STARED IN her rearview mirror and scowled at the bent no-parking sign protruding like a crooked tail from her trunk. Not again. She'd only wanted coffee and chocolate—a brownie, a muffin, she'd even settle for a drizzle over her latte. Chocolate righted the world. And she needed her world to be right because at the moment it was as off-kilter as the no-parking sign.

She scanned the iceplex parking lot for Ty's truck. Or the ice resurfacer. Five minutes. She'd be in and gone in five minutes. Less if Tilda wasn't pouring.

Kelsey grabbed her purse and hurried across the street toward the open sign blinking in the Clipper Ship's window. Inside, Tilda was icing a three-layer chocolate cake behind the counter.

Kelsey glanced at her watch. Amended her schedule. She'd be gone in less than ten minutes.

She approached the counter. "I got my story. So it looks as if I'm heading home."

Tilda twisted the spatula against the side of the cake and spun the turntable to smooth out the icing. "Is it the one you wanted?"

"It's the kind I've made my name on." She'd definitely get to keep her job. Kelsey dropped her purse on the counter. Her gaze jumped from the chocolate cake to the glass-covered dish with the dense brownies inside. She should be finishing her article and hitting the upload button. Instead, she was waffling over chocolate.

"Then, it's been a success." Tilda set the spatula in the sink, then lifted the glass lid and placed a brownie in a paper bag. "You'll earn a front-page spread, become the state's hot topic and have your hometown to thank. Again."

Tilda made it sound as if she'd used the people here. Again. Well, she confessed, she had used people—most harshly, Ty. He was making her choose. *Me or the headline.* She didn't know what she wanted. She'd said goodbye to him, but then again, she hadn't submitted the article, either. She reached inside the bag and pinched off a corner of brownie. The small bite shriveled inside her dry mouth; her stomach pitched and rolled. Nope. Nothing seemed right. "My home is in the city."

"That's just where you park your snow boots, at least for now." Tilda moved over to the latte maker. "Home is where your heart is."

Kelsey tore off another piece of the brownie. Surely the second bite wouldn't be flat. Surely the chocolate would steady her stomach. "First, you'd have to have a heart."

If she had one, she wouldn't have her bags packed and her headlights pointed in the direction of the city. If she had one, she'd have reached for Ty, rather than challenging him. If she had one, Ty would be enough. Her brownie bites collided like pebbles stirred up in the rapids. Except, she was still standing here. In K-Bay.

"So that's the way of it, then?" Tilda turned on the frother and shook her head.

Kelsey gave up and shoved the rest of the brownie in her mouth. Any minute she'd revel in chocolate bliss and make her choice. The frother quieted and she said, "Look, I didn't come to debate hearts and homes and redefine family with you."

Tilda filled a coffee cup and pressed the lid on. "Why did you come, then?"

Because the sign said Welcome. Because

the light was on. Because she didn't want to be alone yet. Kelsey crumpled up the bag and tossed it in the trash. "For the coffee."

"Seems a long way to drive for a simple latte." Tilda picked up a cardboard sleeve. "Ty lives four miles down the road, works across the street and yet he hasn't come inside this place since high school." Tilda twisted the cardboard sleeve up the outside of the cup. "Until today. Ty came in a little while ago and ordered his first hot chocolate in seven years."

Kelsey wondered what Ty was diluting with the hot chocolate. "I'm sure he enjoyed it."

"I'm not sure I care." Tilda handed the coffee to Kelsey. "Important thing is that he came inside here."

So he'd drunk hot chocolate after a very long fast. Maybe he'd just had a seven-year craving. Sipping hot chocolate didn't mean anything. It didn't mean his coming clean about his past represented something significant. Except, there went her reporter's radar. He could have told anyone. He hadn't told Coop or Gideon. He'd told her.

The door opened behind Kelsey. The blast of cold air nipped at her fingers. Coach pulled the door closed and spun to face Kelsey. "Hello there, young lady. Looks as if you're leaving

Ty again, aren't you? I guess I'll have to put up with his moony, mopey self, same as the last time you left him."

Her stomach flipped once, twice, then calmed. It had to be the chocolate finally kicking in.

"You know what the loneliest job in hockey is?" Coach walked over to the end of the counter where Tilda waited, but looked back at Kelsey. "Well, do you?"

She stilled, more than an arm's length away from the door. If she lunged, she'd be out of here, no looking back, no need to look back. Her boots stayed planted. "I'm not well-versed on the sport." Just a certain former player.

"The goalie. When the team loses, it's the goalie that carries that burden alone." Coach accepted a large bag of coffee beans from Tilda. "Good goalies stop pucks. Great goalies get up and keep playing after the initial one goes in. And they keep getting up, no matter how many get past 'em."

Kelsey was the puck. She'd take her shot with her story. And she'd score. She knew it. Ty knew it. And so did Coach. Ty had gotten up the last time, hadn't he? No, he'd stopped playing. What would he do this time? She followed Coach to the door. "What kind of player is Ty?"

Coach shifted the coffee beans and studied her over the bag. "I think you already know the answer to that. Hockey is all about reacting. Knowing how to do so is the key, whatever the situation. Backed into the boards. Down by three goals after the first period. Winning a championship. And most important, knowing you cannot rise up on your own. Alone will get ya nowhere."

Ty wasn't alone. He had Coop, Gideon and an entire town to lift him up. Kelsey held the door open for Coach. "I've never been good at team sports."

"Doesn't mean you can't learn." Coach nodded to her and strode off down the sidewalk.

Kelsey crossed the street, heading to her car. Coach didn't know her. She'd been alone most of her life. Even in a crowd of thousands, Kelsey felt alone. She always had. Still, she couldn't deny the idea of being a part of something tugged at her heart. More than likely it was the K-Bay air, making her breath snag inside her frosty lungs.

Once she returned to the city and her cubicle and her life, everything would switch back to normal. Just as she wanted it. She blamed the wind for the hitch in her throat and her weak conviction.

A woman called her name and Kelsey spotted Stacey Logan crossing the parking lot, coming toward her.

Stacey stopped in front of her and motioned to the SUV beside Kelsey's rental. "Best parking lot in town. Always an open space."

"It's certainly worked for me," Kelsey said. Aside from that pesky parking lot sign. She needed to put a suggestion in Ty's inbox to remove it permanently. Clearly no one abided by the rules. The entire town did not work at the iceplex. And yet everybody seemed to park there.

"You haven't forgotten about the broom-hockey rematch next week, have you?" Stacey dug around inside her purse. "We need you to play on the left wing again."

"I spent more time in the penalty box than on the ice," Kelsey said.

Stacey laughed. "That didn't look to be too much of a hardship."

No, the hardship had been to remember her reason for being here. And to remember what she wanted. The hardship had not been sitting beside Ty, the two of them on their own. "It was fun." That surprised her, then and now.

"I haven't seen Ty smile that often in years."

Kelsey hadn't smiled that often in years, either.

"Please be there, Kels. It's my last real laugh before treatments begin. I need a girls' night. I need to feel strong and in control." Stacey dumped her purse and shopping bag on the hood of her car. "Why can I never find my keys?"

Kelsey glanced at the Phil's Pharmacy prescription jutting out from inside the Lately Lettuce shopping bag, and that snag in her lungs returned. This time it wasn't from the air. "I'll try to rearrange my calendar."

Stacey looked over at her, hope and determination clear in her pale green eyes. She held out her gloved hand, extending her little finger. "Pinkie swear?"

Kelsey peered down at Stacey's hand. She'd never pinkie sworn anything. She'd never been asked. Not in grade school. Not in middle school. Certainly not as an adult.

"I pinkie swore with my mother to never stop fighting this cancer. I pinkie swore with my father I'd live every moment with joy and dignity. And I pinkie swore with the girls I'd always have their backs." Stacey lifted her hand. "Now it's your turn. Pinkie swear, Kelsey, that you won't let us down."

Kelsey stretched her fingers inside her glove. Surely that wasn't a tremor in her hand. It was a simple request. A simple request that shimmied through her, made her chest expand and her smile brighter. Pinkie swears mattered. Kelsey mattered. She hooked her pinkie with Stacey's. "I swear it."

"It's done, then." Stacey hugged her tight and then spun around to rummage inside the shopping bag. She pulled out a green tinted bottle. "Thanks for this, by the way."

Kelsey bent forward and read the label. "Ginger-root extract."

"Summer just told me you helped her find a new supplier of several products for Lately Lettuce." Stacey shook the bottle. "This is a lifesaver and unavailable for shipping here."

"I only gave her the contact information for the owner of a health food chain I know in the city," Kelsey said. In exchange for Summer agreeing to attend the broom-hockey event. Nothing anyone else couldn't have done.

"Well, you saved several of Summer's customers. We owe you." Stacey continued to pull items from her bag. "Charlie was in there, too. He was trying some natural aloe for his skin that Summer recommended after chatting with your supplier."

Kelsey didn't have a supplier. She had connections, she supposed. She'd never really given it much thought. She'd simply made an introduction. Still, realizing she'd helped, well, that made her want to hug Stacey.

Across the parking lot, Charlie and Summer, each carrying a Lately Lettuce bag, walked toward Charlie's work truck. Summer waved to them.

Stacey paused in her search and pointed at Kelsey, yelling, "She's in for next week. Better get ready now, Charlie. The women are taking the boys down."

Charlie laughed and called back, "Not a chance. I've got an insider. I'll know all your plays before you."

Summer hip bumped Charlie. Kelsey chuckled at the deflective move. Charlie whispered in Summer's ear and Summer's face became beet red. Kelsey was pulled away from watching Charlie watch Summer when Stacey shouted.

"Bingo! Found my keys. Which reminds me, I need to tell Coop to find me a car that has remote start. Or even better, a man who can drive me around." Stacey pulled her arm out of her purse and jingled her keys. She stuffed everything else away and faced Kelsey, wrapping her up in a quick hug. "I'm off. Next week the girls are together again to conquer the ice. We should start a broom-hockey league. Call ourselves The Flying Broomsticks."

Stacey tossed her bag and purse on the passenger seat, hugged Kelsey again on her way to the driver's side and drove off.

Kelsey had been hugged more in one day than her parents had hugged her during her entire life. She sipped her latte. It'd gone cold. Ice cold. She got inside her car and started the engine, switching the heat to supersonic blast. In only ten minutes her world had tilted again. How was she supposed to react?

She'd made a pinkie promise to return to K-Bay. The problem was, technically, she needed to leave town before she could come back.

CHAPTER TEN

TY PUSHED A SLED full of fishing equipment down to the lake. A dozen buckets were positioned on the ice and a dozen chairs were opened and waiting. He'd tested the lake for patches of weak ice and replenished his bait supply.

All they needed now were couples. And two matches.

Gideon was up at the house, printing off another set of surveys. Coop had run back into town for s'mores supplies and more drinks. They hadn't expected the group to remain so long at the fire pits after the broom-hockey game. As it was, this event was being held on Ty's property, so curfews wouldn't apply. And he had guest bedrooms with clean sheets waiting if they had to take anyone's keys.

The sound of an engine interrupted the squall of a hawk circling above the trees. The purr was too mild to be Coop's truck. Ty turned around at the familiar thwap of chains against pavement.

He set his hands on his hips and waited for the car to stop in his driveway and his heart to stop racing in his chest.

A puffed-up bundle emerged from the driver's seat. He was beginning to have a certain soft spot for puffy things. The car door shut and still his bundle remained by the car, her hands behind her back.

He remained where he was. Content to wait her out and his racing heart.

She unwound her scarf, letting the ends hang down the front of her coat. "I came to report another accident."

"That so?" he asked.

She nodded—he knew only because the puffball on her pink wool cap bobbed back and forth. She added, "Involving a particular sign."

His lips twitched from the smile that his beard could no longer hide. "Who won?"

"It was a tie," she said.

There was a smile in her voice, too. He hadn't heard that sun-infused tone since she'd visited him at training camp. Could be just a trick of the wind or wishful thinking. He stayed where he was and rubbed his chin. "What do you want me to do?"

"I was sort of hoping you could talk to the sign's owner and get it removed."

"Why would I do that?"

"So I can stop running it over." She lifted one shoulder in a shrug.

Again he knew because that distracting puffball flopped to the side. Her shoulder dropped; the puffball settled back in place.

"Maybe it's you who should move. Maybe you should stop parking there altogether."

"I like that spot." She stepped off the driveway onto the first wide stair that he'd shoveled and salted that morning. The first of the five stairs that led down to the lake. And him. "It suits me."

There it was again. That smile filtered through her light tone. That smile that made his hands sweaty and his knees weak. And made him pray to anyone who'd listen that he wasn't reading this wrong. "You could have texted about the sign. Why are you here, Kelsey?"

"I made a pinkie promise." She held up her hand, flexed her little finger. One corner of her mouth tipped up, one dimple peeked out.

It wasn't a come-hither finger motion. Or the universal sign language for irritating Sunday drivers everywhere. He stayed where he was. But his eyes were locked on that dimple. "Okay."

"With The Flying Broomsticks." Both of her dimples emerged.

Ty's legs wobbled as if he was a kid learning how to skate. He crossed his arms over his chest, searching for balance.

"That's my hockey team." She moved down onto the next step, wrapping the ends of her scarf around her wrists. "Well, I'm part of a team now."

Each roll of her wrist inside the scarf was like a twist inside him. Each step closer was like a surge of adrenaline to his heart. His gaze fixated on her hands. "The Flying…"

"Broomsticks."

If she laughed, he couldn't hear it over the buzzing in his own head. She'd moved again. Almost within his reach, if he stretched.

"We play Wednesday nights over at the iceplex. You should come watch."

There was something different in her voice, as if the sun had set and night reigned. Something that gripped Ty's chest. He grabbed the railing. "To give you pointers on how to improve your game?"

"I think I've got a handle on the keys to

success." She walked to the edge of the step above him.

If he leaned forward he could capture the ends of her scarf. And her. "Care to enlighten me?"

"It's simple, really. You rise when you are part of a team."

"You intend to rise to the top of the broom-hockey league," he said.

"Among other things." She laughed then. Equal parts joy and relief. Light and comfort.

Her laughter bubbled out like a hot spring, washing over Ty and filling him with her own happiness.

She pulled her scarf from around her neck. He anticipated her next move, caught the end as she flicked it toward him. He tugged; she tugged back. "I want to be a team, Ty. Together."

That was when the ground beneath him shifted, as if he'd stepped on the soft patch of ice. Her words clipped him, leaving him weaker than he'd been after his injuries. He pulled himself up onto her step, closing the distance between them. "What happens when we fall?"

"We'll do it together." She reached out until

her hand found his inside the scarf. "You belong to me. And I belong to you."

He'd never imagined he'd hear those words from her. Not when she'd pulled into his drive. Not when she'd walked onto that top step. Not even when she'd tossed him her scarf as if it were the only lifeline from a pit of quicksand. Maybe that was what she was. His lifeline.

He cupped her face; his thumb stroked over her cheek. "Both of us, we're used to playing alone. Going our own way."

"It's a new period. New ice. New game." Her fingers threaded through his beneath the scarf. "Are you in?"

She couldn't know what she'd asked. What she'd said. But he knew.

He leaned down, captured her mouth beneath his and held on. And for the first time ever, his future wasn't buried in shadows.

Kelsey sneaked her arms inside Ty's jacket, wrapped her fingers around his waist and curled farther into him. Her voice had warmed him, but having her in his arms, that spread a peace through his whole body.

He wound her scarf around her neck, but kept interrupting his own progress by kissing her. She didn't stop him. In truth, she pulled him back to her for several drawn-out kisses before letting him continue with the scarf.

"There's no scarf left." Gideon brushed past them on the stairs. "Either take it inside or get down here to finish the setup."

Kelsey rubbed her cheek against his sweater. "I'm not sure you put it on right. Do you think he'll yell if you start all over?"

Ty's laughter ricocheted right through him. He rubbed her shoulders, and then her back. Letting her go seemed like a very bad solution. "I suppose we should help. It was my suggestion after all."

She lifted her head and kissed him. "Tell me how I can help."

"Don't move," he said and held her in place for another round.

Snow splattered the back of his head. Ty reached up and rubbed the spot.

"Kelsey, don't kiss him again or I'm taking aim at you, too," Gideon yelled.

Kelsey peeked around Ty's shoulder. Ty squeezed her. "What's he got?"

"A dozen. Maybe more," she said.

She leaned up on her toes toward Ty. Within seconds, she'd squealed and ducked behind Ty as the snowball hit Ty's shoulder.

"He's serious." Kelsey let go of Ty and

scooped a chunk of snow into her hands. "Gideon Walker, don't you dare throw a snowball at me."

"City girls can't throw."

"I'm not a city girl." Kelsey threw her snowball, packed more snow into her hands and launched another. She arm blocked one from Gideon and rallied again.

Laughing, she glanced over at Ty. "Are you helping or not?"

Ty bent down, stuck his hands in the snow. "We're a team now, aren't we?"

CHAPTER ELEVEN

KELSEY STRETCHED HER LEGS out in a booth at the Bar & Grill and kneaded her shoulder. She already had a bruise from last night's snow-ball war. "Gideon, you pack a mean snowball."

"Sorry. That one was meant for Ty." Gideon glanced up from the nearby table where he sat with his computer and grimaced as he touched the side of his head. "You aren't so bad your-self."

Coach carried over a plate, set it in front of Kelsey and dropped a large cup of coffee in front of Ty. "Word is you carried on all night like a bunch of kids. Playing in the snow until well after midnight."

It was closer to sunrise for Kelsey and Ty. And if she guessed correctly, for another cou-ple who'd departed together.

There'd been magic in the snow angels she and Ty had made, laughter in the secrets they'd shared and sanctuary in the quiet moments. She should want to rest her head on the table and sleep. But it was as if she'd eaten Tilda's entire inventory of espresso beans and washed them down with Coach's pot of coffee that he now held in his grip.

Ty drank half of his cup and winked at her. "We fished, too. It wasn't all play and no work."

Kelsey's toes curled and those espresso beans jumped around inside her like popcorn kernels about to explode. She'd always wondered what it felt like to be giddy.

Coach studied Ty and then looked at Kelsey. He set the coffeepot on the table, his fingers tapping against the plastic lid. "Looks as though you might have found your team. Yet my bell is still silent."

There was no question in Coach's voice. Just the confidence of a man used to being obeyed. The espresso party inside her slowed to a simmer. Kelsey set her fork on the table.

"Coach, give us a minute, will you?" Ty dropped the bacon that he'd stolen back onto Kelsey's plate.

She expected Ty's frown, but not the shadow that shifted across his face. She'd thought they'd stepped into the light finally.

Coach crossed his arms over his chest and remained where he was.

"Coach," Ty said again.

Even his voice was deeper, as if Ty had retreated into a cave. Kelsey reached across the table and curved her fingers with Ty's. He squeezed her hand, running his thumb across her palm, calming her more than words. She said, "It's fine."

Ty shifted forward. "He wants you to…"

She set her other hand on top of their joined ones. "I know what he wants me to do." She looked up at Coach. "And I know what I want to do."

Coach stared her down; she didn't flinch. She wasn't lying. She knew what her heart wanted. What she needed. She also knew there was one more thing, one more detail before the past could be just that: the past.

Her stomach knotted. She squeezed Ty's hand, taking in his strength. "We never talked about my latest story."

Ty's gaze was fixed on her. He tensed beneath her fingers. "It doesn't matter."

"I submitted it yesterday," she said. "Before I came to the lake."

"It'll be fine." He pulled his hands free, rolled his shoulders, massaged his neck. Everything but touch her. Kelsey left her arms extended across the table. A bad feeling crept along her spine.

Ty slid out of the booth and stood beside Coach. He rolled his shoulders again and then held Kelsey's stare. That tremor speared through her core. She couldn't read him. She'd always read him. Always.

But his scar didn't twitch. His eyes didn't narrow. Her arms trembled now. She clutched her hands together on the table and willed him with her eyes to give her something. Anything.

And he did.

"We're a team," he said. "Those were your words."

Even his voice was flat. That wasn't enough.

"We are. That hasn't changed." The quiver was there in her tone. Surely he'd heard it. What was he doing? Why wasn't he sitting? He needed to sit. She needed to explain. "I meant that. I still mean it."

He stared at her, his gaze seeming to dig deep into her soul, searching for… She didn't know what. She waited and waited, never looked away. Sat there and shook as if she'd been buried in the snow all night. Finally he nodded, turned and strode outside. Gideon and Coop rushed after him.

Kelsey ran her palms over the table. Oh God. Oh God. Oh God.

He'd walked out. *Walked out.*

What happened to *team*? What happened to belonging? What happened to them?

The bite of egg she'd swallowed was making her nauseous. She reached for her ice water and stopped. She didn't need any more ice. She rubbed her palms on the table. Back and forth. Back and forth.

Coach cleared his throat and sat on the bench across from her. "He'll be back."

What happened to Coach's confident bellow?

"Will he?" Was that her voice? That strained, high-pitched croak of a whisper?

"You told him you loved him." That certainty returned quickly in Coach's tone. He sat back and nodded. "Love trumps everything."

She shook her head. Now her chin quivered. She hadn't said that. She'd talked about teams. And belonging. And rising. She'd talked about together. She'd never mentioned love.

Oh, God! She fisted her hands on the table.

Coach's eyebrows drew together like twin caterpillars crawling downward. "What were you doing all hours of the night?"

Snowball fight. Fishing. Talking. Another

snowball fight. Kissing. A little fishing. More kissing.

Coach rapped his knuckles on the table. “Don’t answer that.”

She hadn’t planned to.

Coach reached over, covered her hands. “It’ll be fine. I’m going to check on some customers and then we’re going to put together a game plan.”

Game plan. She needed that. But the dash of panic mixed with desperation in his voice told her he might not be the best choice to help her devise one. Kelsey bobbed her head in agreement, willing away the quiver that eased up into her cheeks.

“You stay put.” Coach patted her hand. “I’ll only be a minute or two.”

Kelsey stayed put. For one thing, she didn’t know what to do. And as for the second, the heating vent was blowing on her feet, keeping her body from going as numb as her heart. And third, she prayed Coach would surprise her and come back with her winning game plan.

Coop and Gideon returned nineteen minutes later. She knew because she’d been watching the clock, wondering if she stared long enough if she could reverse time. When that failed, she started setting time limits. If he wasn’t back in ten minutes, she'd leave and find Tilda. Surely Tilda could get her a game plan. His friends returned before the buzzer. Now she had to reset.

Neither Coop nor Gideon came to her booth. Coop offered an encouraging nod, one that a dad would give to his second grader about to do a school performance. Gideon hid behind his computer screen. If only she had a snowball.

Six minutes later, Ty walked back inside. And Kelsey almost slid off the bench. Her heart certainly dropped through her chest, past her stomach to her boots.

Ty stalked toward her. There was more heat, more determination, more everything colliding through his gaze. He came right up to the table, held out his hand toward her.

That incessant tremor snaked one last time through her. Kelsey set her hand in his. And everything quieted, except for her heart. That tripped and stumbled into her throat.

He tugged, urging her out of the booth before pulling her against his chest.

And then into his arms, and everything inside her settled. This was where she needed to be.

"You shaved?" She touched his cheek, fingers covering the full length of his scar.

"No more hiding. Not from you. Not from us." He lifted their joined hands and kissed her knuckles, then each cheek. He pulled away and said, "I love you, Kelsey."

Her heart stumbled again. Everything she'd ever wanted was here. With him. "What about the story?"

His smile was soft, quiet and hinted at shared secrets. It was the smile reserved only for her. The one that both strengthened and weakened her. That one that called her home.

"We're a team," he said. "We'll handle it together."

This man who'd been her headline. Her ticket to a life she'd thought she'd wanted had somehow become her salvation. Was there any greater gift? She brushed her lips over his. "Wait here."

Stepping out of his arms, she raced to the bar as if she'd had an extra helping of those darned espresso beans. Reaching up over the beer taps, she rang the bell and yelled, "Ty Porter, I love you!"

Cheers filled the Bar & Grill. Coach clapped heartily and winked at her as he wiped a finger against the corner of his eye. Ty picked up Kelsey and spun her around once, then told her to give him the words again, as he wasn't sure he'd heard her the first time, even though he had.

Breakfast service resumed only to be disrupted once more when several of the ice fishing group burst into the Bar & Grill. Kelsey studied the group. If she wasn't mistaken, they were still together and still smiling from ear to ear.

Charlie and Summer made up the last of their group. Charlie helped Summer with her jacket and then called out to the customers, "We heard there was a bell ringing going on this morning."

Ty lifted his and Kelsey's entwined hands into the air. "Just missed it."

Charlie seized Ty's shoulder and squeezed. "And here we thought we'd be the first ones to ring the bell before noon."

Ty glanced at Kelsey. She grinned. Another secret to tuck inside her smile. "I told you so."

Charlie reached for Summer, put his arm around her waist. "We'd be the second couple, but what do you say? We're here already with our friends and family."

Summer beamed. "I think it's perfect."

"Together?" Charlie asked. Summer nodded, and the couple stepped up to the bar and together they rang the bell.

Once again, cheers echoed around the tavern. In the midst of the happy chaos, Kelsey watched Gideon pull out his laptop. She nudged Ty and pointed to their friend. “What’s he doing?”

Ty laughed. “Revising the survey.”

* * * * *

For my writing cohorts, Melinda Curtis and Cari Lynn Webb. I couldn't do this crazy job without you.

And my Alaskan little sister, Jessica Bogard, aka Ripley, one of the coolest people I know.

Suddenly Sophie

Anna J. Stewart

Dear Reader,

The right friends help get you through life.

That's definitely the case for Ty, Coop and Gideon, the three heroes in *Make Me a Match*. They bonded from the moment they met and nothing's going to tear them apart: not the secrets they keep, the dreams they have or the opportunities they've lost. Funny how second chances can shake things up.

Gideon Walker feels stuck. But in recent years a bright spot has presented itself in the form of Sophie Jennings. Not that they don't have their issues. Romance is a bumpy road until Gideon is given the chance to get everything he's always wanted—the last thing he expects is to have to match-make for Sophie in order to make his dreams and those of his friends come true.

In a way this novella wrote itself. There are times when you let the characters take the lead, and that's exactly what happened with Gideon and Sophie. Sometimes writing isn't just a job—it's a pleasure.

Much like writing with my BFFs Melinda Curtis and Cari Lynn Webb. We click. After supporting each other for almost a decade we have our own language, our own shortcuts and at times, we're brutally honest with one another. You might think that's not a recipe for success, but I can honestly say I could not traverse this publishing world without them.

After all, great friendships—and romance—are what life is all about.

Happy reading!

Anna

CHAPTER ONE

GIDEON WALKER MISSED the sun.

Some days, today for instance, Kenkamken Bay, Alaska, seemed mired in gray. The low-hanging clouds and soupy mist pressed in on him, making his body sag from a vitamin D deficiency no amount of supplements would remedy.

Straightening the stapler on his desk, Gideon glanced across the room to the glacially slow ticking clock above the giant windows of Kenkamken Bay Savings and Loan. He swore he could hear that clock kick out every second of his mundane life.

Not even the expansive view overlooking Main Street tipped the day into color. Instead, this drizzly Friday afternoon foretold an equally gloomy weekend ahead.

Or it would have if Gideon didn't have a nice new stack of completed dating questionnaires waiting for him to sort through. In the past two weeks, word had spread to outlying towns about Trinity Matchmaking—his, Ty's and Coop's venture into the romance business. What had started out as a bet wagered by their former childhood hockey coach had exploded into a venture Gideon actually enjoyed and found challenging. Who knew they had a talent for helping people find their happily-ever-afters?

Now they were two-thirds toward their goal of matching six couples in time for the Bar & Grill's big Valentine's Day celebration. Thanks to Kelsey Nash ringing the brass bell after breakfast this morning and staking her claim on Ty. Only two more couples were needed to catapult him and his friends out of K-Bay once and for all.

Gideon shifted in his chair, the plastic wheels squeaking as he leaned his arms on the battered desk that had been cloned from the 1960s. How many more days could he stand to stare at the ancient computer screen that had its own ideas as to when it would function properly? A man could only take so many files, so many forms, so many pleading eyes as they looked to him for financial salvation.

He felt like the oldest twenty-five-year-old on the planet. Sure he was young to be a bank manager, but that was what happened when your father was the previous manager, and employment, not to mention employees, were scarce. But the thought of spending year upon year stuck in the same job, behind the same desk in the same town for the rest of his life? Existence wasn't enough and in K-Bay, that was all he was doing: existing. Just like his mother had. Gideon wanted more. He wanted to...*live.*

He didn't see that life happening in K-Bay.

Had it only been seven years since his dream of becoming a big-time sports manager had gone as astray as an overshot hockey puck? Ty's recent confession that his fall from grace had come as a result of illegal steroid use and incredibly bad judgment might have destroyed other friendships, but Gideon understood. As had Coop. The past was the past. It was the future that mattered, and Gideon's future had to lie beyond K-Bay's borders.

If he had to deny one more loan...

Yes, it had indeed been a long, life-sucking seven years.

Speaking of denying...

The bell above the front door tinkled and, as she did every Friday at twelve thirty, Sophie Jennings strode into the customerless bank with her weekly deposit from The Flower

Shop. She shoved her fake fur–lined hood off her head, exposing her plain ruby-cheeked face accentuated by sparkling eyes and long brown braided hair. The smile she aimed at Clara, the only other employee who worked Friday afternoons, dipped slightly as Sophie's gaze skittered briefly over to Gideon before she headed to the window.

His stomach tightened, as it tended to whenever Sophie pinned those searching deep brown eyes on him. In the year since he'd turned down her application for a business loan Sophie continued to be pleasant, as if his decision hadn't derailed plans to expand her store. Maybe it was his guilty conscience that made him think she continued to hold a grudge. Not that Sophie would ever show it. Truth be told, he'd hated to disappoint her, but someone had to look out for her well-being. Her lazy, unemployed, delinquent brother certainly wasn't about to, and Gideon didn't put it past Dillon Jennings to take complete financial advantage of Sophie's generous and caring nature. He couldn't, in good conscience, put her at risk of that.

Gideon sighed and resumed straightening his files—all three of them—on the side of his desk to address once he returned Monday morning. He could hear the friendly chatter between Clara and Sophie, their soft voices filling the room with that touch of color he'd been wishing for moments ago.

As gray as Gideon saw his world, Sophie lightened up any space she walked into with her ebullient and gregarious personality—character traits Gideon both appreciated and worried about. Not everyone was as protective as he was prone to be when it came to Sophie Jennings.

"Hi, Gideon." It wasn't so much Sophie saying his name that caught him off guard but the underlying tone of uncertainty that accompanied her greeting. "Do you have a minute?"

"I have thirty." For the first time that day he willed the clock to slow. He gestured to the chair as he stood, smoothing his tie down his chest. "Please."

She shoved her thick gloves into her jacket pockets and lowered herself into the seat on the other side of his desk. He hoped she wasn't here to apply for another loan. While Gideon knew her business was going gangbusters—despite his previous loan denial—he didn't relish the prospect of rehashing his refusal and her disappointment. Then again, he wouldn't mind seeing the dormant gold flecks in her eyes spark against a challenge. "What can I do for you?"

"I, um." She tucked a nonexistent strand of hair behind her ear and tugged the sleeves of her down jacket over her hands. "I heard you're the man to see about finding a date."

For an instant, he forgot how to breathe. "I'm sorry?"

She stared at the floor as her cold-pinked cheeks flamed. "This matchmaking thing you have going on with Coop and Ty? I was wondering if you could fit me in?"

"You want my help finding a date?" That came out ruder than he intended.

She pinched her lips into a straight line. "You guys have had some nice success stories and I was at the Bar & Grill this morning. Kelsey Nash looked pretty happy to be ringing that bell. Things have eased up a bit now that Mom's gone, and other than Dillon..."

"I heard he was arrested again." He purposely kept his tone even. "Shoplifting this time, wasn't it? I'm sorry." He wasn't, actually. As far as Gideon was concerned, the farther away Sophie could get from her brother the better. Putting the twenty-one-year-old behind bars for a while would probably be the best thing for Sophie.

Sophie sighed. "I know you don't approve of him. Or of my defending him, or even my bailing him out, but he's the only family I have left. I promised our mother I'd look out for him."

"I doubt she'd meant for you to risk your livelihood, not to mention your future, to do so." Her loyalty was admirable, but at some point it was going to turn around and bite her. "I'm sure you already realized, but turning down your loan had more to do with my not trusting your brother than you. He's a liability, Sophie. One I couldn't let the bank take a chance on. Not even for someone as reliable as you." That spark he'd been hoping to flame earlier flared in her eyes and he added, "I factor a lot of elements into loan consideration. That's not to say you couldn't readdress the issue with a new manager if and when you want to reapply."

Coward. Why didn't he just tell her he'd turned her down for her own protection? Because that would open the door to something he didn't want to chance: that Sophie Jennings might actually understand and appreciate his actions. They were friends. Sort of. That had to be enough. Didn't it? "But that's not why you're here. So." He leaned his arms on the desk and changed the subject. "You want in on Trinity Matchmaking. Why?"

She looked at him for a long moment and he watched her struggle against the shift in subject. When she spoke, he felt a knot loosen in his chest. "I'd like to find someone to spend time with, maybe have a future with. It's a little lonely around here. You know?" Her tight smile brushed against the edges of his heart. "K-Bay is where I belong—it's my home. I'm not going anywhere, especially now that the business is doing better and I'm looking to expand." The unspoken "despite your best efforts" hovered between them. "It would be nice to find someone who feels the same. Unless I'm not a good candidate that—"

Was Gideon hearing correctly? Sophie? Insecure? Little Miss Optimism seemed to be on vacation today. "Of course I—we—could. Try, that is. I'm sure you're a fine candidate." Was there a hole Gideon could crawl into until he got his thoughts in line with his mouth? "I happen to have some extra questionnaires in my briefcase." He leaned down and pulled out the stapled packet they'd been handing out for the past few weeks. "You know we have a Valentine's Day party coming up next week. And some other events planned. You up for those?"

Given the problems they'd had finding willing female participants, he should be feeling excited to include Sophie.

"After twenty-four years of postponing a social life," Sophie said as the tension on her face subsided and she accepted the papers, "I'm up for anything. I can have this back to you later today."

"I'll be at the Bar & Grill tonight. How about you drop it off then? I'm working on matches this weekend." Matches that had just taken a left turn off a cliff.

"Great." She jumped to her feet and clutched his questionnaire against her chest. "I'll see you tonight. Thanks, Gideon. I appreciate your help."

Gideon blinked as she left the bank, hurried across the snow-strewed street and disappeared behind the flower-laden window boxes, ribbons and bows of her shop.

Sophie Jennings wanted him to find her the perfect man. The hair on the back of his neck prickled. Someone from K-Bay? Not a single appropriate person sprang to mind. Not with the rough-and-tumble, grizzled men who had an aversion to razors and romance. He loosened his tie so he could breathe. Even if he expanded their questionnaire topics a hundred-fold, he wasn't sure anyone could be a match for someone as special and unique as Sophie.

But she deserved the same shot at happiness as everyone else who'd come to them. Gideon bit the inside of his cheek. He just never anticipated being the person responsible for finding it.

"RATE IN ORDER of preference. Skydiving, kayaking, hiking or playing pool?" Sophie nibbled on the end of her pencil and winced. "Is this thing for real?" Wasn't there a fill in the blank for "other" or "none of the above"? Maybe Gideon and his friends' matchmaking service wasn't such a good idea after all.

Gideon. All this time she'd suspected he'd been less than forthright when he'd told her he couldn't approve her loan. Maybe it was naive, but she didn't think her brother had entered into the equation. Dillon wasn't perfect, but what did Gideon think her brother was going to do? Dip into her bank account and siphon off the loan money?

Her brother was still reeling from their mother's death a year ago and his proclivity toward finding trouble, something that had begun to manifest after their father took off years ago, had only gotten worse.

But you didn't turn your back on family. No matter how bad things got.

Sophie swallowed hard. Or what your brother did.

Yeah, that was probably exactly what Gideon thought: that it was only a matter of time before Dillon was irredeemable. But Dillon knew where the line was. He knew how far he could go. She gnawed on her lower lip, unconvinced.

Whether he knew or not wasn't the point. It wasn't any of Gideon Walker's business.

Falling into her mother's lifelong pattern of denial, Sophie put her brother out of her mind and focused on something else. Something distracting. Less stressful. Like this dating questionnaire.

Not all the questions could be so… She flipped to the next page as the confidence she'd clung to faded. "If I had to choose an animal guide, which would it be? Bear, fish, wolf or bird? Oh, wow." She dropped the pencil and rested her head in her hands. All that was missing was being asked what kind of tree she would be.

Regret settled like a dormant rose in winter. She couldn't possibly be desperate enough for social interaction to entrust her dating life to a group of lifelong friends whose list of activities were relegated to whatever sporting season it was…could she?

"Stop it." She sat up and straightened her shoulders, giving herself a shake as she refocused her positive energy. This was an opportunity, and if there was one thing Sophie had learned a long time ago, it was to grab hold of those and see them through to wherever they led. Life was an adventure and meant to be embraced. Besides, interspersed with the ridiculous questions were actual reasonable inquiries. There was a place to fill out her interests, what she liked to do for fun and what her plans were for a family.

"This could be worse. He could have asked what my favorite hunting target… Ah." Question fifteen. Sophie couldn't help it. She laughed. "So wrong again. I wonder if aphids would be an acceptable answer." The darn bugs could be a menace to her flowers, especially given how warm the winter months had become.

"You're talking to yourself again, boss," Melanie Singer sang as she waltzed past Sophie's office door with an overgrown bonsai in her hands. "If you aren't going to share with the rest of us—"

Since the "us" consisted of Sophie, Melanie—

her newlywed assistant manager—and a part-time delivery driver currently out on the job, it was no secret Sophie was suffering through a serious dating drought. What else could one call the inch-deep dating pool of K-Bay? She'd known most, if not all, of the residents her whole life and none of them, save for one, had ever captured her romantic attention or made her stomach do that tarantella she'd read about in books. A schoolgirl crush, she told herself for the umpteenth time; a schoolgirl crush that continued to squeeze her heart every Friday around noon. A schoolgirl crush that had taken a serious beating last year when grumpy Gideon had denied her loan request in such a cool, detached way she'd felt as if a winter storm had blown over her and encased her heart in ice.

A year later and she still remembered the overwhelming impulse to grab hold of his bloodred tie—it must have been a Thursday—and choke some life into the number cruncher. Sometimes he seemed wound so tight Sophie wondered if he trimmed his beard—when he'd had one—one whisker at a time.

She only ever saw him crack a smile when he was out with his friends, and even then she suspected getting his lips to curve took an act of Congress.

Why her heart sought to flutter like an overactive butterfly whenever she stepped into the bank was beyond her. But it did. Every week.

Friday. Blue-tie day. Her favorite day, as blue brought out the hint of exploding spring in his eyes.

For now, Sophie didn't see the harm in venting her social-agenda frustration to her employee. Besides, she had enough blackmail material to use on Melanie dating back to high school that would ensure her friend's silence. Not that there was any reason for silence. Hard to keep a secret in K-Bay.

Sophie pushed up from her desk, took a moment to straighten her paperwork and put the collection of scattered pens back into the flowerpot holder. She knocked a reverent knuckle against the memorial photograph of her mother and stopped in the doorway, the questionnaire in her hands. "I talked to Gideon Walker today."

"Did you?" Melanie perched on a tall stool in front of the bonsai, a pair of tiny manicure scissors in her hands poised to trim the tiny shrub into compliance. "You didn't ask for another loan, did you? It took you months to recover the last time he turned you down."

"Don't exaggerate. And this didn't have anything to do with money." But Melanie brought up a good point. The fact that she'd had to ask Gideon of all people about finding a date almost stopped her cold. She could have approached Coop or Ty this morning at the Bar & Grill, but they'd both looked…occupied. That left Gideon, and seeing as she was going to be at the bank anyway…

If she'd ever doubted the universe was determined to make her its comic relief, she now had solid proof.

Stuffy Gideon probably disapproved of Sophie's tendency toward taking chances, but what was the point in living if you weren't going to go after life with a bit of gusto and purpose? That didn't mean she didn't learn from her mistakes. She'd readjusted her plans and now she was poised to make The Flower Shop better than ever. Thanks to Gideon, she'd scrimped and saved enough in the past year to put a decent deposit down on the building next door. Take that, Mr. Blue-Eyed Grumpy Pants.

"For your information," Sophie told Melanie, "I asked Gideon about the matchmaking service he and Ty and Coop are running."

Melanie's green eyes went horizon wide. "Wow. Asked as in…?"

"He gave me paperwork to fill out." Sophie

waved it in front of her, half wishing it would disappear altogether. "You should see some of the questions they're asking. They're so… masculine." Not that she didn't appreciate a good hike now and then, but it certainly wasn't on her list of most romantic outings. Now, a picnic under the moon and stars, or maybe a walk around Aberdine Lake would be nice. Then again, there wasn't anything like getting sweaty, dirty and smelly to see if you'd really met your match.

"Well, they are guys," Melanie said with a shrug. "But because of them, most of the men in town are looking mighty fine these days." Melanie's grin mirrored Sophie's as she thought about the recent trek a good portion of K-Bay's men had made to Mike the barber. Who knew there were so many handsome faces lurking under all that…fuzz. "It's not as if Ty and Coop had a clue about women before they got together with—" Melanie broke off as the front door chimed and Mr. Felenti, one of their weekly regulars, hobbled into the store.

Dowager humped with a trembling hand clutching an ancient carved cane, the old man was one of Sophie's favorite people in K-Bay, despite his overpiqued curiosity and penchant for good-natured gossip. Somewhere between eighty and infinity, there truly wasn't a more charming person in town.

"You want me to—" Melanie started to stand.

"I've got him." Sophie set the questionnaire down on the metal worktable and glanced at the calendar above the order desk. A twinge of sadness slipped around her heart but didn't dim her smile. "It's his anniversary," she whispered to Melanie as she went to greet her customer. "Mr. Felenti, good afternoon. Happy anniversary."

The stooped old man's raisin-wrinkled face stretched into a wide grin as his eyes welled. "Would have been sixty-two years today, missy. Tell me that wouldn't have been a K-Bay record." His gnarled fist reached out and clasped Sophie's hand. "My Edie did so love any reason to celebrate."

And now Mr. Felenti celebrated anniversaries alone by taking his wife a bouquet of flowers and sitting on the bench he'd had placed near her grave; a flask of Edie Felenti's famous hooch for toasting in his jacket pocket.

"Do you have anything specific in mind you'd like to take her?" Sophie nudged him toward one of her two-door refrigerated floral cases along the far wall. "Other than baby white roses," she added. Edie Felenti had loved miniature roses.

Her heart sighed at the thought of spending that many years with someone. Loving someone. Mr. Felenti clanked his way across the showroom and stared into the displays behind the glass. “Lovely, as always.” But he shook his head and dismissed the selection of prearranged bouquets and filled vases. “I don’t see anything that looks like my Edie.”

“How about I have Melanie fix you a nice cup of tea and I’ll put something together for you. Come on.” She caught his arm and led him over to one of the chairs on the other side of the work counter. She’d always liked the idea of customers being able to see what she and Melanie did when it came to arranging, maintaining or creating the perfect floral accent for their chosen occasion. Flowers were social, and she liked making the choosing of them a social event.

“I’ve got lemon-zinger tea, Mr. Felenti,” Melanie called as she abandoned her bonsai. Meanwhile Mr. Felenti hefted himself onto the high chair and hooked his cane on the edge of the counter.

“Sounds zesty.” Mr. Felenti cackled. “Two sugars, please. Don’t tell Doc Maxwell,” he said to Sophie as she gathered up a handful of baby's breath. "He's been going on about my blood sugar."

"He's just concerned. We want you around as long as possible, you know." Sophie touched the back of his hand before she wound her way through the displays of vases and stuffed animals, Mylar balloons bouncing along with a rainbow of less-expensive items. She tried to keep a good gift selection in stock, from artist offerings of jars and boxes to delicate jewelry designed and handcrafted by a trio of sisters who lived just outside town.

She ducked inside the larger floral case, the blast of cool air reminding her of her quick walk to the bank and the surprised expression on Gideon's face when she'd asked him about finding her a romantic match.

She shouldn't care one whit about what Gideon thought. As if he sat in that sterile bank of his, thinking of ways to irritate or get under her skin. She doubted Gideon Walker gave her two winks of thought aside from her Friday-deposit visits.

She'd hold what was left of her family together. She had to. She'd promised their mother. She just never expected that promise to have to include a secret stash of cash she could use for bail money if needed. The peanut-butter jar on top of the refrigerator—safest place for it given Dillon's peanut allergy—was her failsafe. Her brother had a good heart, but his last bail had been set so high, she'd almost come up short for her rent at the store. Maybe someday he'd realize that and make the changes he needed to, but until then, she would plan ahead.

She plucked out five pristine white miniature roses out of their container before adding some pittosporum, freesia—she stopped to take a deep sniff—and lavender. At the last minute, she collected a few healthy vines of ivy.

This time of year she all but bounced on her toes in anticipation of spring. Sure, winter flowers were lovely, but she couldn't wait for her greenhouse at the back of the property to start producing those that she currently had to ship in from other parts of the Lower 48. Winter had the same flattening effect on her bank account as it did her plants. But things would turn around quickly enough once the chill eased.

She found Melanie and Mr. Felenti with their heads together when she returned to the counter, realizing too late they were commiserating over her dating questionnaire. *Uh-oh.*

"You throwing in with those hockey boys?"

Mr. Felenti said as he jabbed a crooked finger at her negligible answers. "Don't know what got into their heads thinking about matchmaking. Darn silly business, if you ask me."

The K-Bay matchmakers were indeed serving as one of the more unusual mysteries about town these days, but given Sophie saw a few more happier couples circling the Bar & Grill—Ty and Coop with their new significant others included—what did she have to lose?

"It would be nice to meet someone with similar interests," Sophie said while trying to find a way to snatch the papers out of Mr. Felenti's hands without being rude. "This place eats up a lot of time. I'm happy to take a shortcut."

CHAPTER TWO

"IT'S A LITTLE spooky how well you've taken to daddyhood." Gideon lowered himself into the chair across from Coop Hamilton, a man he'd known for nearly as long as he'd been alive. Ever the serial dater, Coop had fallen fast—and hard—for Nora Perry, a whip-smart, determined woman who called life as she saw it.

Little Zoe, all big eyes and soft baby-fine blond curls, had been a life-altering surprise, the result of Coop's brief encounter with Nora. Though looking at his friend, he'd never seen Coop seem so... What was the word? *Content.* "Nora's got you on Zoe duty, huh?"

The combination of clacking pool balls, frying oil and on-tap beer sent his senses to singing and his stomach to growling. The brass bell hanging over the bar seemed larger of late, as if taunting him with its desire to be rung to signal a match made in...K-Bay.

"She drove Dad to his doctor's appointment today. They stopped for dinner on the way back." Coop's expression carried a hint of disappointment that disappeared when he looked down at his daughter. "I'm afraid they might be plotting something."

"I wouldn't be surprised." Gideon reached for a spiced peanut as he signaled Coach for a beer. He watched Ty Porter stroll in from the kitchen where he'd been working, a lazy smile on his scarred face and—was that a skip in his step?

Of course it was. It wasn't every day a woman rang a bell and declared her love, very publicly, for a man. Lucky son of a gun.

"At least with our new jobs—" Gideon raised his voice so Coach could hear his boast "—you'll be able to flesh out that bank account of yours and not rely on how many cars you sell in a week. Financial stability is only two couples away."

Coop shrugged, his lack of enthusiasm pressing heavily on Gideon's shoulders.

Gideon prided himself on being a practical kind of guy. Logical, reasoned. He didn't subscribe to the notion of love at first sight or dreamlike happily-ever-afters. The only time he'd ever felt the spark witnessed recently in his friends was courtesy of Friday afternoons at the bank. Observing the emotional upheaval and surrender of his two best friends had both entertained and terrified him. So much was changing, and yet he couldn't imagine losing himself to anyone that fast.

An image of Sophie's beaming face burst into his head.

Or could he?

Gideon clenched his hand. He was leaving and the last thing he needed—or wanted—was to put Sophie in the position of choosing between him and staying. Growing up he'd seen his mother having to make that choice, sometimes daily. She'd left her socially overflowing life in Anchorage to follow his father to K-Bay and become a staid banker's wife; a life that had ended far too soon thanks to one too many martinis and a midnight drive. Gideon only remembered seeing his mother smile in photographs taken from before K-Bay. Gideon set his jaw. Sadness. Depression. Regret. For what? For *love*?

Sophie Jennings belonged here. All the more reason to help her find someone appropriate in K-Bay. A guy who was safe, secure and interested in giving her everything she wanted in the place where she felt at home.

Coop and Ty seemed so mired in domestic bliss, Gideon was determined to cement their successful futures by fulfilling his part of the bet. Two matches, he reminded himself. That was all that stood between them and…their dreams.

Gideon thanked Coach for his beer as he stared down at the froth streaming over the edge of the glass.

"Hey, someone's crashing the party." Ty pointed to Gideon's beer to indicate to Coach that he needed one of his own. "My shift's done, Coach, and by the way, did you lower the age requirements in this place?"

"That little one is more than welcome," Coach said with a wink. "She's got better manners than the three of you put together."

"Kelsey finally get tired of looking at you?" Gideon asked Ty as his stomach growled for more than peanuts, pretzels and salt.

"She's working on that new website of hers. Wants to get the blog up and running by Valentine's Day, and apparently my hovering over her shoulder with suggestions isn't productive. No need to rush home just yet." Ty grinned, leaned across the table and held out his hand to Zoe. She wiggled excitedly and grabbed hold, then stuffed Ty's fingers in her mouth. "Now, that's a grip. I'm impressed." Ty chuckled and scrubbed a hand over his recently shaved beard that used to hide the scars of his youth.

Zoe wasn't the first female to slobber on Ty, but she might just be the last. Ty was as far gone over Kelsey Nash, onetime reporter and reputation ruiner turned dream come true, as Coop was over his instant family. It all made Gideon feel not only like a third wheel, but that he wasn't even on the same vehicle.

"I'm thinking she's going to have a wicked slap shot once I get her on skates." Coop jostled Zoe in his arm just enough to make her giggles echo through the bar. "What do you think, Zoe? You want to play hockey with your dad one day?"

"Mmfha!" Zoe blinked curious eyes up at her father.

"Jeez, let the kid start walking before you put her on ice," Gideon said. All this baby stuff shifted him to this side of nervous. Time to get to work. "Now, look, I've got a new round of questionnaires to go through." He reached for his laptop. "We've got more than a decent shot at winning this bet. As usual, we need a few more female applicants to start matching up couples." His gaze strayed to the door in anticipation of Sophie's arrival. Gideon took a long drink of beer. The idea of seeing Sophie twice in one day filled him with more anticipation than the start of hockey season.

"As you said, I need that job now that I have a family to support. Not that I'm relishing telling Dad about the possibility of us moving out of K-Bay." Coop shoved Ty's hand away from his daughter and glared at him. "Get your own. She's mine."

"Hey, she needs to get to know her uncles. Come on." Ty held his arms out for her. "Hand her over."

"Guys—" Gideon sighed.

"Yeah, yeah." Coop hefted Zoe up and over the table, her pink winter romper with what Gideon thought were ears on the hood making her look as if a pastel bear had gobbled her up. Coop frowned when she settled into Ty's arms as easily as she had his, but then his expression shifted and a knowing smile crept over his mouth. "Listen, Nora and I could do with a date night. You and Kelsey want to babysit?"

"Can we please talk about your social life after we get this matchmaking business settled?" Gideon pleaded and looked to Coach for support as he delivered Ty's drink. Zoe aside, he longed for the days he spent with Coop and Ty lounging at the bar with nothing better to do than commiserate about…nothing. "Coach, come on. Help me out."

"No can do," Coach said with a slow shake of his head as he, too, fell under Zoe's charming spell. Coach tickled her under her chin. "You three made the bet, you three see it through on your own. You know, it might be time to work on a more expansive kids' menu for this place."

It was all Gideon could do not to gnash his teeth to dust. "It's as if you two are okay leaving your future in my hands. That the case?"

"He's got a point. We both saw what can happen with Gideon's plans." Ty settled Zoe into the crook of his arm. "But first, we order. Burgers? Applesauce?"

Gideon grunted his agreement. He'd have gone with raw bison meat on a stake if it meant getting these guys to focus.

"Extra cheese on mine," Coop said.

"Done and done," Coach told them and disappeared behind the bar.

"Everyone good?" Gideon ground out. "Drinks okay? Zoe, you happy?"

Gideon took her gurgle as a yes.

"What's our current ratio of applicants?" Coop asked and drank down the last of his water.

"We're about two to one, men to women. No big surprise," Gideon answered. "Our next group outing is in a week—"

"February the thirteenth," Ty said. "Fingers crossed this Polar Dip idea of yours doesn't go, um." He cringed and glanced at Zoe. "Feet up."

"It's not going feet up," Gideon grumbled. He wasn't worried they'd fail. Not much anyway. "We'll win the bet and this time next year we'll be settled down south. Did we finalize the bus rental?"

"Booked and deposit paid for thanks to the applicants' registration fees. We're renting a bunch of chairs, too. Coop and I will go early to set up. You can babysit the couples on the journey there."

"A lot of women love nothing more than to sit and sip hot chocolate and watch a bunch of nearly naked men jump into freezing water," Coop said.

"Proves which is the smarter sex," Gideon quipped.

"That's a reality show I'd watch," Ty said. "At least the weather is supposed to be clear. You really believe this is a good date idea? Will we need liability insurance?"

"If we didn't have it for the ATV trip, we should be fine. And I'm looking at this as a test-of-character outing," Gideon said, loosening his tie. Ah, now it felt like Friday. "How each reacts to the other during this trip can either solidify or destroy a potential relationship." Listen to him, as if he'd actually taken Psych 101 in college.

"I hope I'm not too late to be included." The female voice that broke into the conversation stopped Gideon cold. Seeing Sophie standing beside the table, bundled in that down jacket of hers, eyes as steady as a forest of dormant redwoods, had him shoving to his feet and sloshing his beer over the edge of his glass. "I didn't mean to interrupt," she said, backing away as beer dribbled along the table.

"You're not," Gideon said. Without looking he knew Ty and Coop well enough to suspect they were exchanging confused expressions. "We were just going over details for the bus trip. We're calling it the Polar Dip Date."

"Hmm." Sophie pressed her lips together, but it didn't stop the smile from appearing on her face. "I've often thought ice water and men in bathing suits was a combination for romantic success."

"Clearly she's never seen our swim trunks," Ty said. "Mine have glow-in-the-dark smiley faces."

"Mine don't," Coop said.

Sophie laughed. "Here's my questionnaire." She handed over the papers Gideon had given her with something akin to a wince. "I did the best I could. I'm betting there won't be many who share my opinion of *Lumberjack Loons*."

The fact she even knew about the Alaskan-based reality show quirked a smile on his lips. "I wish you the best of luck matching me, fellas."

"I'm sure we'll find you someone." Wow. How coherent of him. His stomach was doing all kinds of flip-flops. It was as if his plan to leave town had kicked his fledgling attraction to Sophie into overdrive.

"Your little girl looks a lot happier than when I saw you changing her diaper at the grocery store checkout, Coop." Sophie circled the table and dipped down beside Ty as one of Coach's waitresses swooped in and cleaned up the spill Gideon had made. "She's beautiful." She reached out and caught Zoe's foot in her hand.

"Her name's Zoe. She looks like her mother," Coop said, and earned a heartfelt sigh from Sophie.

"I was relieved you had some questions about family and future plans on your questionnaire," she said to Gideon as he lowered himself into his chair. Her eyes flicked to his tie, and a smile emerged on her lips as she met his gaze.

"Yeah, well, it seemed appropriate." His fingers itched to flip through her answers and see what her plans included.

"That's code for he'll be handing out new forms in a few days," Coop said. "So, Sophie. Entrusting us with your foray into the dating world. We're honored."

"You've made me curious," Sophie said and backed away as their burgers were served.

"Can we get you anything?" Coop asked, aiming a sidelong glance in Gideon's direction. "Why don't you join us?"

"I already ate, thanks. But I can take her off your hands while you eat if you want." She held out her arms.

"That's an offer I'll gladly accept." Ty hefted Zoe into the air and Sophie grabbed hold, placing the little girl over her shoulder in an effortless motion. Gideon stared and realized apart from the questionnaire, she'd barely looked at him.

"So tell us, Sophie," Ty said as he dug into his dinner. "What is it you're looking for in a man?"

"You mean me telling you what my favorite type of boat is doesn't give you enough information?"

"Sometimes we like to explore things a bit further." Coop blew on a thick fry and, breaking it in half, held it up to Zoe.

"Ah, no." Sophie pushed his hand away. "She's too young and that's too hot."

"Bah!" Zoe protested and dropped her head onto Sophie's shoulder.

"Still learning," Coop grumbled, but Gideon thought the hint of red on his friend's face was wildly entertaining.

"I'm surprised Gideon didn't ask for a follow-up consultation," Ty said and barely flinched when Gideon's boot found his shin. "I mean, he does like to be thorough when it comes to matching up our applicants."

"I want someone steady." Sophie sat Zoe on her lap, facing the table, and wrapped her hands around the baby's torso. "Reliable. Considerate." She ducked her head and rested it gently against Zoe's for a brief moment. "Someone who wants to make a life here in K-Bay. I don't mean I expect you to find me a husband," she added and glanced at Gideon as if she'd just admitted to some wild, inappropriate fantasy. "But I need someplace to start.

Someone to start with. Get my feet wet, so to speak, in the dating game."

"Gideon's great at starting things," Coop said. "If anyone can help you find someone, he can. Right, Gid?"

"Right." Gideon managed a shaky smile and dropped her paperwork on top of the others. "Yeah, nothing I want more than to help you find your perfect someone, Sophie."

But even as he said the words, he knew he was lying.

CHAPTER THREE

"OH, DILLON." SOPHIE'S PUB- and baby-induced good mood evaporated the second she stepped foot inside her front door. Dillon sat exactly where he'd been this morning, glued to the sofa, a video game controller in his hand, and a collection of beer bottles and energy drink cans scattered around his feet.

Gideon's earlier comments came back at her with the force of a slingshot.

She marched to the kitchen and reached over the sink to shove open the window. Taking a good breath of fresh air and shivering against the cold, she tried to ignore the pile of food wrappers, empty microwave containers and dirty dishes.

"Dillon, I thought we talked about—" She returned to the living room, list in hand.

"Can't talk now, sis. About to level up." Dillon angled his controller this way and that as he sent virtual grenades lobbing toward the heads of his online opponents.

Sophie bit her lip. She hated conflict of any kind and usually avoided it like the plague, but enough was enough. He was an adult. It was time for him to start acting like it. "Was it really too much trouble to take out the trash?"

"I'll do it in a minute!" The frown marring his features was so reminiscent of their father—a man she had few good memories of—she almost lost her breath. Dillon's thick brows pinched together as more explosions echoed from the flat-screen television. The TV was the only new indulgence Sophie had given in to in the past two years in an effort to pinch every penny. The set had been a blessing when it came to entertaining their mother, but if Sophie had even suspected how much time it was going to suck out of her brother, she would have chucked the thing after coming home from the funeral.

"Ah, man!" Dillon threw the controller down and glared at her. From his saggy posture on the sofa, she'd give him to the end of the year before he looked more like a sci-fi gelatinous mob boss than the long-distance runner he'd been once upon a time. "Now look! It's as if the whole day was a waste."

"I guess it's trash time, then." Despite the open kitchen window, the air in the house continued to hang heavy and stale. No doubt because he hadn't ventured outside unless it was for a beer run.

"Quit nagging me," Dillon spat with an exaggerated roll of his eyes that only accentuated his scraggly hair and overgrown beard. "I'm going."

She followed him into the kitchen. "I spotted a couple of new help-wanted signs in town. The Clipper Ship is looking for a busboy and the hardware store—"

"I'll find something on my own," he said as he turned on the faucet and started dumping his pile of trash into a bag. "I don't need your help."

"You need someone's." Sophie hugged herself, fighting the urge to disappear into her room. Not this time. Not tonight. "It was your choice not to take that partial scholarship to UCLA," Sophie reminded him with as kind a tone as she could muster, despite her disappointment. "You made a deal with me and Mom when you turned that down. You said you'd get a job and contribute around here."

"That scholarship wouldn't have paid for anything other than tuition."

"You wouldn't have been the first college student who had to work to cover living expenses. And I would have helped where I could." Of all of their father's less than admirable traits for Dillon to acquire, he'd gotten a double dose of the lazy, entitled gene. The idea of working hard never occurred to either of them. "You should have at least tried. But this, what you've been doing since Mom died—" She stopped as his jaw tensed. He'd already tuned her out. "There's something out there for you, Dillon. I wish you'd try to find it." *And stop spending your free time getting busted for misdemeanors.*

"Easy for you to say," Dillon grumbled, splashing water over the edge of the sink. "You've always known what you wanted to do."

"That doesn't mean it's been easy." She was more than happy to regale him with how much effort it had taken to get The Flower Shop off the ground. Or how much farther she could be on her chosen career path if she didn't have to carry him, as well. Guilt settled, easing the urge to lash out at him. Instead, she said, "What would Mom say if she saw you now?"

"She'd ask how much the bail was and go back to watching her shows."

Sophie swallowed hard, banking the tears that burned behind her eyes.

That her brother would say such a thing so casually only proved how far off track he'd gotten. Every second that passed proved Gideon Walker right. It only added to her frustration. Shame rolled over her in thick, heavy waves. She'd fallen into the same pattern as their mother, coddling him, making excuses for him and trying to make life as easy as possible. But life wasn't easy.

Maybe it was time he understood that.

"This can't go on, Dillon." She didn't want to pull the trigger on her backup plan, but the more time that passed, the more she came to accept there was only one solution. If only it wasn't so hard.

"There's more to life than work," Dillon said with a dramatic sigh and a drop of his chin to his chest, his arms wrist deep in suds. "Not that you'd know about that."

"I beg your pardon?" She blinked at him.

"All you do is go to work and then come home and rag on me. I don't see you having any kind of life."

"Asking you to clean up after yourself isn't ragging." But his accusation felt like carte blanche to do so. Sophie felt her spine stiffen as resolution set in. A sharp dose of reality was what Dillon needed. "I'm going to expand my social life just like you're going to get it together and find a job. This house doesn't pay for itself. Either step up or I'll be making some changes." The words came out in a rush, as if she'd purged herself of a long-held tension, and could now breathe easier. She walked to the sink and ruffled the back of his hair, just like she used to when he was little. But he shied away, as if her touch had burned him.

Sophie tried to ignore the sharp stab at her heart. "Thank you for cleaning up. Good night, Dillon."

"Yeah. Night."

Sophie trudged up the stairs, dragging her oversize purse with her, banging it against the wall as she ducked into her bedroom. Exhaustion descended as soon as she sank onto her mattress. It was all she could do to reach over and click on the bedside lamp.

This room served as her refuge, the one place she'd always felt at peace no matter what happened outside the door. The soft colors, the stacks of paperbacks in the corner for when she had time to read, the conglomeration of pictures of her, Dillon and their mother before everything got so...challenging. Sophie sighed.

Dillon was correct about one thing: she didn't have much more than work and home, but that was why she'd ventured into scary matchmaking territory and talked to Gideon.

Gideon.

Sophie let out a growl of frustration and threw herself back on the bed, staring up at the popcorn ceiling. Gideon Walker had his foibles, but being distant with the truth wasn't one of them. If anything, the man was too honest, as evidenced today by his heavily voiced opinion about her brother.

All this time she thought Gideon had turned down her loan request because he considered her an unworthy investment or, worse, that she was not bright enough to run a successful business. Today he'd made it pretty clear that wasn't the case.

His admission should have made her feel better. Instead, it made her sad.

How her mother expected Sophie to do what she couldn't and keep Dillon out of trouble, Sophie couldn't fathom. But the deathbed promise she'd made wasn't something she could forget.

She rolled onto her side, her gaze falling to the starry night outside her window. Everyone in town knew what a troublemaker Dillon was. At least Gideon had been honest and said what she was sure dozens of other people were thinking. She had seen a glimpse of the real Gideon tonight at the Bar & Grill, though, when his handsome face had cracked an occasional smile. He was…different from how he was at the bank. Friendlier. Fun.

Maybe she needed to cut him some slack.

And maybe Gideon was the person who could find a soul mate for her.

CHAPTER FOUR

GIDEON SIPPED HIS COFFEE, courtesy of Tilda at the Clipper Ship Coffee Shop. The small dining area in the far back was a hidden gem in town and served a bracing coffee. The early-Saturday-morning zing of caffeine did his system a world of good given the restless nights he'd had since inputting the data from the latest questionnaires. He'd be lucky if his laptop didn't go on strike.

"Am I reading this right?" Ty asked with more skepticism on his face than Gideon had seen in a while. "You're matching Sophie Jennings with Peter Ellingsworth, Jack Travis and then Manfred Dellison?"

Gideon shrugged. The less he said the better. He didn't want to admit—vocally at least—that he'd kept Sophie's questionnaire out of the program and plucked a few outliers from the male applicants to pair her off with. All three of those men were…well, safe. They'd treat her with kindness. And if there happened to be an emotional connection, wasn't it better to make one with a schoolteacher, a supermarket manager or a…

Ty frowned. "Is there a glitch in the software you wrote? Manfred works for a pesticide manufacturer. Sophie's a florist. You don't see a conflict there?"

Another shrug. What Gideon did see was a socially awkward borderline geek with a penchant for collecting odd goggles and stalking Alaskan wildlife in the moonlight.

It took every ounce of control Gideon had not to grimace behind his coffee mug as he thanked Tilda for her excellent sense of timing in bringing over his breakfast, the clang of her wristload of bracelets a welcome distraction. No one did smoked-salmon-and-cream-cheese omelets quite like the Clipper Ship, which was why he only allowed himself to indulge a couple times a month. And the paprika-spiced potatoes and homemade buttermilk biscuits? Superb.

"Sophie can talk to anyone about anything." Gideon avoided Ty's gaze and dug in. "Peter or Jack might be a better choice."

"I thought Peter didn't want kids. And did you even read Manfred's answer to 'What's your greatest achievement?' This guy had a hand in creating one of those pesticides linked to the decline in the bee population. You do know flowers need bees to thrive, right?"

"I aced biology. Unlike some people." Gideon tried to lighten the mood. Anything to keep Ty distracted from asking what Gideon was sure was headed his way: probing questions about his feelings for Sophie. "There's always Jack Travis as backup, and you can't find anything wrong with him."

"The guy is as boring as glue," Ty said. "I'm falling into a coma just thinking about their date. Do you have something against Sophie?"

Gideon choked on his omelet and almost spit out a caper. Sputtering, he reached for his napkin as his eyes watered. "What?"

Ty set the printout aside and welcomed his own stack of boysenberry pancakes dripping with butter accompanied by a thick slab of bacon. "I wouldn't match a warrior princess with Manfred," Ty said. "Let alone someone as sweet as Sophie. Just seems an odd pairing to me."

"Look, all I'm trying to do is get us enough matches to win that bet. You want to go through the forms and see if you can do any better—"

"No, no. I've spent my time there in purgatory, thanks." Ty held up one hand in surrender. "We've trusted you this far with the logarithm. We know you won't let us down."

Guiltily, Gideon swallowed a bite of potato and ignored Ty's skeptical expression. It wasn't as if he was sabotaging Sophie's chance at happiness. He was showing her what K-Bay had to offer, and compared to some of the other men—men he wouldn't trust within three feet of K-Bay's flower princess—she'd do perfectly fine.

Other people in K-Bay who were looking for matches didn't have to rely on Sophie, even if Sophie was relying on Gideon. And if by not putting her info into the system it caused a few, well, problems, there was still time to fix them.

One thing he did know was that reading Sophie's questionnaire had him leaning away from the idea of their friendship toward… something that could never be.

Sophie was homegrown K-Bay. Her feet may as well be tied to the tree roots in the town's foundation.

And Gideon was all but packed and ready to leave for good.

"Hey!" Ty waved his fork in front of Gideon's face. "Where did you disappear to?"

"Nothing. Nowhere." Gideon tried to push away the realization that there would soon come a day when he wouldn't see Sophie stepping through the door of the bank to brighten up his afternoon. All this time he'd been focused on what waited for him outside K-Bay. He'd never stopped to think what—or who—he might be leaving behind. "There are ten couples on that list for the Polar Dip so far. Odds are someone out of that group has to ring that bell, so I'd guess we're just about home free by Valentine's Day."

"From your lips." Ty didn't sound as enthusiastic at the prospect of winning the bet with Coach as he had only a few days ago. Or maybe Gideon was projecting his own doubts onto his friend. "But back to Sophie for a second."

Gideon's appetite waned. "Must we?"

"Don't mess with her too much," Ty warned in an oddly protective tone. "I know you haven't been overly fond of our local florist, but there are plenty of people who are, me included. She might not be as fragile as Eleanor Clambert, but it took a lot of nerve to put her heart out there, and the last person who should be taking another swipe at her is you. Unless you have other ideas?"

"I've never taken a swipe at Sophie."

"You turned her down for that business loan last year," Ty reminded him.

Gideon shook his head. Didn't anyone see he'd only refused her because he was protecting her? "That was different. That was dollars and cents. And I didn't want anyone taking advantage of her."

Ty arched a brow in that silent way he had of absorbing information for future use.

"She wasn't a good financial risk," Gideon added. He didn't have any trouble imagining what Dillon Jennings would do to get in between Sophie and the money she needed for her shop. Gideon wasn't about to let her be that vulnerable when someone completely unreliable was lurking over her shoulder.

He didn't regret it. Much.

"If you're not careful," Ty said, "those risks you don't believe are worth taking are going to bite you in the butt. All the more reason to be careful with these matches, Gid. One wrong move and disaster will strike. And take all of us and our futures with it."

"SOPHIE?"

On Tuesday morning, Sophie glanced up from the third of twenty centerpieces for a wedding in neighboring Denali, her hands wrist deep in floral foam, baby's breath and delicate purple irises.

"Hello. Manfred, isn't it?" She smiled at the slight, gawky, bespectacled man coming in the door and set the arrangement aside. She remembered him—barely—from high school. At least she thought she did. Sophie wiped her hands on her apron and approached. "How can I help you?"

He cleared his throat, wide eyes circling the store like a fish in a bowl. "Gideon Walker contacted me. I believe you and I have a date to plan for this evening."

"Oh!" The nervous smile that took over the entirety of Manfred's face told her she was about to become the three-strikes-you're-out member of the matchmaking club. "Oh, I didn't realize he'd have another one for me so soon." She'd barely recovered from Sunday night and Peter Ellingsworth, and the dinner that wasn't. He'd spent more time complaining about having to dodge his ex-girlfriend's phone calls than he had talking with Sophie. She'd begged off to the ladies' room but wasn't gone ten seconds before he was on his phone—with said ex.

Her coffee date with Jack Travis yesterday morning had started with more promise, but that had soon gone awry when a clumsy barista had tripped next to their table and her tray full of mochas and espressos had landed in Jack's lap. He'd leaped to his feet instantly and caused the guy sitting behind him to… Well, the entire café had suffered a severe domino-like collapse. The last Sophie had seen of Jack, he'd been waddling down the street, plucking his pants away from tender areas, a string of curses echoing in the morning air.

And now…Manfred.

"Um." She shoved her hands into her pockets and rocked back on her heels. She should have checked her cell phone, apparently. Assuming Gideon had given her a heads-up. "So did you have something in mind you'd like to do?"

"I was thinking we could go nocturning."

Sophie's mind went completely blank. A stilted laugh accompanied her next words. "I'm afraid I'm not sure what that is."

"That's because I made it up," Manfred said after letting out a noise Sophie could only identify as a snort. He pushed his glasses farther up his nose. "You see, you put on these night-vision goggles and go into the woods to look for creatures. Opossum, raccoons, all kinds of bugs and stuff. I've always wanted to go with someone and maybe make a contest out of it. You know, see how many different species each one of us finds? Like a wildlife scavenger hunt."

"Couldn't we do the same thing by staking out some backyards?" Raccoons and the occasional bear or moose were frequent visitors in many backyards, especially if one forgot to lock down their cans for the night. She'd be happy to skulk around and knock a few lids off for good measure.

"Could." Manfred's grin was back. "This is more fun. More…adventurous. Your questionnaire mentioned something about adventure, right? What do you say? I can pick you up after dark. What's your address? You live up on Eskaleut Lane, right?"

"Um." Harmless, she told herself. Manfred was harmless, just…odd. Small-town problems. She seemed to be attracting odd like bees to pollen. "I'm working late tonight, actually. How about we meet at the Bar & Grill about eight?"

"Excellent. I'll make sure to clean your goggles for you. See you tonight!"

Sophie stared at the glass door for a good minute after Manfred left. Her faith in Gideon's matchmaking abilities had officially waned.

Was her personality so bad, had she answered that questionnaire so wrong, that these were the three men K-Bay had to offer her? Or maybe they'd overstated what they had to offer. Yeah. She could buy that. Guys exaggerated. About everything. Of course, there was one other possibility. "Gideon has gone and lost his mind." Or he had it out for her. Again.

"What's that?" Melanie asked as she returned from her coffee break and handed over a steaming latte to Sophie. "You look a little pale. What's going on?"

"Nothing." Except Manfred wasn't nothing. "I have another date. Tonight."

"Who with this time?" Melanie's eyebrows disappeared under her bangs.

"Um." Sophie sipped her drink and walked away, disappointment and embarrassment surging through her. "Manfred Dellison."

"Manny the Maniac?" Melanie tripped over a seam in the linoleum and caught herself on the counter. "Are you serious?"

"He was just here," Sophie explained with more than a little trepidation in her voice. "And do people really still call him that? It's been years since high school." But she did have to wonder how she'd forgotten.

"Of course. He develops poisons for a living." Melanie shuddered. "That's more than a little icky. I wouldn't let him near your drink."

"Oh, stop. Manfred's not dangerous," Sophie argued around a too-tight throat. "Unless you're an insect. Why did they call him that anyway?" Even if Gideon did think she was a ditz, he wouldn't have set her up with anyone unstable. Sophie nibbled on her lower lip. Would he?

"Something about how he walks around town at all hours of the night. Wearing these funky night-vision-goggle things. Reminds me of a stalker in one of those horror movies. Seriously, that's who Gideon matched you with? Girlfriend guy and coffee pants weren't enough?"

"I guess not."

"Are you going?"

"Uh-huh." Sophie swallowed and turned pitiful eyes on her friend. "Manfred looked so excited, so happy. I couldn't very well say no. And besides, I can't give Gideon the satisfaction of not seeing this through. He already thinks I'm flighty. I don't want to give him the impression that I'm not trying or grateful for his efforts." Despite where his efforts were leading her. She was beginning to understand how Gideon must really see her.

Melanie frowned. "I've never heard anyone, least of all Gideon, call you flighty. Flirty maybe." She waggled her brows and cocked her head. "Maybe Manfred will have something to say about that. Where are you going? What are you doing?"

"Have you ever heard of nocturning?" *Please, please...*

"Not even a little."

"Then, do me a favor. Keep your phone on tonight. I might be sending out an SOS." Sophie knew one thing for sure. She'd be spending most of the night praying Manfred didn't live up to his nickname.

CHAPTER FIVE

GIDEON'S NERVES WERE getting to him.

He didn't mind these group dates anymore, but solitary sentry duty at the Bar & Grill while most of the couples were in full date mode was annoying.

Ty had skived off instead of joining him, as had Coop, who seemed more than content to stay home with Nora and Zoe than venture out to see how effective the latest round of matches were. Ty and Coop had better get their behinds over to the rink tomorrow night to help with broom hockey. Those men-versus-women matches were getting…nasty.

As for tonight? The majority of those meeting for drinks and dinner seemed to be having a good time and had sequestered themselves in booths. Some couples ventured elsewhere to find their own entertainment.

Watching Sophie accept a pair of science-fiction-movie-reject night-vision goggles from Manfred put a frown on Gideon's face. He hadn't been able to look away from her from the second she'd opened the door. Her wide-eyed expression might have brought an amused smile to his face if his envy hadn't asserted control.

Gideon clenched his jaw, loosened his tie and grabbed hold of his beer. After her disastrous first two dates he didn't anticipate much could go wrong for her with Manfred. Then again, Gideon didn't expect to see her looking so nervous. Gideon abandoned his stool as Manfred escorted her out of the bar. Where were they going? He didn't imagine Manfred, of all people, would venture too far away from the familiarity of the bar.

Had Sophie bothered to glance his way he might have considered stepping in, or at least asking where the couple was headed for the night, but he swore she was purposely avoiding looking in his direction.

Unease unwound like a garter snake in his chest. The idea of Sophie being out of his sight didn't sit well, and his apprehension increased over the next hour.

"I'm sensing a bit of uncertainty here," Coach said as he set a second beer in front of Gideon. "What gives? You worried about Sophie?"

Truth be told, Coach was right. He couldn't stop thinking—or worrying—about her. Not that he was about to admit it. "Why would I be—?"

Coach held up a hand to cut off his denial. "You nearly toppled the table the other night standing up when Sophie joined you. Tell me the last time you did that and I'll change topics right now."

"I was being polite," Gideon explained, unsure why the thought of people knowing he cared about Sophie unnerved him so much.

Coach scoffed. "Sure. We can call it that. But I've never seen your head turned so fast or so completely before. Sophie Jennings, huh?" Coach grabbed a glass and wiped it down with his towel. "You're putting a lot of faith in the universe's sense of humor given how you almost derailed her future business plans."

What was it with everyone and Gideon turning down Sophie's loan application? "I told Ty and I'll tell you, it was a good decision. She was a risk."

"She's a risk, all right." Coach grinned. "Though right now, I'd say Manfred's a bigger one. Odd combination those two, wouldn't you say?" Leave it to Coach to echo exactly what Ty had said the other morning at breakfast.

"Manfred needed someone kind. A test run, so to speak." But Gideon's attempt to justify didn't ring true even to his own ears. Okay, maybe his motives weren't quite so honorable when it came to finding a match for Sophie. There wasn't enough self-confidence in Manfred for him to hit on a tree trunk, let alone Sophie. The very idea he'd try to kiss her was enough to make Gideon want to beat his fists against the wall of the Bar & Grill.

"Manfred Dellison needs more than a test run," Coach said. "He needs a refresher course in human interaction. He's taking her nocturning."

"What's that? Like a walk in the moonlight?" Maybe Manfred had more romance in him than Gideon assumed.

"It's Manfred's version of a wildlife scavenger hunt." Coach's frown deepened. "What do you think the night-vision goggles were for?"

The beer he'd drunk churned in Gideon's stomach. "You mean he's taking her out on a midnight hike in the woods? I thought maybe he'd just show her the moon."

What kind of idiot takes a woman hiking in the dark and calls it a date?

What kind of idiot fixes up a woman he's interested in with anyone like Manfred? A man who didn't want to admit she'd wiggled her way into his heart, that was who. Which meant Gideon had to find a way to wiggle her out again. But first he needed to make sure she was okay. "Any idea where they're headed?"

"From what I was able to glean—" Coach arched a brow "—sounded like Windhawk Forest. Could be tricky, though. Lots of potential to go off the path around there. Hope he's leaving a trail of bread crumbs."

Yeah, Manfred didn't strike him as the practical sort. Gideon grabbed his jacket and shoved his cell phone into his pocket. "Do me a favor, Coach. Call Ty and tell him I had an emergency."

"ARE YOU SURE you're all right?" Sophie stumbled over the strewn branches of nature gone wild as she tightened her arm around Manfred's slim waist. His arm draped heavy around her shoulders. He didn't look as if he weighed much, but then she was sinking ankle deep in mud, so looks were definitely deceiving. "I thought you told me you'd been on this trail hundreds of times."

"Maybe not hundreds," Manfred panted. Despite the slightly offensive aroma of nervousness and sweat, he hobbled on his uninjured leg rather impressively. "And maybe not this late. Man, I took a heck of a tumble, didn't I?"

"Like a circus performer on debut night," Sophie said and tried not to wince as her body ached with Manfred's added weight. "Are you sure this is the right direction?"

"Uh, yeah." He flipped a switch on his goggles that sent a narrow beam of light shining down the obscured path between thick trees. "See the mark on that trunk right there. I made that—" He lifted his arm from around her shoulders to point, but his unsteadiness caused them both to crash to the ground.

The thud knocked the wind out of her and she waited a few seconds before moving against the half-frozen ground. She sighed and stared up through the canopy of branches.

Maybe venturing into the matchmaking world hadn't been her best idea.

Even under three layers of clothes she shivered. Her fingers were numb, as she'd lost her gloves a good half mile ago when she'd helped drag Manfred out of the shallow ravine he'd toppled into. Toppled. Sophie bit her lip to stop from laughing.

He'd somersaulted so fast and so far he could have been mistaken for a hedgehog on amphetamines.

"I'm okay," Manfred insisted, but the strain in his voice was either embarrassment or he'd robbed himself of whatever lung capacity he possessed. "Just give me a second—"

"Sophie! Manfred!"

Sophie shot up. "Gideon?" She reached back and slapped her hand against Manfred's jacket, jabbing at him to pay more attention. "Manfred, I think that's Gideon."

"Great," Manfred groaned. "Nothing I was hoping for more than to have to be rescued from my first date by Captain Fantastic."

The sympathy that had abandoned Sophie two minutes into nocturning resurfaced as she heard footfalls through the woods. She shifted on the ground and tried to see him in the darkness. "Your first date? Oh, Manfred, why didn't you tell me?"

He flicked on the high beam again and forced her to turn away for fear of being blinded. "Would you have gone out with me if I had?"

"Of course." And the fact this was his first date explained so much about his enthusiasm when it came to their outing. He'd been trying to impress her. "But, Manfred, you went a little overboard. Dinner would have been nice. Talking. Getting to know each other."

"I thought you wanted adventure. Excitement. Isn't that what women want?"

"Not all of us," Sophie said. "I mean, yeah, I guess I kind of do." She had included that in her questionnaire under "comments." "But that doesn't mean you have to do things you're not comfortable with just to get a date. You're a very nice guy, Manfred. Some girl is going to realize that and then you'll be set for life."

"But not you, huh?" Manfred pushed himself up and flicked off the light. She couldn't see his face any longer, not without seeing spots exploding in front of her eyes, but she could hear the resignation in his voice. The same tone she'd used herself on more than one occasion.

A tone she'd used most recently when she'd thought about Gideon.

It didn't seem to matter what she did or who she was with, the idea of Gideon always managed to sneak in. How was that even possible given what little he thought of her?

And now the man was hoofing toward them in person; the perfect ending to yet another painful day. She heard him continue to holler their names and she called back, directing him by snagging the goggles off Manfred's head and turning on the light to wave it in the air.

"You and I both know, Manfred," Sophie said as she heard Gideon's steps along with the snapping of twigs and scattering of brush, "we aren't a great match. Bees aside—"

"I didn't know about the damage that pesticide would cause," Manfred interrupted. "When I found out about the effects, I started on a workaround that would keep the pesticide effective and not harm the bees."

"You did?" Sophie's heart opened another crack.

"I did. And it's almost done. We're running some more tests to be sure, but I'm going to fix it."

"That's great, Manfred. I'm glad you told me."

"Sophie, do you think—" He stopped and for a moment, Sophie wondered if the excitement had gotten the best of him and he'd passed out.

"Do I think what?" She found his hand and squeezed her frozen fingers around his.

"I realize we won't have another date, but maybe...maybe we could be friends?"

Sophie smiled and wished he could see it in the darkness. "We're already friends, Manfred." And it was time to get her friend some help. No matter who it had to come from. "Gideon, we're over here!"

It was a good thing she knew he was on his way, otherwise his appearance—all gloomy, brooding shadows—might have scared ten years off her life. The flashlight in his hand blinded her all over again.

"Sophie, are you okay?" He was at her feet in a breath and she felt his grip around her arms, hauling her up. His hands assessed her as he ran them up to her shoulders, down to her wrists. For an instant, she thought he might pull her into a hug, but as quickly as the hope appeared, it vanished. "Manfred, what were you thinking dragging her out here like this? Remember? We talked about dinner and a movie."

"We did. I thought this would be more fun."

"He's hurt," Sophie whispered and felt the instant warmth of Gideon's touch through her clothes. Suddenly, the February freeze didn't seem so bad. Not if Gideon was around to keep her warm in that nice wool trench coat of his. "Not seriously, I don't think. What are you doing here?" she asked as he hefted Manfred to his feet.

"Coach overheard your plans," Gideon said. "Did you really think this nocturning of yours was a good idea?"

"If it's any consolation, I don't anymore."

Manfred chuckled and Sophie found herself smiling again. He really was a cute guy, but despite his postulations of being an avid nocturnist, he'd ventured way out of his comfort zone. "I'm sorry, Gideon, but it's not going to work out between me and Sophie."

"Not for lack of trying," Sophie added to soften the blow. "If we get you back to your car, Manfred, do you think you can drive home? Or do you want to go to the emergency clinic?"

"No need to add another level of mortification to my evening, thanks," Manfred said. "I can drive. And home sounds like a grand idea. I see a heating pad and ice packs in my future."

"We'll follow you to make sure you get home okay. Right, Gideon? And then you can drive me home." Sophie made sure her voice didn't leave any room for argument.

Gideon looped Manfred's arm around his neck and started back down the path. "Sure thing. I'm really sorry about this, Manfred."

"Don't be." Manfred laughed. "I think this might just be the greatest night of my life."

CHAPTER SIX

"HE ACTUALLY IS a sweet man." Sophie scooted closer to the window of Gideon's truck to keep an eye on Manfred as he limped across his icy lawn and hopped up the three steps to his front door. He gave them a wave before disappearing into the house, the porch light flickering on with a snap and buzz that indicated the fixture was more of a bug zapper than for illumination. Poor little bugs.

"Nice guy or not, you could have been seriously hurt." Gideon made a U-turn, tires crunching in the gravel, and headed down the three-mile stretch of road toward town. "I can see where his judgment might have been impaired, but I thought you had more sense than to go gallivanting through the forest in the dead of night."

"Gallivanting?" Sophie's cheeks flamed. "I didn't want to offend him. And who goes into the woods at night wearing a tie? Honestly, Gideon, do you ever loosen up?"

"Manfred was supposed to be safe."

"Safe?" The urge to apologize evaporated as Sophie plucked a thin dried branch out of her hair. "What do you mean, *safe*?"

"Safe as in you shouldn't have gotten hurt."

"I didn't get hurt." She shifted around to look at him, that uneasy, quivering feeling fluttering in her stomach again. "Manfred did. And in case you didn't notice, Gideon, despite whatever else you think of me, I am a grown woman capable of making her own decisions."

"Believe me, I am well aware."

Didn't he sound positively thrilled about it. Sophie pursed her lips, the urge to grab that ridiculous Tuesday yellow tie and strangle him with it making her palms itch yet again. "I knew what I was getting into when I signed up for the matchmaking. I didn't expect Prince Charming right out of the gate." Good thing, too, since she hadn't even found Prince Tolerable yet. "There's no liability issue, if that's what has you worried."

"That's not it." The way he ground out each word, as if they were glass under his heavy boots, didn't do anything to alleviate her nerves.

"Then, what is it? I can't seem to win with you, Gideon. First you imply I'm too stupid to understand how my own business works, and now I'm too fragile to go romping around in the woods with a character from the *Proton Patrol*."

"I love that show." A smile cracked his stony face. "But that's not what this is about. And why would you ever believe I thought you were stupid?"

"History." She exhaled sharply. "I don't need or want your protection, Gideon. If that's what's going on in your head, you kick that sexist, controlling idea aside right now."

"I don't have any intention of controlling you. As if I could."

"Then, what is it? One minute you're nice, the next you're surly, not to mention grumpy, too." She flopped back against her seat and glared at him. "Admit it, already. I drive you nuts. You can't stand me."

She gasped and grabbed hold of the door handle as he screeched the car over to the side of the road and slammed on the brakes. He unhooked his seat belt as he shoved the car into Park and turned toward her.

"What on earth—" Sophie panted as her heart hammered against her ribs. "Gideon—"

He reached across the seat and gripped her upper arms, dragging her toward him. Before she could process what was happening, he kissed her. Not one of those tentative flirty kisses that, when done right, made a woman smile and blush. No, this was a fireworks-going-off-in-her-brain type of kiss. She couldn't think straight, couldn't do anything but hold on to him and take the wild ride.

When he lifted his mouth, his breathing was stable. She could feel the tension coiled in his body, as if he were trying to stop himself from doing something…something she just now realized she'd always wanted him to do.

"I don't kiss stupid women, Sophie." He brought up one hand and trailed a finger down the side of her cheek. "I don't think about kissing stupid women every hour of the day, and I certainly don't go racing off to Windhawk Forest to search for them in the dark. Tie and all."

"But you came after me." She should have kept the thought to herself, but all she could think, all she could say was "You kissed me."

"Yeah. I did." He pushed her away and settled back in his seat, shifting the car into Drive again, and resumed their journey into town. "That was probably a mistake."

"Oh." That wonderful, warm, fuzzy cloud she'd been drifting on vanished and she plummeted back to earth. Her throat tightened and her eyes burned, but she straightened her shoulders and folded her hands. "Okay."

"Not that way, Soph." Gideon sighed and shook his head. "I can't seem to do or say anything right when I'm around you. I meant I shouldn't have started something that can't go anywhere. I'm not staying in K-Bay, Sophie."

"It was a kiss, Gideon." The words constricted in her throat. "You didn't put a ring on my finger." That Gideon, Ty and Coop dreamed of futures beyond their hometown was one of the worst-kept secrets in K-Bay. Until this moment, she didn't understand how much that mattered to her. Or how serious he was about leaving. Her stomach ached. Deep down where she thought it would never stop. "But thank you for clarifying."

"Sophie—"

"Do me a favor? Could you take a bit of a risk with whomever you match me up with next? I'd actually like to begin a social life and not have it end before it starts."

Instead of smiling at her attempt at humor, he frowned. "I'll see what I can do."

"Thank you."

"You're welcome."

Sophie pressed her lips into a straight line, giving up the last word. She reached over and dug her fingers into the knot of his tie, loosening it with more strength than she realized she had. He caught her hand when she sat back, gave her fingers a quick squeeze, and for an instant, she hoped they understood each other. But then his hand left her and went back on the wheel.

Pressing her fingers to her lips, she could still feel the warmth of his kiss on her mouth.

Something that, in all honesty, she wished she didn't know.

"I'LL BET SOPHIE'S still pulling twigs out of her hair," Coop said, laughing once Gideon finished regaling him, Ty and Coach about Sophie's date with Manfred when he got back to the bar that night. He left out the part about their argument. And that he'd kissed her.

The silent drive to her house had culminated in her slamming his truck door so hard his teeth rattled. The fact that he could smell the trace hints of her perfume—all flowery and fresh—grated on his last nerve.

His life could now be divided into sections: before he'd kissed Sophie Jennings and after. After was going to be a very long, very lonely time, and ever since the wager had been made, he'd never been tempted until now to back out and see if maybe there was a future in K-Bay after all. With Sophie. Except he couldn't—wouldn't—do that to his friends. They were in this together.

"I'm trying to figure out why you paired Sophie and Manfred to begin with." Coop compared the questionnaires in front of him. "I'm not seeing any overlap in their answers. Was there a computer glitch? Or did you get bored letting the computer do the work and wanted to try this yourself?"

"Yeah, well, they were two of the last to submit and I…I screwed up, okay?" There, he'd said it. He didn't say he'd screwed up purposely. It would take far more than the gallon of coffee he'd since ingested to admit that; coffee that would probably keep him up the rest of the night so he could dwell on his agonizing drive to Windhawk Forest. When he'd prayed and hoped that he wouldn't find Sophie at the bottom of some ravine.

"You know the funny thing?" he told his friends as they glanced around the Bar & Grill at the few couples still mingling. "She wants me to match her again. I swear that girl can smile through anything. Nothing gets her down." Come to think of it, her request had come with a significant amount of fire behind the words, as though she were challenging him.

Sophie challenged him all right. Because of her he'd taken his eyes, however quickly, off the prize.

"Tell me you're going to be more careful with who you pair her with on the Polar Dip," Ty said. "I told you—"

"Does it look as though I'm in the mood for an 'I told you so'?" Gideon growled.

"That's what friends are for." To Ty's credit, he refrained from uttering another word on that topic.

"I didn't hear any bells ringing tonight," Coop said. "But that doesn't mean we won't soon. From what we saw there are some promising matches being made. I bet by the time we get back from the lake that bell will be chiming like the cathedral in Anchorage."

"Don't ring your bells too soon, boys." Coach ambled up to their section of the bar and refilled Gideon's coffee and Coop's soda. "You've got a long way to go to claim your winnings."

"Those jobs are as good as ours," Gideon said with a finger jab at their former coach's chest. "You be ready to pay out like a slot machine."

"I've got my ears open," Coach said. He angled a look at the brass bell over the bar. "From where I'm sitting, you lot have some work to do to land two more couples. Things might seem fine and dandy to you right now, but earlier I saw at least one beer get tossed in someone's face, one parachute call be implemented and one young lady duck out the bathroom window and run home. At least, that's where I assume she went."

"Ah, man." Gideon slumped lower on his stool. "Tina Charlotte I bet." That girl would run from her own shadow. "Who deployed his parachute?"

"Jed Parker's phone went off about fifteen minutes into his date with Eleanor Clambert. Begged off, stating problems at the mill."

Coop frowned. "Didn't he get fired from the mill last month?" His confused gaze landed on Gideon. "Dude, what were you thinking? Eleanor needs special care and attention. She's, well, gentle." As gentle as any woman who worked six days a week with a group of loud, demanding toddlers could be.

"I wasn't thinking." Shame joined the other emotions washing over him like a cold shower. Eleanor was one of the shyest people in all of K-Bay. The fact she'd ventured into dating at all should have been cause for a town celebration. Unfortunately it looked as if Eleanor was taking the brunt of the aftereffects of him pulling not one, but three potential matches out of the algorithm in an attempt to find Sophie someone "safe." "Chalk tonight up to complete stupidity. But I'll fix it. I swear." He had to. His friends' futures depended on it.

"Poor Eleanor can't catch a break," Ty said. "That's the seventh person we've tried with her. She wants to find someone so badly. You can see it in her eyes."

"I've got enough guilt, thanks." Gideon took a slug of coffee and winced. "Between her and Manfred..."

Gideon sat up as if a bolt of lightning had struck him. He reached for the questionnaires, shuffling through the pile until he found Eleanor's and the one Coop had been reading earlier.

"Between her and Manfred what?" Coop asked. "Seriously, we can't afford another gaffe like the one tonight."

"No, this is good, I swear." Gideon flipped to the second page and tapped on question seven. "It might take some convincing, but I might have found Manfred's perfect match."

"Now he finds it." Ty finished his beer. "What makes you think—"

"He told Sophie this had been his first date."

"Seriously?" Coop's eyebrows shot high

enough to disappear beneath his hair. "He's what? Our age? Twenty-five?"

"Twenty-four," Gideon corrected. "Sophie's age. I'm guessing with a nickname like his, dates were difficult to come by."

"And yet you set him up with Sophie," Ty marveled. "What am I missing?"

If he wasn't seeing it, Gideon wasn't going to show him. He doubted his friends would take kindly to his jeopardizing their bet with Coach for the sake of his reluctant feelings for Sophie. "Give me a second." He pulled out his phone and called Manfred, issuing yet another apology and offering to find him another potential match. A good one. Manfred's enthusiasm was almost contagious and almost made Gideon forget the evening's earlier disaster. "Great. Yeah, tomorrow night. I'll have Coach set a special table. Eight o'clock. What?" He frowned. "No, twenty minutes on, twenty minutes off. Alternate between heat and ice, and if the swelling hasn't gone down in the next few hours, call Doc at the clinic. No, it's no trouble. Talk to you soon." He clicked off. "One potential relationship salvaged. Tomorrow I'll get feedback from the other matches and we'll go from there. We'll have a final list of pairings for the Polar Dip in a couple of days."

"And just who is going to be bachelor number four for Sophie?" Coop asked, sliding Sophie's questionnaire in front of Gideon. "And should we perhaps buy her protective gear, or hire a bodyguard for her?"

"Don't worry. This will be different. I know just the guy. New to town, moved here after his divorce. I met him at the bank last month when he opened his account. As far as I could tell, he's completely normal and nice. Exactly what Sophie ordered. All I need to do is get him to fill out a questionnaire."

SOPHIE STARED DOWN at the empty peanut-butter jar in her hand, the extra twenty-dollar bill she was about to add to Dillon's bail fund shaking in her fingers. Her disastrous date and kissing encounter in Gideon's truck faded into memory.

"Dillon!" She tried to remember the last time she'd yelled so loud that she hurt her throat. "Dillon!" She headed out of the kitchen but stopped short when he skidded in front of her, the irritated look on his face so commonplace now she barely noticed. She held out the jar. "Where is it?"

"Where's what?"

"Don't lie to me. The cash that was in this jar." She set it on the table. "Where is it?"

"You mean your fun-cash stash?" Dillon's face softened, but she didn't for one second believe he was in a teasing mood. He was gauging her reaction to see what he could lie about next.

"Is that what you think that was? Fun money?"

"What else would you leave it around here for?"

She took a deep breath and let it out slowly. "Where is the money, Dillon?"

"I needed a new chip for my gaming device. And some new controllers and, well..." He shrugged. "You know. Stuff."

"You spent almost a thousand dollars on *stuff*?" In a flash, everything Gideon had ever said about her brother, all the gossip about town, everything she'd worried was true and that she'd ignored, coalesced. "Did it ever occur to you I was setting that money aside for something important? Or for you?"

"Then, I just used it early." Dillon walked to the fridge and pulled out an energy drink, popped it open right in front of her and shrugged as if nothing had happened. "You're off the hook, sis. Thanks."

"I'll remind you that you said that." The sadness overwhelmed her. Her heart hurt, like a wrung-out washcloth. She'd failed him. Both she and their mother had. Years of excusing his behavior, enabling his antics, had left him completely irresponsible. Now it was time for her—and him—to pay the price. "I'm not going to replenish that money, Dillon." The statement felt like the first crack in a window. "I worked hard to earn that extra cash so I'd have it when we needed it." There would be no more trying, no more hoping for the best. She wouldn't see it. Not with her brother. "I'm going to be making some changes around here," she called as he left the kitchen.

"Whatever!"

Sophie sank into the chair at the table, the same chair her mother had occupied for so many years. The chair Sophie had avoided sitting in since her mom's death, as if she were afraid of dislodging a ghost. But the time had come to do what needed doing. For both her and Dillon.

She dialed, hands trembling, and hoped it wasn't too late at night to get the ball rolling. "Alice, hi. It's Sophie Jennings. You have a few minutes? Yeah? Great. Listen." She swallowed the tears and soldiered on. "I was wondering if you could tell me what it would take to put my mother's house on the market."

CHAPTER SEVEN

"HOW YOU DOING, CARL?" Gideon grabbed hold of the pole behind the driver's seat as the ancient school bus coughed and sputtered its way out of town and threw off enough exhaust to warrant the EPA asking for new regulations. "Think we'll make it there in one piece?"

"Roxanne will hold together." Carl Sheffield, a K-Bay institution for longer than Gideon had been alive, clutched the wheel with white knuckles, enough to leave Gideon cursing Ty's choice of transportation. What were those weird vibrations coming from under the bus where Gideon assumed the shock absorbers should be? *Roxanne* gave an odd backfire that caused its occupants—all twenty-five of them—to jump high enough to bounce. "Hear me, baby? Hold together." Carl's muttering did nothing to ease Gideon's mind.

Lake Wakanaba was a good hour outside K-Bay. Who knew how long it would take to get there in this contraption and what shape they'd be in when they arrived? During the planning stage, Coop and Ty had agreed with him that extra time the couples spent together could bolster potential matches, hence their choice of venue for the Polar Dip.

However, getting everyone safely back to K-Bay seemed less than guaranteed at this point. Gideon wouldn't be able to relax until they were at the Bar & Grill, and he had a nice large beer in his hand.

"Coop and Ty are already setting up at the lake." Gideon bent over so he could tell Carl the plan for the day. "I don't anticipate being there very long. Maybe a couple of hours."

"Don't make no never mind to me," Carl said as his spring-loaded seat bounced in time with Roxanne's rumblings. "You just tell me where and when and me and my girl will be ready."

"Great." Gideon slapped a hand on Carl's shoulder, quickly looking away from the windshield as Carl took a too-wide turn onto the highway.

He grabbed the clipboard off the top of his backpack that he'd left on the seat behind Carl and faced his group. Many of them looked as uncertain as he felt given their method of transport to Lake Wakanaba. Gideon swallowed hard. All the more reason to get their minds on each other instead of the upcoming mountain roads.

"Good morning, everyone." He injected an overabundance of enthusiasm as he scanned the crowd. "Thanks for getting up so early. Everybody get their coffee okay?"

Grumbles and heads nodding was all Gideon got. The level of excitement was about equal to that of a funeral procession. He felt his gaze being pulled toward the back of the bus, where Sophie was wedged between the window and Chase Peterson, his final choice when it came to finding her someone suitable.

He'd exchanged greetings with Sophie this morning, but their conversation didn't hold any of the banter he'd enjoyed prior to her evening with Manfred. Kissing her the other night might have fulfilled a long-held desire on his part, but the wall his actions had put between them might never be scaled.

She stared out the window, bag clutched against her chest, but he could see the muscles in her jaw working, as if yet again she was forcing herself not to look in his direction. He reached up to straighten his tie before he remembered he wasn't wearing one. Answering Sophie's challenge about loosening up had him feeling as if he were missing something.

"So." He cleared his throat and had to yell over the din of Roxanne's engine. "You are all new couples today, unless otherwise requested," he added when Manfred held up his hand. A hand that was firmly clasping that of Eleanor Clambert. At least he'd been right on that front. Eleanor and Manfred had hit it off immediately, and despite everything else going on around Gideon, that gave him something to smile about—and be proud of.

That was what happened when he paid particular attention to a problem. Things worked out.

"What I'd like each of you to do is tell your date one thing about yourself that isn't on your questionnaire. Something that might surprise even me. We've got at least an hour's drive ahead of us, so let's make the most of it and get to know each other. I'll make you aware when we're about there."

He headed to the back of the bus as the muted conversations began, some accompanied by nervous laughter. The smell of exhaust got worse the farther back he went, and he wondered if he'd ever see a school bus again without wanting to choke.

He took his time, making sure conversation was happening, making check marks next to those couples on his list who seemed to have an easier time of things than others. He kept his ears especially open as he reached Sophie and Chase, and tried not to notice how Sophie's smile lit up her entire face. Her gaze skittered to his before she ducked her chin and shook her head, murmuring an answer to some question Chase had asked her.

She'd asked him to take more care, take more of a risk for her, and he had. Chase was a good guy coming off being blindsided with divorce papers from his childhood sweetheart. But it hadn't taken much of a push to get him to fill out one of Gideon's forms. Chase had agreed it was time to get out there again, and thankfully, he looked good on paper. Being the floor manager of one of the mills in town meant he was steady. Secure. Responsible. All things Sophie needed—and said she wanted—in her life.

Seeing them together on paper was one thing. Seeing Sophie smile at Chase was another. Gideon had to change his mind on where to sit and threw himself into the spot directly behind Sophie and Chase.

Sophie turned her head, eyes narrowing as

she caught sight of him, but Gideon busied himself scribbling nonsensical notes on his clipboard and planned to listen to every word.

"So, Sophie." Chase focused curious blue eyes on her and smiled as she struggled out of her down coat. The stifling air in the bus fogged the windows. She gave him a grateful smile when he lent her a hand.

Chase had that new-Hollywood look about him with piercing eyes and a jaw she could break a cinderblock on. Not that she was a good judge of men, but given the envious looks she'd received since climbing onto the bus ahead of Chase, she'd hit the jackpot when it came to handsome. "What deep dark secret are you keeping to yourself?"

She couldn't help it. She laughed. "I'm a pretty shallow pool," she admitted as the back of her neck prickled. What was Gideon doing sitting right behind her? There were plenty of other empty seats on the bus.

"Come on," Chase teased. "I bet there's something fun about you we don't know. Like maybe you have secret fairies to help keep those flowers of yours happy so they magically bloom all year round?"

Sophie chuckled. "I only have one helper,

and trust me, she's not very magical." Melanie would probably disagree. "Um." She squeezed her eyes shut and tried to think of something. "Oh, okay. When I was a little girl, I used to ask my mom and dad to put twinkle lights up on my ceiling so I could pretend I was sleeping under the stars."

"That's cute," Chase said. "And did they?"

"No." Sophie barely registered the bitterness anymore. "They were always going to. But then my mom got sick and Dad took off. I found a box of lights in the garage a few years later. It was something." It was a reminder that sometimes you didn't get what you asked for—you had to make things happen yourself. "What about you?"

"Oh, you wouldn't believe me if I told you."

"Try me," Sophie prodded. "You seem normal enough. Just don't tell me you know where there are buried bodies at the lumber mill."

"No, no bodies. Not human anyway."

Sophie's smile dipped.

"Okay, here's the gist." Chase leaned over and she caught a whiff of his aftershave, something with citrus that made her nose itch. "I have a side hobby."

"Okay." And it had to do with...bodies?

"So go ahead. Confess." *Oh, wrong choice of words.*

"I'm a taxidermist," he whispered.

Sophie managed a silent O as she blinked.

"Crazy, huh?" Chase leaned back and crossed his arms over his chest and grinned. "Birds are my specialty. I don't kill them, mind you, but I do go looking for carcasses on my days off. I find it challenging, finding all the materials I need to match them just right. You'd be surprised what you can order on the internet. You know, the right glass eyeball makes all the difference..."

Sophie spun in her seat and glared at Gideon when she heard him snort. He covered his mouth as if he were coughing, those gorgeous blue eyes of his seeming torn between laughter and apology before he closed them and shook his head.

CHAPTER EIGHT

WHEN THE BUS bounced onto the unpaved road leading to Lake Wakanaba, Gideon took pity on Sophie and got to his feet. “Hey, Sophie, I could use some help if—”

“Happy to!” She shot up so fast she just missed cracking her head on the roof of the bus. “Sorry, Chase. I’ll be, um, back, okay?”

“Sure.” Despite appearances, Chase didn’t seem to be the sharpest tool in the shed. Near as Gideon could tell, Chase hadn’t noticed Sophie’s complete lack of interest in his hobby. “I can help, too,” Chase offered. “If you need.”

“It’s covered for now, thanks.” Gideon stepped back to let Sophie go ahead of him. “I am so sorry,” he whispered as they reached Carl. “I swear I didn’t know.”

“Might be time to revamp those questionnaires of yours.” Sophie sighed and dropped into the seat next to his backpack. “And maybe it’s time I admit defeat. I don’t have to date. I could be the lonely cat lady of K-Bay. I've always wanted a cat."

She was joking, right? The image of Sophie as a reclusive feline fancier sliced through his heart.

"Let's not go making drastic life choices just yet." Gideon attempted to keep the tone light. "There's probably a few more questionnaires—"

"Shouldn't we have parked back there?" Sophie asked as she pointed to the sign Carl had passed.

Gideon cursed. "Hey, Carl, you missed the sign."

"Nah. Saw it," Carl insisted and pointed ahead. "I know a special spot closer to the lake. Great view from the get-go. Trust me." He squinted and leaned forward to peer through the dirt-spattered window. "Only a little ways to go."

Different gears ground under the bus as the tires and brakes strained. "Ty and Coop should have set up by the dock by now," Gideon said. Why did he have a bad feeling about this? "I've been trying to call them, but the cell reception—"

"Please tell me there's a bathroom close by." Nadine groaned and crossed her legs. She wiggled in her seat, her lashes coated so thick with mascara you could hear her blink. "I drank too much coffee."

"There's a bunch of porta-potties down a path," Carl called over his shoulder. "I'll show you as soon as I park. This time of year, we're nice and early so they shouldn't be, um, full yet. Save for fishermen, of course."

"Of course," Sophie said with a flinch. "I'll be refraining from ingesting any more liquids for a while."

"Okay, folks, listen up." Gideon stood tall and faced the crowd. "As soon as Carl parks in his special place, I'll have those who need restrooms get off first. When you exit—" he took a step back to peer out the fogged-up door and pointed to where he spotted Ty and Coop at the edge of the lake "—head on over to Coop and Ty. They've got a drink and snack station set up along with chairs, blankets and hopefully anything else we'll need for the next couple of hours. The weather's supposed to be pretty nice, actually, so no one should freeze." And now the windup… "Those of you men willing to take the Polar Dip, stand by for instructions. Ladies, you're certainly welcome to put a toe in the water, too."

The laughter he received in response to his teasing was either a good sign or they were mocking him. In either case, at least it had broken the nervous tension.

"I've also got some extra towels stashed under the bus in case anyone forgot theirs. Manfred?"

Manfred pressed his glasses farther up on his nose. "I'll need one. I was distracted this morning."

Eleanor giggled and her face went fire-engine red as she clung to him.

Gideon stopped himself from smiling. "Noted. Hey, Carl, Coop's trying to get our attention."

"Almost there." Carl jammed his foot on the brake and the bus shuddered to a stop. When he cut Roxanne's engine, Gideon swore he heard the bus let out a sigh of relief. "The bathrooms are down that little trail right there—"

"Gotta go!" Nadine shoved past her date and hopped out of the seat, followed by a number of other women, who were bundled up in their down jackets and scarves despite the weather report for clear skies and unseasonably warm temps.

"Be careful, please," Gideon warned. Carl opened the bus door and the women piled into the aisle.

"I can hear Coop calling your name," Sophie

said. She stood and joined him, touching his shoulder as she rose up on tiptoe. "He doesn't look happy."

"Coop always looks like that." Then again, Coop was running toward them at a pace he hadn't seen since their high school hockey days. "Hang on." He held out his hand to Nadine, but she wasn't about to wait. She ignored him and dashed down the steps and off the bus.

"Whaaaa!" Her scream was quickly followed by a squelching splash. The bus lurched to one side. The women behind Nadine didn't have the chance to reach for something before they also toppled out of the bus and out of sight.

"Stop them!" Sophie hollered and grabbed one woman's arm. "Stacey, wait." Too late. Stacey went flailing after them.

Gideon pushed in front and stared down at the four, five…no, six women currently slopping around in one of the deepest mud puddles—*please let that be mud*—he'd ever seen. Nadine's shriek of horror had him covering his mouth to prevent himself from laughing.

"Holy—" Chase had come up the aisle followed by some of the other men. "Let us through. We'll help them out." Before Gideon could argue, Chase and his fellow Galahads hopped out of the bus, but instead of helping, they ended up knee-deep in mud, slipping and sliding around the women they couldn't grab hold of.

"It's like wrangling greased pigs," Sophie whispered with a hint of a giggle against Gideon's back. The rest of the bus's occupants gathered at the windows, laughing and shrieking in sympathy.

"Why didn't you park back at the lot?" Coop yelled from the far side of the mud puddle, which Gideon now realized had been camouflaged with ice-caked winter grass.

"Stop!" Gideon yelled to the jostling group and shoved his clipboard at Sophie. "Everyone stop moving right now! Carl, start Roxanne. We're headed back down that path."

He bent and unlaced his new boots, tossing them under his seat before he stepped off the bus and sank ankle deep. Calf deep. Knee deep. Oh, no.

Everyone had stopped moving at least, but they were all clearly waiting for his instructions. As if he knew what to do. Coop stood at the far end of the pit—nothing puddle about this thing now—hands on his hips, his shoulders shaking so hard with laughter even Gideon started to grin.

"What the—" Ty abruptly halted beside Coop. "Gideon, I thought we discussed the parking lot—"

"Now is really not the time," Gideon called out and took careful steps toward his mud people. "Stand up, everybody. Feet flat, stop flailing like overactive windmills and stay where you are."

More squeals erupted as feet went out from under people. Mud sprayed as people struggled to adjust. By the time they'd crawled, stooped and clawed their way to where Coop and Ty were standing, there wasn't an inch of bare skin—or clean clothes—showing.

Gideon slogged his way back to the bus, eyes narrowing as he caught sight of Sophie standing in the open door, eyes alight with humor as she doubled over laughing.

"You think this is funny?" Gideon asked as he dragged his legs through the mud.

She nodded and tears sparkled in her eyes. "I think it's hilarious. Gideon Walker, methodical planner, control freak extraordinaire, is stuck in the mud." She cackled and the sound shot straight through him. "Where's my phone?" she added as he got hold of the bus and hauled himself forward. She squealed as he wrapped his hand around her wrist and gave her a jerk forward. "Don't you dare!" she cried. But as she attempted to pull away, he tugged harder, his feet slipping out from under him. He felt himself falling back…with Sophie's wrist in his grasp.

"Gideon!"

He came up sputtering in time to see most of her face go under. He shifted up as quickly as he could and held her against him. "You idiot!" she shrieked and slapped at him.

"Sophie, I am so sor—"

And then he saw her. Saw Sophie. Still laughing. Swiping streaks of mud across her cheeks and nose, sputtering sludge.

"You got her?" Coop called over to him as he finished pushing the last of the white knights onto firm ground.

"Oh, he's got her," Ty said. "Carl! Get that truck moving to the parking lot. Slowly! And don't run over those two fools."

"Tell me you brought a change of clothes," Gideon said as Roxanne roared to life and Carl shifted the bus into Reverse.

"I'm always prepared." Sophie grinned and shifted off him, but he lifted his muddy hand and stroked the side of her face, staring into her eyes. "What?" She blinked at him, her white teeth brilliant against her dirty face.

"Nothing," he whispered. "Nothing except… I'm sorry." He watched as understanding crept into her eyes. He wasn't talking about the mud.

"I know." Her smile was sad, though. "Guess what? I think I might want to jump in the lake after all."

Sitting frozen in the mud, Gideon became certain of two things. One, he had no business being a matchmaker, and two, he'd just fallen head over heels in love with Sophie Jennings, Queen of the Mud People.

GIDEON GRIMACED AS the last of the couples trudged off the bus—Nadine and her extra-muddy lashes included—later that afternoon looking completely spent, but with smiles on their faces. Total disaster averted.

They'd stayed at the lake longer than expected, mostly to accommodate Ty racing to the closest convenience store thirty minutes east to buy trash bags for muddied clothes, extra towels, thermal blankets, sweats, T-shirts and a couple of bottles of whiskey to top off still-steaming coffee back at the lake.

Thanks to Sophie parading around in her mud suit looking as proud as if she were wearing a golden tiara, moods and attitudes shifted and improved. Within minutes, more people than expected were diving into the chilly lake—clothes and all—to join in the fun. Trinity Matchmaking's Polar Dip was destined to be talked about for weeks, maybe months to come.

"Send me any cleaning bills," Gideon told the couples as they filed out of the bus and into the Bar & Grill for a promised meal and recovery time. "Sophie, stop." He hurried over to where she was lugging sopping piles of filthy towels and discarded blankets. "You've done enough. Coop and I will take care of that."

"Yeah, yeah," Coop grumbled as he sidled up to the bus, having parked his car. "If I'd known today would entail this much hard labor, I'd have hired out. You." Coop pointed at Gideon. "No more outing planning for you. You're done."

"We're done," Gideon corrected. Tomorrow was Valentine's Day. He was officially tapped out of romantic ideas for fledgling lovebirds. Well. Maybe he had one or two ideas left. "Sophie, can I talk to you for a minute?"

She blinked at him, making a kind of tsking sound with her tongue when Coop gently pushed her aside. "Sure."

Gideon led her around the side of the building, his stomach dropping into a strange little jig he'd never felt before. "Look, I admit today was a bit of a disappointment."

"It turned around." She smiled up at him, her damp hair hidden beneath the wool cap Gideon always kept in his bag. She'd been the first one into the lake, and while her clothes had taken a beating, she'd managed to emerge as fresh faced as ever. Shivering perhaps, but smiling nonetheless, proof she could come out of anything unscathed. "About me and Chase." She inclined her head toward the door. "I recognize you did try this time, but let's face it. That's four strikes. I'm out."

Gideon's usual frown returned. "Come on."

She let out a laugh but for the first time in memory, it didn't sound genuine. She sounded…disappointed. "There haven't been any sparks with the guys you've matched me with, Gideon. Let's be honest."

Guilt niggled once again. "Yeah, well, I—"

"You and I both know what happened between us in the truck the other night was a fluke. A mistake," she stated as if he needed reminding about what he'd said. "Fine, there were sparks, but that's probably because I irritate the heck out of you and kissing me was the only way to shut me up. Right?" Was that expectancy on her face? Did she want him to deny it? To tell her she was wrong, that it was more than irritation and a desire for silence that had him taking her into his arms?

"Actually." Gideon cleared his throat. "I do have one more match for you. If you're willing to take one more chance." Just as he was doing right now by asking her.

Sophie dropped her head back and groaned. "Gideon, you're killing me. This was me saying let me drop out of this social experiment."

"No, I got that." And he hated the fact he'd let her down, hadn't taken her wanting to find someone as seriously as he should have. He'd been playing with her, but he was ready to stop with the games and play for real. If only to see if she shared a fraction of his feelings. "I promise, come to the Bar & Grill tomorrow night. Eight o'clock. I won't disappoint you again. It'll be perfect. Please?"

"All right." Did she have to sound so put out? "Eight o'clock. Got it." She gave his arm a quick squeeze and him an even quicker smile. "It was nice to see you loosen up." She flicked a finger against his bare collar. "You look good non-buttoned-down. I'm going to head home, take a quick shower and check in at the store."

"Great. I'll see you later," he called out as she walked away. Coop arched a brow in his direction. "Shut up."

"Did I say anything?"

"You didn't have to. I have a plan."

"That's what I'm afraid of." Coop dropped a heap of dripping towels at his feet. "Just remember not all your plans work out. No way am I taking these home. My washing machine will explode and that's only after Nora kills me."

"I've got it. But first I need to talk to Coach about using the roof tomorrow night."

"You finally going to do something about that girl?" Coop asked as Gideon headed inside the tavern.

"Looks like."

For now, he wouldn't think about what came next, or how he'd be letting his best friends down if he changed his mind about leaving. All that mattered for today, for tomorrow night, was Sophie.

Whatever happened after…would be up to her.

CHAPTER NINE

"OKAY, HOW COULD you have gone on that trip," Melanie asked her late the next afternoon, "and still be smiling now? I'm hearing yesterday's Polar Dip was a catastrophe."

"Hurricanes and typhoons are catastrophes," Sophie corrected and brushed her fingertips over a lacy bunch of baby's breath. "And certainly I'm smiling. I just paid off the last of the mortgage on this place and made a down payment on the vacant shop next door. Expansion, here we come. I'm going to start interviewing contractors next week." Was she bouncing on her toes? Walking on air? Maybe both? It felt like both. It was as if a hive of bumblebees had taken up residence in her chest and had her buzzing around doing their bidding. "And yes, the lake adventure was definitely not what anyone expected. You did miss a show, though." She'd probably be scrubbing mud out of her ears for the next week. "It turned out okay. I heard a few couples already planning second dates on the bus ride home."

"Will you be seeing Chase again?" Melanie blinked wide-eyed at her.

"No." Sophie shuddered. "It's not his fault. I'm sure there's a woman out there who would appreciate his many talents."

Sophie glanced at the clock on the wall for the hundredth time. Just after six. "Gideon asked for one more shot at finding me a decent match. Would you mind closing up tonight?" But first she had a quick stop to make.

"Nah. Elliot's out of town," Melanie sulked about her recently acquired husband and rested her chin in her palm. "Nothing else to do except feed the cat."

"Maybe after this evening I'll ask to borrow Mr. Puffins. I might need some cat practice."

"Oh, speaking of properties, that reminds me. Alice from Parkhouse Real Estate called. She said she'd have the paperwork ready for you by Monday."

"Great, thanks." Time to bite the bullet and dive into her own life, and out of the one she'd been stuck in.

"What paperwork?"

"I'm selling Mom's house." Sophie slipped off her apron and grabbed her jacket and bag.

"More later. Right now I need to run. See you in the morning."

She hurried across the street, and at the corner raced up the two blocks to Amare Street. She spotted Mrs. Turnblat standing at the living room window of her two-story cottage. Sophie gave her a quick wave and stepped through the wooden gate, carefully latching it behind her before hopping up the steps onto the wide porch. Beautiful. Perfect. Giddiness descended.

"Hi, Mrs. Turnblat," she said as the old woman, gray hair sparkling atop smiling eyes, opened the door. "Thanks for letting me see the house before you put it on the market."

"My pleasure, dear. Come in, come in. Can I get you some tea?"

"No, thank you. I have a date tonight," Sophie whispered as if it were a secret. "I don't want to be late." Mainly because she wanted to get it over with. There was a reason no one had lit the spark inside her that she'd been supposedly waiting for.

Gideon already had, whether he'd intended to or not.

"Well, then, let me give you the tour. Will it just be you living here?"

"Yes," Sophie said, pushing aside the guilt at leaving Dillon to live his own life. "Yes, it'll just be me."

"I KNOW, I KNOW." Gideon heard Sophie's words and got up from his seat at the elbow of the bar as she hurried into the tavern at ten minutes after eight. "I'm sorry I'm late," she said, shrugging out of her coat. "Crazy day. Lots of changes. Wow." Her eyes went wide as she smiled at him. "You cleaned up nice." She reached out and tugged on his tie. "Black tonight. Special occasion?"

"Somewhat. You look beautiful." Gideon tried to remember a time Sophie wasn't stunning. Whether it was jeans and a T-shirt or the pretty pink-flowered dress that flittered around her knees in lacy ruffles, she never ceased to turn his head. "Doesn't she look nice, guys?"

"Yes, she does," Coop said. A sly smile appeared on his friend's face. "No mud tonight, Sophie?"

"Not tonight." Sophie patted her cheeks after she draped her purse and jacket on the bar. "I save the Eau de Sludge for special occasions. So." She tapped her fingers on the edge of her bag. "Where is this perfect match you went on about?"

"Ah, upstairs, actually. On the roof." Gideon cast a sideways glance at Coach, who, after knocking his hand against Coop's and then

Ty's arm, gestured for them to follow. "This way, please."

"Great. Oh, wait until I tell you what I did today," she said, the sound of her heels tapping not only against the hardwood floor but also against his heart. "I think you'll actually be proud of me—" Her phone rang. "Hang on a second. I should have turned that off."

Her answering the call stopped Gideon from telling her he'd always be proud of her, that he wanted to make her proud of him. She skittered to a stop in the back hall by the staircase. "Dillon?" She plugged her free ear and bent forward as if she couldn't quite hear. "Dillon, where are you?"

The change in stance was instantaneous and, for a moment, chilled Gideon to the bone. Her carefree expression turned icy as her lips thinned and she took a deep breath.

"What's wrong?" Gideon asked and touched her arm, trying to shake off the rejection when she turned away from him. "Is he okay?"

"Yeah, I'll be there as soon as I can."

"What's wrong?" he repeated.

Sophie ended the call and shoved the phone into a pocket. "Dillon's been arrested. Again."

"And he called you. Again." The disapproval in Gideon's voice made Sophie cringe.

"Don't start on me about my brother, Gideon. I'm well aware of his faults. I don't need you to remind me or judge."

"I wasn't," he argued. Then realized that was a lie. "What are the charges this time?"

"He's upped his game again. Possession with intent to sell. He just keeps getting deeper and deeper into trouble. I'm sorry, I really am, but I need to go." She hurried back to the bar and grabbed her jacket and purse.

"Of course." All the effort he'd made to plan the perfect evening, the favors he'd called in, the hours he'd spent practicing what he wanted to say to her, they all vanished as she turned and headed to the door.

"I know," she called over her shoulder. "Whoever this guy is, I don't expect him to wait for me. So if that means I lose this chance, that's that."

"Wait a minute. Sophie, hold up." He managed to reach her and spin her around once they were in the vestibule. He moved her out of the way to let a group of teens inside. "Okay. This isn't any of my business, but how much longer are you going to protect Dillon from the consequences of his actions? He has to stand on his own sometime."

"Believe me, I know." Sophie looked down

at where his hand was holding her arm. "And you're right, it isn't any of your business. I can't talk to you about him. Not when you're convinced he's a complete loser."

"He's your brother. I get that." Gideon tried to appease her. "But he can't be your life. At some point you need to live your own. Come upstairs with me, Sophie. Please."

"Whatever's waiting upstairs is a fantasy, Gideon. What Dillon's dealing with right now is real and I need to get to him. I'm sorry if you don't understand that, but he's the only family I have left. I have to take care of this."

"Then, let me come with you—"

"No. I'm sorry, but you're hardly impartial where Dillon's concerned and I need to handle this by myself. But thank you for offering," she added.

"So you're just going to walk away from something potentially wonderful to fix somebody who doesn't want to be fixed?"

Sophie frowned at him. "However I feel about Dillon, I made a promise to my mother. I said I'd be there and I'm going. I don't break my promises to anyone. I keep my word."

"And what about your word that you'd go on this date tonight?" He knew he was sounding childish, that he should tell her the truth, but her rejection stung, whether she knew she was walking away from him or not.

"That's different," Sophie said and pointed up. "I didn't promise *him* anything, Gideon. I'm sorry, but I've got to get to the sheriff's office. Good night."

Gideon stared after her, unable to move as she got into her car, backed up and disappeared into the night.

She'd really done it. Chosen her deadbeat brother over him. Over a chance at the happiness she claimed she wanted.

Maybe he was wrong about this. Maybe Sophie wasn't the one. Maybe she wasn't ready.

But Gideon was. He'd actually thought about giving up his shot at the big time, considered abandoning the dream he, Coop and Ty had had for most of their lives, all to stay here in K-Bay with her.

And yet she couldn't even commit to one evening. What did that tell him? Maybe it was better that she didn't realize what he was willing to give up. For her. For them.

Yeah, Gideon had gotten it all wrong. He glanced at the sky, shook his head and kicked at the old stump near the bench outside before heading back into the bar. But it was going to be up to Sophie to make things right.

"SHERIFF TOMLINSON, HELLO." Sophie walked into the station a little over a half hour later, anger and frustration nibbling at her heels as she folded her hands on top of the counter. "Thanks for letting him call. Your office must have me on speed dial by now."

"Sophie, sorry to drag you into this," the older man said as he lifted his substantial girth out of his chair. "Dillon insisted on you being his one phone call."

"Yeah, well, he keeps forgetting his lawyer's number," Sophie lied. "Any idea what the bail's going to be?"

"Pretty high, I'd imagine. His past arrests are going to factor in this time, nothing I can do about it."

Sophie shook her head. "No, I understand. Of course. Would it be possible to see him?"

Sheriff Tomlinson's beady eyes went as wide as they could. "You normally just want to hang out until the bail's set. You sure?"

Oh, she was sure. "I'll explain when I'm finished with him."

"Follow me." The sheriff lifted the pass-through and led her into the back room where the holding cells were located. The drab, dull formerly apricot-painted walls looked like bruised fruit under the fluorescent lights.

"Sophie." Dillon leaped off the thin mattress and raced over to the door, wrapping his fingers around the steel bars. "You must have taken the long way."

"I was on a date," she fudged the truth and nodded for the sheriff to leave.

"Wait! Where's he going?" Dillon extended an arm as if he could snatch the sheriff back. "He's supposed to let me out. Didn't you post bail?"

"No, I didn't." She'd practiced what she might say to Dillon during the drive over, but looking at him in that cell for the fifth time in less than a year, she knew no amount of rehearsal would help. She couldn't sugarcoat what she needed to say. What Dillon needed her to do. She took a deep breath. "And I won't even after it's set."

"You won't post my bail?" Dillon screeched like a barn owl. Sophie cringed. "Why do you think I called you?"

"Because you always call me," Sophie said and forced herself to keep her arms at her sides. She would not cower, she would not fold and she would not cross her arms over her chest in an effort to protect herself. "But I'm done, Dillon. There's no money for bail."

"There's always money for— Wait." Dillon's

eyes narrowed. "This is what you were talking about the other night? The peanut-butter money?"

"That was your bail stash," Sophie confirmed. "There's nothing else to be used."

"You've got the shop for collateral. Or your car or Mom's hou—"

"Enough!" Sophie almost flinched at the sound of her own voice echoing back at her. "Enough, Dillon. You've taken advantage of me for the last time. I won't run to your rescue anymore. You're an adult, and I warned you this day was coming. You're going to see these charges through. You're going to accept whatever punishment they hand out to you, and when you get out, you can look for a new place to live."

"You're kicking me out?"

"I'm selling the house," Sophie said. "Mom left it in my name because she knew you'd squander whatever cash she left you, and she was right. Your share of the insurance money is gone, isn't it?"

"You can't do this," Dillon said in lieu of an answer. "You promised Mom—"

Tears burned her throat, but she squeezed her fists tight, focused on the pain of her nails digging into her palms instead of the grief crushing her heart. "I promised Mom I'd watch out for you, but I can't anymore, Dillon. It's not doing either of us any good. I could put up with a lot, excuse a lot, but this is where I draw the line. I'm tired. I love you. You're my kid brother, but until you grow up and accept responsibility for your actions, I don't want to see you. I'll pack up your stuff and put it in storage. You can pick up the key with Sheriff Tomlinson when you get out."

"Sophie, wait, please!" Dillon stretched out his hands and for an instant, she saw the happy, carefree, loving little boy he'd been. Temptation struck, urging her to give him another chance, but it would only be another opportunity for him to hurt her and pull them backward. She was worn-out with crying herself to sleep over him. "Sophie, I can do better, I promise."

"Then, do better," she said, hand on the door before she pushed it open. "But not for me. For yourself. Goodbye, Dillon."

She closed the door behind her, covering her mouth as she sobbed. She could hear him calling for her, the sound of her name ringing in her ears as she headed back to the reception desk. The expression on the sheriff's face was all she needed to see. "You heard?"

"You did your mom proud, Sophie," Sheriff Tomlinson said, patting an awkward hand on her back. "You did what she never could. He'll know it's for the best one day."

"Yeah, I hope so." She swiped a finger under her eye. "Would you do me a favor?"

"I'll let you know how he's doing and what's going on."

Relieved he understood, she smiled. "Thanks. I think I'm going to get a drink." And maybe cry on Gideon's shoulder.

If he was still willing to provide her with one.

CHAPTER TEN

"YOU REALLY GOING to waste all this on us?" Ty asked. Gideon popped open his second beer of the night and sat back in the metal patio chair he'd hauled up to the Bar & Grill's roof. "There's some fine food here, Gid. Lots of ambiance and romance."

"Listen, guys, no offense." Coop sat on the edge of the third-story railing and piled on the jokes. "But neither of you is my type. Maybe I'll give Nora a call."

"Go ahead. It's all paid for." Gideon toasted the night sky. "I'll take Zoe off your hands while you two romance. And you two." Gideon stared at Ty, who already had his phone out. "Yeah, yeah. Go ahead. Kelsey, too."

"Boy, Mr. Crabby is in fine form tonight." Ty grinned, but the teasing helped push Gideon over the edge of feeling sorry for himself.

How could he blame Sophie for something she wasn't aware she'd done? She didn't know he'd been the one she was meeting tonight. It probably wouldn't have made a difference if she did know. Sure, part of him was hoping she'd figure it out, but this was where taking a risk had cost him dearly. He'd done too good a job over the past few years convincing Sophie he didn't like her. There was no way for her to believe he'd fallen head over heels.

Why else would he be sitting under twinkling electric star-shaped lights beneath the real night stars and wishing he'd chosen his words with more care?

"You know, the fact she's so loyal to Dillon is actually a good thing," Coop said after he finished texting Nora. "I mean, you know she cares about family."

"Even criminal members," Ty added. "Coop's right. You can't blame her for standing up for the only family she has."

"No, I can't. And it's probably just as well anyway. That bell is going to ring at least two times tomorrow night at the Valentine's party. I know it." He felt it in his bones. "Which means in a matter of weeks the three of us, and your significant others, will be bound for the Lower 48 and working to get a winning team for Coach."

The silence that fell was like a two-ton explosion, the way it sounded in Gideon's ear.

"What?" he asked his friends, who were suddenly intent on looking anywhere other than at him. "What am I missing?"

"Nothing," Ty said a little too quickly. "It's just, things are now more complicated than they were. Nothing that's not fixable, but—"

"Picking up and leaving might not be so easy anymore is what Ty's trying to say," Coop put in.

"Maybe not for you," Gideon said, trying not to envision his dream crashing for the second time in his life. He'd let himself believe Sophie might just be a part of it. Now even his friends were having second thoughts. "We made a pact, remember? We made a bet. And I've done a lot to make sure we won it."

"But we haven't won yet," Ty said before taking a long drink of beer. "Let's wait until we do before we start packing, okay?"

"That sounds about right," Coop said, checking his phone. A few seconds later, he frowned. "Oh, hey. Um, Nora's calling me. I need to take this downstairs. Ty, you want to come wait for Kelsey?"

"Huh?" Ty blinked before glancing down at his phone. His face took on a similar confused expression before he hid a quick grin. "Right. Kelsey, um, doesn't like dark stairwells. They give her the creeps. Later." Ty smacked Gideon's arm before he and Coop headed downstairs, leaving Gideon alone on the roof, with the dinner he'd arranged for Sophie and the twinkling lights of her childhood dream mocking him.

"HEY, COACH." SOPHIE HAULED herself up onto one of the few empty stools at the Bar & Grill and waved him over. "Can I get a very large, very dry white wine?"

"Sure thing." Coach put down his phone and smiled. If he was surprised at her reappearance he didn't show it. Then again, Coach was as unflappable as they came.

"Is Gideon around?" Her stomach clenched as she asked and then accepted the wine he set in front of her. "I think I owe him an apology."

"You're right on that count," Coach said in a tone that had her doing a double take.

"Excuse me?"

"What's the deal with Dillon?" he asked instead. "You bail him out again?"

"No, as a matter of fact," Sophie replied and wondered how the rumor mill spun this fast in K-Bay. "I did not. I left him in jail to get himself out of trouble for a change. Why?"

"No reason. Just wishing I'd made a bet earlier this evening. I would have won a fortune. Gideon's upstairs on the roof."

"Don't tell me he's with my mystery date. I'll be back for that," she muttered, gesturing at her wine before moving toward the staircase.

How many ways could she apologize to Gideon? She wasn't in any hurry to tell him he was right about Dillon, but she was anxious to admit she'd taken his advice and was letting Dillon deal with his own mess this time. After a quick stop in the ladies' room, she resumed her path to the staircase and found Ty and Coop coming down.

"Hi, guys."

"Sophie." Ty grinned one of those all-knowing-but-I'm-not-telling kind of smiles that eased the harshness of the scars on his face. "You looking for Gideon?"

"Upstairs?" She pointed.

"Yep. We'll see you guys later." Coop shoved Ty onward as Sophie headed up to the roof.

She hesitated for a moment outside the door, free hand poised over the knob as she practiced her apology once more. "Come on, go out there and get it out of the way," she whispered, and after doing a brief dress check, she turned the knob, pushed open the door and stepped—

Into the fantasy dream of her childhood.

Thousands of tiny blinking and flickering lights were strung across the expanse of the roof, creating a canopied effect above the black wrought iron table and chairs. Along one side sat a narrow table filled with firelit chafing dishes and a silver ice bucket chilling a bottle of wine.

And there, staring out across the K-Bay horizon, sat Gideon, his back to her, a beer bottle dangling from between his fingers. Gideon. And no one else.

Sophie tried to call out to him, but the words lodged somewhere between realization and hope. She pressed a hand against her heart. There was no mystery date. There was no perfect match.

There was only him.

She dipped out of her shoes and strode barefoot across the chilled roof, dashing as the cold sank into her toes. When she reached him, she bent down and set her purse—her phone turned off—on the ground and stood directly behind him.

"Someone went to an awful lot of trouble tonight," she said and tried to keep the tears out of her voice.

Gideon was up like a shot, spinning to face her, eyes wide and his cheeks turning pink in the most fascinating expression of embarrassment she'd ever seen. "Sophie."

"Hi." Oh, he looked so handsome in his crisp tailored white shirt and dark slacks, his once-pristine tie unknotted and hanging loosely around his neck, the top two buttons of his shirt undone.

"You came back." He didn't look as if he quite believed it.

"I did."

"Where's Dill—"

"In jail. I didn't bail him out, Gideon."

He sighed. "I'm sorry."

"No, you're not." She reached up and touched his face. "I wasn't going to bail him out. Not tonight. Not ever again. But I needed to tell him that to his face. I cut ties." And maybe one day the thought of what she'd done wouldn't hurt so much. "Until he gets his act together anyway. And yes, before you say it yourself, you were right." About so many things.

"I wasn't going to say that," he argued. "What— Why— How—?"

She could really have fun with this, drawing out his unease, but she didn't want to. She only wanted one thing right now and she was tired of waiting.

She walked forward and wrapped her arms

around him, snuggling her cheek against the warmth and strength of his chest. "I realized this was where I belonged. With you."

"With me?" She felt one arm go around her while he set his beer down. Next thing she knew, he was holding her so tightly she didn't care if she never breathed again. "Are you sure you want me?" he asked.

"Well, it's not as if anyone else worked out." She chuckled. "Despite you giving it your best shot." She leaned her head back and looked up at him as a knowing smile curved his full lips.

"Actually..." he hedged and shrugged. Grinned.

"I knew it!" She slugged his arm, laughing. "You didn't try, did you? You didn't want me to find anyone else."

"No." His smile was the most beautiful smile she'd ever seen. Because it was all for her.

"And all this time you didn't think I was flighty or a bad businesswoman? All this time you liked me?"

He looked offended that she'd even thought it. He smoothed a hand down her hair. "Sophie Jennings, you're the most capable person I've ever known. You just scare the life out of me sometimes with the chances you take."

"Like asking to borrow money when my brother probably would have stolen it?"

He nodded. "Like that."

Her heart swelled. "You were looking out for me even then? Because you cared about me."

"Guilty."

"So can you officially remove my name from the dating database now?"

"I already did. Except—"

"Except what?"

"Sophie, you being here, right now, with me, saying these things." He took a deep breath. "It's what I wanted to happen, but I meant what I said the other night in the truck. I'm not staying. We're not staying. Tomorrow night, we'll have an opportunity we can't pass up."

"You mean the bet you, Ty and Coop have with Coach?"

He frowned. "How did you—"

"You think I have that flower shop just for flowers? Mr. Felenti told me all about you guys getting a shot at professional hockey careers. What does that have to do with you and me?"

"Because K-Bay is your home. You belong here."

"Maybe." She shrugged. "But remember that annoying habit I have of leaping before I look? I've got a few more good leaps in me."

"I didn't want you to have to choose and give up something you want. And the store—"

"How about we take what comes down the road together and deal with it then?" He was such a worrier. She'd have to work on that. "There's no point being concerned about something until it's here. There's always the option of turning the store over to Melanie. I've got lots of choices, Gideon. Nothing's written in stone."

"You mean it?"

"I mean it. You know what else I mean?" She stretched up on her toes and pressed her mouth to his. "I love you, grumpy banker man."

"I love you, too, flower girl."

This time, when he kissed her, she held on, smiling against his lips until she gasped and stepped back.

"What's wrong?"

"Nothing." She pressed her finger against his mouth. "Just don't let me forget later."

"Forget what?"

"To ring the bell."

EPILOGUE

CLANG! CLANG! CLANG!

Cheers erupted, toasts were made, glasses clinked.

The trinity of matchmakers didn't move.

"Well." Coach sagged in his chair, as he pinned each of them with his trademark stare. "Looks as if you boys will be headed to the Lower 48!" He slapped a hand on Gideon's back.

"Looks like," Coop said without much enthusiasm. "Dad will be thrilled."

"It'll be hard for him, leaving," Ty added. "He's lived in K-Bay his entire life."

"We all have," Gideon put in.

"You boys have a lot to discuss, so I'll leave you to it." Coach beamed. "I'm proud of you three. Doing what you said you would. Taking charge of your lives and your futures. I look forward to seeing what's down the road for each of you, but I don't suppose any of you will be around here from now on."

"No, I suppose not." Gideon winced as he stared down at his beer.

"What's with the frown?" Sophie rejoined them, having surrendered a fussy Zoe to her mother. Gideon turned his face so she could stare at him nose to nose. "My ringing that bell is good news. That's six, right, since Manfred and Eleanor from earlier tonight also count. You guys get your jobs with a hockey club now."

Ty choked on his beer. "She knows?"

"Most of the town knows," Sophie said with her cheeky grin and a roll of her eyes. "You may not have realized it, but there were a lot of people pulling for you. Me included."

"Explain that to me," Coop said. "Moving for Nora won't be that big of a deal since she was moving here anyway, but K-Bay is your home. You have a business. Roots."

"K-Bay is a home," Sophie corrected. "Like I told this guy last night." She leaned her head against Gideon's arm. "I'm ready for whatever comes with him."

"Don't tell me you're all having second thoughts about finally getting those dream jobs," Kelsey said as she and Nora arrived.

"Not...exactly." But as Nora placed their daughter in Coop's arms, the expression on his friend's face told Gideon what needed doing. Confirmation from Ty only took a quick glance.

After nearly thirty years, the three of them understood each other well enough to not need words. Not even when it came to deciding the future all of them—or none of them—wanted.

"K-Bay is a good place to raise a family," Gideon said in a clear effort to ease into the decision. "This town is small, it's safe and it's—"

"It's home," Ty said. "Being a rink manager is pretty good. I like the kids. The hours are predictable and I can still play."

"And I'm good at selling cars," Coop stated. "When I have customers."

"The bank isn't going anywhere." Now that he thought about it, the job was a good deal. Given his growing expertise with questionnaires, he could take a new tact when it came to applications and understanding people's motivations. Maybe he could loosen the reins a little. And trust more.

"As long as you aren't using us as an excuse," Sophie said with a touch of admonition in her voice. "You're not, are you?"

Gideon, Coop and Ty took one more look at each other. And shook their heads.

"I want to stay," Coop admitted.

"Me, too. Gid?" Ty arched a brow in his direction.

"I want roots," Gideon said as he slipped his arm around Sophie. "I want them here. The question is—"

"Who's going to tell Coach?"

"Tell Coach what?" Coach stood next to them and tossed a thick, glossy, green folder into the center of the table. "I thought for sure you'd be celebrating."

"We need to talk to you about the bet," Gideon began.

"We aren't taking the jobs," Coop blurted. "Easier to just put it out there. We want to stay in K-Bay. With our families."

"Huh." Coach scrubbed a hand across his whiskered face and inclined his head. "I'm a little disappointed, boys. I handpicked this team for you three. It needs special attention since it's going to be relocating. Before you make a final decision, why don't you see exactly what you're passing on?" Coach called over his shoulder, "Coming! Got drinks to deliver. I'll be back."

"No fair." Gideon stared at the folder as if it were about to let loose a plague. "It's as though he's torturing us."

The table went silent until Sophie slapped

her hand down on the folder and pulled it toward Gideon.

"You know you're dying to see what's inside. Go ahead. Open it."

Gideon flipped open the folder. Sophie leaned closer, read along with him. Whether her smile mirrored his own, he could only imagine. "The K-Bay Ice Pirates."

"The what?" Ty snatched the file away so he and Kelsey could read it. "I'll be—"

Coop huffed. "Read out loud, please."

"Coach is moving his best team to K-Bay. Look." He pulled out an official press release on letterhead dated one week from today. There were their names in the Ice Pirates' colors, black, white and green: Head Coach Ty Porter, Vice-President of Marketing Cooper Hamilton, Vice-President of Finance Gideon Walker.

"Can I get an exclusive interview with the new staff?" Kelsey asked, the expectant look on her face pulling shocked smiles and nods from everyone at the table.

"You did it," Sophie whispered to Gideon as she pressed her lips to his cheek. "Looks as though you won after all."

Gideon nodded, his ears ringing with shock, but as he turned and looked at Sophie, he knew he'd already won. "You prepared for that new adventure?"

She kissed him hard and he felt her smile against his mouth, a sensation he didn't think he'd ever tire of.

The bell chimed again, and as Gideon and his friends looked over, they found Coach watching them, a grin on his face. "Welcome home, boys. Welcome home."

* * * * *

MONTANA
MAVERICKS